AMERICAN HUMORISTS SERIES

DISSERTATIONS

BY MR. DOOLEY

WITHDRAWN

Finley Peter Dunne

LITERATURE HOUSE / GREGG PRESS

Upper Saddle River, N. J.

Republished in 1969 by
LITERATURE HOUSE
an imprint of The Gregg Press
121 Pleasant Avenue
Upper Saddle River, N. J. 07458

96 794

Standard Book Number–8398-0375-3
Library of Congress Card–72-91077

Printed in United States of America

THE AMERICAN HUMORISTS

Art Buchwald, Bob Hope, Red Skelton, S. J. Perelman, and their like may serve as reminders that the "cheerful irreverence" which W. D. Howells, two generations ago, noted as a dominant characteristic of the American people has not been smothered in the passage of time. In 1960 a prominent Russian literary journal called our comic books "an infectious disease." Both in Russia and at home, Mark Twain is still the best-loved American writer; and Mickey Mouse continues to be adored in areas as remote as the hinterland of Taiwan. But there was a time when the mirthmakers of the United States were a more important element in the gross national product of entertainment than they are today. In 1888, the British critic Grant Allen gravely informed the readers of the *Fortnightly*: "Embryo Mark Twains grow in Illinois on every bush, and the raw material of *Innocents Abroad* resounds nightly, like the voice of the derringer, through every saloon in Iowa and Montana." And a half-century earlier the English reviewers of our books of humor had confidently asserted them to be "the one distinctly original product of the American mind"—"an indigenous home growth." Scholars are today in agreement that humor was one of the first vital forces in making American literature an original entity rather than a colonial adjunct of European culture.

The American Humorists Series represents an effort to display both the intrinsic qualities of the national heritage of native prose humor and the course of its development. The books are facsimile reproductions of original editions hard to come by—some of them expensive collector's items. The series includes examples of the early infiltration of the autochthonous into the stream of jocosity and satire inherited from Europe but concentrates on representative products of the outstanding practitioners. Of these the earliest in point of time are the exemplars of the Yankee "Down East" school, which began to flourish in the 1830's—and, later, provided the cartoonist Thomas Nast with the idea for Uncle Sam, the national personality in striped pants. The series follows with the chief humorists who first used the Old Southwest as setting. They were the founders of the so-called frontier humor.

The remarkable burgeoning of the genre during the Civil War period is well illustrated in the books by David R. Locke, "Bill Arp," and others who accompanied Mark Twain on the way to fame in the jesters' bandwagon. There is a volume devoted to Abraham Lincoln as jokesmith and spinner of tall tales. The wits and satirists of the Gilded Age, the Gay Nineties, and the first years of the present century round out the sequence. Included also are several works which mark the rise of Negro humor, the sort that made the minstrel show the first original contribution of the United States to the world's show business.

The value of the series to library collections in the field of American literature is obvious. And since the subjects treated in these books, often with surprising realism, are intimately involved with the political and social scene, and the Civil War, and above all possess sectional characteristics, the series is also of immense value to the historian. Moreover, quite a few of the volumes carry illustrations by the ablest cartoonists of their day, a matter of interest to the student of the graphic arts. And, finally, it should not be overlooked that the specimens of Negro humor offer more tangible evidence of the fixed stereotyping of the Afro-American mentality than do the slave narratives or the abolitionist and sociological treatises.

The American Humorists Series shows clearly that a hundred years ago the jesters had pretty well settled upon the topics that their countrymen were going to laugh at in the future—from the Washington merry-go-round to the pranks of local hillbillies. And as for the tactics of provoking the laugh, these old masters long since have demonstrated the art of titillating the risibilities. There is at times mirth of the highbrow variety in their pages: neat repartee, literary parody, Attic salt, and devastating irony. High seriousness of purpose often underlies their fun, for many of them wrote with the conviction that a column of humor was more effective than a page of editorials in bringing about reform or combating entrenched prejudices. All of the time-honored devices of the lowbrow comedians also abound: not only the sober-faced exaggeration of the tall tale, outrageous punning, and grotesque spelling, but a boisterous Homeric joy in the rough-and-tumble. There may be more beneath the surface, however, for as one of their number, J. K. Bangs, once remarked, these old humorists developed "the exuberance of feeling and a resentment of restraint that have helped to make us the free and independent people that we are." The native humor is indubitably American, for it is infused with the customs, associations, convictions, and tastes of the American people.

PROFESSOR CLARENCE GOHDES
Duke University
Durham, North Carolina

January, 1969

FINLEY PETER DUNNE

Finley Peter Dunne was born on West Adams Street, Chicago, in 1867 and died on Long Island in 1936. At the age of seventeen, after graduation at the bottom of his high school class of fifty, he was hired as a reporter by the Chicago *Herald*. He rose rapidly in the profession, and was a city editor at the age of twenty-one. Part of his success was due to the fact that he was the first reporter to realize that the public wanted full narrative descriptions of baseball games, not just the final scores. In 1900, Dunne went to New York to become Editor of William C. Whitney's *Morning Telegraph*. His next position was that of part-owner and Editor of *Collier's Weekly*. When that review was sold he retired to Long Island, and turned out practically no work after 1911. Dunne was married in 1902 to Margaret Abbott.

Most of the "Dooley" sketches appeared between 1893 and 1905. Dunne wrote more than seven hundred of these "marvelous little satires, each perfectly constructed, with a twist at the end as incomparable as the last line of a sonnet" (Henry Seidel Canfield). Martin Dooley (first called Colonel McNeery) is a Chicago Irishman, a philosophical bartender who comments in a rich brogue upon the contemporary social and political scene. This dialect is not only witty and pleasing to the ear, but was probably the only way Dunne could get his ideas in print in his censorious age. It was no light matter to attack figures such as Andrew Carnegie, McKinley, Queen Victoria; or the chauvinism of the Spanish-American War; or the Business Ethic, or Social Darwinism. Sociological commentary and the muckraker's hatred of oppression and injustice appear behind the *persona* of the jester. Of the Negro, Dooley says, "He'll ayether have to go to th' north an' be a subjick race, or stay in the south an' be an objick lesson." And of Manifest Destiny: "I have seen America spread out fr'm th' Atlantic to the Pacific, with a branch office iv the Standard Ile Comp'ny in ivry hamlet." The Dooley sketches were read by nearly everyone in public life, probably with more apprehension than amusement by those whom he attacked. Lloyd Morris describes Dunne's appeal as being like "a social plumb line. It not only struck the plain people at the bottom but reached to the intellectuals at the top. He was a favorite of such improbable readers as Henry Adams and Henry James." Another critic remarked that "if all the newspaper files and histories were destroyed between the years 1898 and 1910, and nothing remained but Mr. Dooley's observations, they would be enough" to reconstruct the life of those years.

Dunne's satires belong to that rarest of literary genres—the newspaper column that remains as topical today as it was when written. His remarks on stuffed shirts and hypocrites in finance and politics, war profiteers, and the gutter press—as well as lighter topics such as weight-reducing, the American family, and novel-reading as escape—are still pertinent. His philosophical dissertations such as "The Pursuit of Riches," in which life is compared to a Pullman dining car, where you never get what you order, but "it's pretty good if your appetite ain't keen and you care for the scenery" are good reading regardless of one's political or social views. It is hoped that all of his works will find their way back into print, for Dunne was second only to Mark Twain as an American humorist.

Upper Saddle River, N. J.   F. C. S.
May, 1969

THE KING IN HIS
SHIRT-SLEEVES

Dissertations
by Mr. Dooley

By the Author of
"Mr. Dooley's Philosophy"
"Mr. Dooley's Opinions," etc.

London and New York
Harper & Brothers Publishers
1906

Contents

Contents

DISSERTATIONS
By Mr. Dooley

THE KING IN HIS SHIRT-SLEEVES

"I SEE be th' pa-apers," said Mr. Dooley, "that th' King iv Biljum has been havin' throuble with wan iv his fam'ly."

"Th' poor man," said Mr. Hennessy. "What was it about?"

"Oh, faith, th' usual thing," said Mr. Dooley. "She marrid some wan th' king, her father, didn't like. Th' man iv her choice was not her akel. He was on'y a jook or a prince or something like that—a good-fellow, d'ye mind, sober, industhrees an' affictionate, but iv lowly exthraction. But that ain't what I wanted to talk to ye about. Th' throubles iv a king with his fam'ly ain't anny more inthrestin' thin th' throubles iv a plumber or a baseball player. It's th' same thing—th' food, th' cost iv th' new tile, th' familyar face at breakfast, th' girl runnin' off an' marryin' a jook or a clerk in a butcher-shop. What I've been thinkin' about is how long th' kings can stand havin' all these things known about thim.

[3]

" Whin I was a boy, if a king fell out with his
folks, no wan knew iv it but th' earls an' markesses
an' jooks that overheerd th' row while they were
waitin' on th' table. They didn't say annything,
but wrote it down in a note-book an' published it
afther they were dead. Whin th' king passed th'
butther-plate so high to his wife that it caught her
in th' eye, it was a rile secret. Whin his rile spouse
pulled his majesty around th' room be th' hair iv
th' head, th' tale remained in th' fam'ly till it got
into histhry. Whin wan iv th' princesses threatened
to skip with a jook, th' king touched th' spring iv
th' thrap-dure, an' her rile highness, Augoostina
Climintina Sofia Maria Mary Ann, wint down among
th' coal an' th' potatoes, an' niver was heerd iv
again.

" But nowadays 'tis diff'rent. Th' window-shades
is up at th' king's house as well as ivrywhere else.
Th' gas is lighted, an' we see his majesty stormin'
around because th' dinner is late, kickin' th' rile dog,
whalin' th' princes iv th' blood with a lath, brushin'
his crown befure goin' out, shavin' his chin, sneakin'
a dhrink at bedtime, jawin' his wife an' makin'
faces at his daughter. Th' princess called at th'
King iv Biljum's house yisterdah an' insisted on seein'
th' ol' man. A stormy intherview followed. ' I told
ye niver to darken this dure again till ye left that
loafer iv a husband iv ye'ers,' says his majesty. ' I
come here to get me clothes,' says her rile highness.
' If ye don't give thim up I'll call next time with a
constable,' she says. ' Don't make me f'rget me sex
an' lay hands on a woman,' says his majesty. ' Clear
out iv this befure I cease bein' a king an' become a

parent,' he says. Her rile highness had a fit iv
hysterics at this, an' th' king tore around th' parlor,
knockin' over chairs an' kickin' at th' furniture.
Half an hour later th' princess emerged, followed be
th' king in a smokin'-jacket. At th' dure he hollered
at her: 'Ye'll stay away fr'm here if ye know what's
good f'r ye.' 'I'll have th' law on ye,' says th'
princess as she wint off on her bicycle.

"An' there ye ar-re. Th' times has changed, an'
th' kings lives in th' sthreet with th' rest iv us. It 'll
be th' death iv thim. No wan respects annybody they
know. To be a king an' get away with it, a man must
keep out iv sight. Th' minyit people know that a
king talks like other people, that he has th' same kind
iv aches that we have, that his head is bald, that his
back teeth are filled, that he dhrinks too much, that
him an' his wife don't get along, an' that whin they
quarrel they don't make a reg'lar declaration iv war,
but jaw at each other like Mullarky an' his spouse,
their subjicks say: 'Why, this here fellow is no
betther thin th' rest iv us. How comes he to have
so good a job? Down with him!' An' down he
comes.

"Ye take this here King iv Biljum, Hinnissy. I
know all about him, f'r Dorney had th' room next
to him whin he was in Europe. an' he heerd him
snore! Think iv that! Think iv hearin' a king
snore an' meeting' him th' nex' mornin' an' bowin'
to him! If this King iv Biljum knew his own business he'd on'y come out iv th' house wanst a year, an'
thin he'd have his face veiled. Instead iv that he's
all over th' wurruld. He's in th' rubber business.
He's th' rubber king. If ye buy a garden hose, see

[5]

that th' name iv Leepold, King iv th' Biljums, is on th' nozzle. He makes gum shoes, nursin'-bottles, raincoats, combs, an' teethin'-rings. Ivry week he has to set down with th' boord iv directors iv his rubber comp'ny an' hope f'r rain.

"He takes his pleasure befure all th' wurruld. If ye go into a hotel annywhere in Europe, Dorney says, ye can see him settin' in a rockin'-chair smokin' a seegar an' chattin' with th' dhrummers. 'Who's that old la-ad with th' whiskers?' says Dorney to th' clerk. 'That's ol' Leepold, King iv Biljum,' says th' clerk. 'He's our star-boarder,' he says. 'Who's that ol' fool cuttin' up with th' chorus girls at th' next table?' says Dorney to th' waither at th' res-thrant. 'It's Leepold, King iv Biljum,' says th' waither. 'He's in here ivry night. I guess his home life ain't very atthractive.' 'Th' King iv Biljum in his autymobill ran into a milk-cart yisterdah on th' bullyvard,' says th' pa-apers. 'In th' altercation that followed, th' lowly milkman walloped his majesty severely. . . . Th' King iv Biljum wint up in an airship yisterdah an' aftherwards took dinner with Santos-Dumont, Colonel Tom Ochiltree, Tod Sloan, an' Chansy Depoo. . . . Th' King iv Biljum an' Maddymozelle Toorooro, th' Spanish dancer, danced a fandango at th' Caffy de Paree las' night. His majesty paid f'r all breakage. . . . Ivry afthernoon th' King iv Biljum can be seen on th' bullyvard. Th' statement that th' droop in his right eye is permanent is not correct. . . . Th' King iv Biljum was seen in a smokin'-car in th' limited thrain yisterdah, in his shirt-sleeves, playin' siven-up with a few frinds. Whin th' thrain stopped f'r lunch his majesty hopped out, et a dish iv baked beans, a section iv grape-pie an' a cup iv coffee, an' had a pleasant chat with th' cashier, who used to wurruk at th' Palace hotel an' knows him well. It was "Leep" an' "Mame" with thim to th' delight iv th' hangers-on at th' station, who are very fond iv both iv thim.'

"An' so it goes. Now, supposin', Hinnissy, that ye was a Biljum, whativer that is, an' Leepold was ye'er king. Ye see him on th' sthreets ivry day snortin' around in an autymobill, with dust in his whiskers an' cinders in his eyes that makes him wink ivry time a nurse-girl goes by; ye see him dhrinkin' at th' bar, bettin' on th' races, feedin' himsilf with common food, quarrellin' with his wife, kickin' his daughter out-iv-dures, an' mannyfacthrin' rubber boots. Wud ye bow down to him whin he come out iv th' concert-hall with th' sixtet? Wud ye fling ye'er caubeen in th' air an' holler, 'Long live th' King,' or 'Veev th' roy,' or 'Hock Leepold,' or whativer 'tis up to a Biljum to holler at such a time? Ye wud not. Ye'd say to ye'ersilf: 'Well, if that fellow's a king, so'm I. I think I'll move him over an' take th' job mesilf. He's a nice ol' man, runs an autymobill pretty well, is a succissful flirt, an unsuccissful husband, a five-cints-on-th'-dollar failure as a father, an' a pretty good mannyfacthrer iv hose. He's all iv these things. But as a king, is he worth th' wages? I guess not!' An' whin Leepold come out some mornin', it 'd not be ye'er hat that come off but his.

"Th' thruth is, Hinnissy, that th' kings have got to take a brace. If ye have anny kings among ye'er frinds, tell thim I said so. Th' king business is like a poker-game. It's been goin' on f'r a long time, an' whiniver it put its money in we lay down thinkin' we was up again' a hand full iv kings an' queens. But th' minyit they'se a show-down, th' bluff is over. Thin we see that th' hand that we were afraid iv is composed intirely iv sivins, sixes, an' dooces, with maybe wan jack that looks like a king on'y to near-sighted people. A show-down is death to rilety. Tell ye'er frinds to stay in dures an' niver show their faces at th' window, an' maybe we won't get on to thim."

"I don't know anny kings," said Mr Hennessy.

"Well, I wudden't thry to," said Mr. Dooley. "It wud be all right f'r ye, but ye'er wife mightn't like it."

ROYAL DOINGS

ROYAL DOINGS

"GR-REAT throuble among th' crowned heads iv Europe," said Mr. Dooley.

"What's goin' on?" asked Mr. Hennessy.

"Oh, ivrything that people get arrested f'r," said Mr. Dooley. "Dhrunkenness an' disord'ly conduck, assault an' batthry, riot an' elopemints. Th' King iv Biljum has fired his daughter fr'm th' house again, an' she's down at th' newspaper office dictatin' th' sad story iv her life. Th' Czar iv Rooshya is unaisy in his head, an' sets all day long while an American hypnotist makes passes in front iv him. Th' Impror iv Germany has been sayin' nasty, spiteful things about th' King iv England behind his back, an' if they iver meet some wan is goin' to th' flure. Th' King iv Spain is lookin' f'r his august mother to slug her f'r wantin' to marry again. An' th' happy Hapsburgs are batin' polismen, shootin' thimsilves, an' runnin' off with ladies iv th' chorus.

"Ivrywhere on th' continent iv Europe 'tis th' same thing. Ye see yon palace raisin' its lofty head in yon garden? Think ye, Hinnissy, that all is happiness an' contint within thim yon marble walls? It ain't so. In that stately pile th' dishes is passin' through th' air th' same as in th' humble abodes iv th' poor. His impeeryal majesty is dhraggin' her

2   [11]

impeeryal majesty around th' gr-reat hall iv state
be th' hair iv th' head. Th' oaken walls resounds with
cries iv: ' Let go iv me ear.' Occasionally a king
comes out iv th' goolden dure pursooed be crowns,
sciptres, ol' masthers, carved furniture, an' books.
Who is that woman at th' window iv th' palace?
'Tis her serene altess Sophia Maria Victorine Lino-
lea Bejabers Bezaza Carebella Deliria Maud, Crown-
Princess iv Weisenbrod, whoopin' f'r th' polis. Th'
coort news an' th' polis news is th' same thing: ' Her
majesty took th' air in th' garden where she met his
majesty, after which she took th' count.' ' Th' queen
was seen dhrivin' yisterdah. Her eye is much betther.' ' Owin' to th' state of her majesty's rile tem-
per, his majesty rayceived th' cabinet Thursdah in
th' coal-cellar. Her majesty disturbed th' council
be hollerin' down th' furnace-pipes an' poundin' on
th' flure. Th' chanceller iv th' exchequer on lavin'
th' residence through th' laundhry shute was felled
be a pianny stool.' ' It is announced that her majesty
has eloped with th' coort plumber.'

"An' so it goes. Th' papers are filled with rile
throubles. A poor dimmycrat 'ain't got a chanst.
He cud bate his wife all night an' niver be noticed
be th' press. Home-made elopemints receive no attintion. Lave me tell ye about th' romance iv th'
Crown-Princess iv Saxony. It's wan iv th' mos' romantic things I've seen lately. Not bein' a romantic
speaker, I can't tell it to ye th' way I ought to, but
I'll tell it me own simple way. Manny years ago,
wan iv th' ladies iv th' Hapsburg fam'ly marrid th'
Crown-Prince iv Saxony. Th' house iv Hapsburg
is th' rough-house iv Europe. Th' fam'ly is gay

[12]

dogs, an' Sophy J. Hapsburg inherited their thraits. She met th' crown-prince some time afther they were marrid, an' f'r thirty or forty years they lived together happily, but not f'r long, an' raised a large or German fam'ly. But th' bloom soon come off th' peach. In less thin a quarter iv a cinchry, Sophy begun to tire iv th' dull, monotynous life iv th' Saxon coort. She saw that Ludwig was not th' man she expicted him to be, but a coorse nature, who cud not undherstand th' gropin's iv a rayfined spirit. Whin she got to be fifty or sixty years iv age, she got onto the fact that she had a soul.

" Whin a woman discovers she has a soul, Hinnissy, 'tis time she was sint to a rest-cure. It niver comes till late in life, an' ye can't tell what she'll do about it. She may join a woman's club, an' she may go on th' stage. 'Tis sthrange how manny ladies with wan leg in th' grave wud like to see th' other in th' front row iv th' chorus. Ludwig did not know what was the matther with his spouse. He had niver suffered fr'm annything that he cudden't thrace to food or dhrink. He had no soul. Men sildom have. Whin ye see a man with a soul, side-step him. Profissor Giron had a soul. They was no soulfuller person thin Alphonse Giron in all th' land iv Saxony. Although on'y a poor young man, hired f'r to tache bad language, which is Fr-rinch, to th' childher, he was full iv wicked impulses. He didn't have much else, but he had a soul. Th' outcome was certain. If a woman with a soul doesn't lose th' soul pretty quick an' get back her common-sinse, she'll lose both. Wan day, whin Ludwig was down at th' brew'ry, Sophy packed a few things in a bag. Alphonse

[13]

helped himsilf to Ludwig's cigars, an' they wint to
th' deepo an' took th' nine-nine. They're in a hotel
in Switzerland now, talkin' to rayporthers an' fixin'
up th' allimony. Alphonse thinks it ought to be
lib'ral. He wud scorn to discuss details, but he feels
Ludwig ought to raymimber th' past an' dig deep.
Sophy thinks so too, but she knows if Ludwig is
close about it her an' Alphonse can go to Paris an'
make a livin' writin' pothry. They'se money in
pothry if you know how to get it out. They ixpict to
start up shop in Paris in about a month. Alphonse
told th' bar-tinder at th' hotel so. They're gr-reat
frinds, Alphonse an' th' bar-tinder, an' often spind
th' afthernoon together while Sophy is up-stairs talkin' about her soul. Nobody hears much about Ludwig or th' childher. But he's holdin' out sthrong
again' givin' up too much money.

"Ain't it a wondherful romance, Hinnissy?
Thank Hiven, th' days iv chivalry ain't entirely
passed whin a woman iv th' rile house iv Hapsburg
can turn her back on th' glitter iv th' coort an' th'
care iv th' childher an' skip out with a kindhred soul
about th' age iv her oldest. I've niver been so excited
about annything in me life. I've looked f'r news about
it in th' pa-aper ivry day, an' me frinds iv th' press
have not disappointed me. Happy Sophy! Happy
Alphonse! What a good time they're goin' to have
whin Alphonse goes out with a pome an' comes home
with a parcel iv pig's feet! It's a beautiful, thrillin'
story."

"I don't see annything beautiful about it," said
Mr. Hennessy. "It's just a crazy-headed ol' lunytic
iv a woman runnin' away fr'm her childher."

Royal Doings

" Hinnissy," said Mr. Dooley, sternly, " ye f'rget Sophy's station. Whin an ol' crazy-headed lunytic iv a woman skips out 'tis a crime; whin an ol' crazy-headed lunytic iv a duchess does it, it's a scandal; but whin an ol' crazy-headed lunytic iv a princess does it, it's a romance."

ORATORY

ORATORY

"**D**ID ye iver make a speech?" asked Mr. Hennessy.

"I did wanst," said Mr. Dooley. "Ivry thrue-born American regards himsilf as a gr-reat orator, an' I always had a pitcher iv mesilf in me mind standin' befure a large an' admirin' bunch if me fellow-pathrites an' thrillin' thim with me indignation or convulsin' thim with me wit. Manny times have I lay in bed awake, seein' mesilf at th' head iv a table, poorin' out wurruds iv goolden eloquence fr'm th' depths iv me lungs. I made a pretty pitcher, I must say,—ca'm, dignified, a perfect masther iv mesilf an' me audjeence. Th' concoorse shrieked with laughter wan minyit, an' rose to their feet in frenzied applause th' next. In all me dhreams I wore a white necktie an' a long-tailed coat, because I have a theery that all thrue eloquence comes fr'm th' tails iv th' coat, an' if ye made an orator change into a short coat he wud become deef an' dumb. As I sat down afther me burst iv gleamin' wurruds, th' audjeence rose an' cheered f'r five minyits, an' Sinitor Beveridge, th' silver spout iv th' Wabash, who was to follow me, slinked out iv th' room.

"So wan day, whin th' Archey Road Improvement Comity give their grand banket, an' th' chairman asked me to make a few appropriated remarks in place iv Chancy Depoo, I told thim I wud toss off some orathory just so th' boys wud not be disappointed.

"I didn't write out th' speech No great orator who has niver made a speech needs to. I merely jotted down a few interruptions be th' audjeence; like this, Hinnissy: (Great Applause) (Loud an' continyous laughter), (Cries iv 'Good,' 'Hear, hear'), (Cries iv 'No, no,' 'Go on'), (Wild cheerin', th' audjeence risin' to their feet an' singin', 'For he's a jolly good fellow, which nobody can deny').

"An' havin' arranged all these nicissry details, I wint to th' banket. I knew ivry man there, an' thurly despised thim. There wasn't wan iv thim that I considered me intellechool equal. At wan time or another ivry wan iv thim had come to me f'r advice. But somehow, Hinnissy, th' minyit I looked down on what Hogan calls th' sea iv upturned faces dhrinkin', I begun to feel onaisy. I wasn't afraid iv anny wan iv thim, mind ye. Man f'r man they were me frinds. But altogether they were me inimy. I cudden't set still. I had come with an appytite, but I cudden't eat. I had a lump in me throat as big as an apple. I felt quare in th' pit iv me stomach. I noticed that me hands were moist. I thried to talk to th' man next to me, but I cudden't hear what he said. Wan orator afther another was peltin' th' audjeence with remarks out iv th' *Fourth Reader*, an' I cudden't listen to thim. All th' time I was thinkin': 'In a few minyits they'll detect ye, Martin Dooley, th' countherfeit Demostheens.' Th' room swam befure me eyes; there was a buzzin' in me ears. I had all th' symptoms iv Doctor Bunyan's customers. I thried to collect me thoughts, but they were off th' reservation. I wud've

gone out if I thought I cud walk, an' I was goin'
to thry whin I heerd th' chairman mention me name.
It sounded as if it come out iv a cheap phonograft.

"I f'rgot to tell ye, Hinnissy, that in thinkin' iv
me gr-reat effort I had rehearsed a few motions to
inthrajooce th' noble sintimints that was to bubble
up fr'm me. At th' mention iv me name, an' durin'
th' cheerin' that followed, I was goin' to lean forward
with me head bowed an' me hand on th' edge iv th'
table an' a demoor smile on me face that cud be
thranslated: ' Th' gr-reat man is amused, but wudden't have ye know it f'r wurulds.' Whin th' cheerin' throng had exhausted its strenth I intinded to
rise slowly, place me chair in front iv me, an' leanin'
lightly on th' back iv it, bow first to wan side an'
thin th' other, an' remarks: ' Misther Chairman, a-a-
and gint-elmen: Whin I see so manny smilin' faces
befure me on this suspicious occasion, I am reminded
iv a little incidint—' An' so on.

"Well, glory be, Hinnissy, I can hardly go on
with th' story. It was twinty-five years ago, but I
can't think iv it without a feelin' at th' end iv me
fingers as though I had scraped a plasther wall. At
th' mention iv me name I lept to me feet, knockin'
over all th' dishes an' glasses in me neighborhood.
I stepped on me neighbor's toes an' bumped into
th' chairman, who was still tellin' what he wanted me to think he thought iv me. I rolled me napkin up into a ball an' thrust it into me pants pocket.
I become blind, deaf, an' dumb. I raymimber makin'
a few grunts, fightin' an imaginary inimy with me
fists an' dhroppin' in me chair, a broken four-flush
Pathrick Hinnery. I've niver got me repytation

back. Most iv th' people thought I was dhrunk.
Th' more charitable said I was on'y crazy. Th' impressyon still remains in th' ward that I'm a victim iv
apoplexy.

" Well, sir, 'tis a sthrange thing this here oratory.
Ye see a man that ye wudden't ask to direct ye to th'
post-office get on his feet an' make a speech that wud
melt th' money in ye'er pocket. Another man comes
along that ye think a reg'lar little know-all, an' whin
he thries to make a speech to a Sunday-school class
he gives an imitation iv a victim iv croup, delusions
iv pursuit, an' Saint Vitus's dance. If he don't do
that he bombards his fellow-man with th' kind iv a
composition that they keep boys afther school f'r.
Carney made wan iv that kind at this banket. Carney has a head as hard as a cocynut. He wanted a
new bridge built acrost th' crick, an' he was goin' to
talk about that at th' banket. On th' way over he
tol' me about it. He argyed so well that he convinced me, an' I'm wan iv th' most indignant taxpayers f'r a poor man that ye iver knew. I thought
whin he got up he wud say somethin' like this:
' Boys, we need a new bridge. Th' prisint wan is a
disgrace to th' ward. Curtin's horse fell through it
last week. By jimuneddy, if Billy O'Brien don't
get us a new bridge we'll bate him at th' prim'ries.'

" That wud have gone fine, f'r Curtin was a loud
an' pop'lar fish-peddler. But what did Carney do?
He niver was within four thousan' miles iv a swing
bridge acrost th' Chicago River. Says he : ' Gintlemen:
We ar-re th' most gloryous people that iver infested
th' noblest counthry that th' sun iver shone upon,'
he says. ' We meet here to-night,' he says, ' undher

that starry imblim that flaps above freemen's homes
in ivry little hamlet fr'm where rolls th' Oregon in
majestic volume to th' sun-kist wathers iv th' Passyfic to where th' Pimsicoddy shimmers adown th'
pine-culad hills iv Maine,' he says. 'Th' hand iv
time,' he says, 'marches with stately steps acrost th'
face iv histhry, an' as I listen to its hoof-beats I hear
a still, small voice that seems to say that Athens,
Greece, Rawhm, an' E-gypt an' iver on an' upward,
an' as long as th' stars in their courses creep through
eternity an' twinkle as they creep, recallin' th'
wurruds iv our gr-reat pote, " Twinkling stars ar-re
laughin' love, laughin' at you an' me," an' a counthry, gintlemen, that stands to-day as sure as to-
morrah's sun rises an' kisses th' flag that floats f'r
all. Now, gintlemen, it is growin' late, an' I will
not detain ye longer, but I have a few wurruds to
say. I appeal fr'm Philip dhrunk to Philip sober.'
That ended th' speech an' th' banket. Th' chairman's name was Philip. Th' second Philip that Carney mintioned was not there.

" I guess a man niver becomes an orator if he has
anything to say, Hinnissy. If a lawyer thinks his
client is innocint he talks to th' jury about th' crime.
But if he knows where th' pris'ner hid th' plunder,
he unfurls th' flag, throws out a few remarks about
th' flowers an' th' bur-rds, an' asks th' twelve good
men an' thrue not to break up a happy Christmas,
but to sind this man home to his wife an' childher,
an' Gawd will bless thim if they ar-re iver caught in
th' same perdicymint. Whiniver I go to a pollytical
meetin', an' th' laad with th' open-wurruk face men-
tions Rome or Athens I grab f'r me hat. I know

he's not goin' to say anything that ought to keep me out iv bed. I also bar all language about bur-rds an' flowers; I don't give two cints about th' Oregon, whether it rolls or staggers to th' sea; an' I'll rap in th' eye anny man that attimpts to wrap up his sicond-hand oratory in th' American flag. There ought to be a law against usin' th' American flag f'r such purposes. I hope to read in th' pa-aper some day that Joe Cannon was arrested f'r usin' th' American flag to dicorate a speech on th' tariff, an' sintinced to two years solitary confinemint with Sinitor Berridge. An' be hivens, I don't want anny man to tell me that I'm a mimber iv wan iv th' grandest races th' sun has iver shone on. I know it already. If I wasn't I'd move out.

"No, sir, whin a man has something to say an' don't know how to say it, he says it pretty well. Whin he has something to say an' knows how to say it he makes a gr-reat speech. But whin he has nawthin' to say an' has a lot iv wurruds that come with a black coat, he's an orator. There's two things I don't want at me fun'ral. Wan is an oration, an' th' other is wax-flowers. I class thim alike."

"Ye're on'y mad because ye failed," said Mr. Hennessy.

"Well," said Mr. Dooley, "what betther reason d'ye want? Besides, I didn't fail as bad as I might. I might have made th' speech."

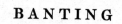

BANTING

BANTING

"I SEE th' good woman goin' by here at a gallop to-day," said Mr. Dooley.

"She's thryin' to rayjooce her weight," said Mr. Hennessy.

"What f'r?"

"I don't know. She looks all right," said Mr. Hennessy.

"Well," said Mr. Dooley, "'tis a sthrange thing. Near ivrybody I know is thryin' to rayjooce their weight. Why shud a woman want to be thin onless she is thin? Th' idee iv female beauty that all gr-reat men, fr'm Julius Cæsar to mesilf, has held, is much more like a bar'l thin a clothes-pole. Hogan tells me that Alexander's wife an' Cæsar's missus was no lightweights; Martha Wash'nton was short but pleasantly dumpy, an' Andhrew Jackson's good woman weighed two hundherd an' smoked a pipe. Hogan says that all th' potes he knows was in love with not to say fat, but ample ladies. Th' potes thimsilves was thin, but th' ladies was chubby. A pote, whin he has wurruked all day at th' type-writer, wants to rest his head on a shoulder that won't hurt. Shakespeare's wife was thin, an' they quarrelled. Th' lady that th' Eyetalian pote Dan-ty made a fool iv himsilf about was no skeliton. All th' pitchers iv beautiful women I've iver see

3

had manny curves an' sivral chins. Th' phottygraft iv Mary Queen iv Scots that I have in me room shows that she took on weight afther she had her dhress made. Th' collar looks to be chokin' her.

"But nowadays 'tis th' fashion to thry to emaciate ye'ersilf. I ate supper with Carney th' other day. It was th' will iv Hiven that Carney shud grow fat, but Carney has a will iv his own, an' f'r ten years he's been thryin' to look like Sinitor Fairbanks, whin his thrue model was Grover Cleveland. He used to scald himsilf ivry mornin' with a quart iv hot wather on gettin' up. That did him no good. Thin he thried takin' long walks. Th' long walk rayjooced him half a pound, and gave him a thirst that made him take on four pounds iv boodweiser. Thin he rented a horse, an' thried horseback ridin'. Th' horse liked his weight no more thin Carney did, an' Carney gained ten pounds in th' hospital. He thried starvin' himsilf, an' he lost two pounds an' his job f'r bein' cross to th' boss. Thin he raysumed his reg'lar meals, an' made up his mind to cut out th' sugar. I see him at breakfast wan mornin'. Nature had been kind to Carney in th' matther iv appytite. I won't tell ye what he consumed. It's too soon afther supper, an' th' room is close. But, annyhow, whin his wife had tottered in with th' last flap-jack an' fainted, an' whin I begun to wondher whether it wud be safe to stay, he hauled a little bottle fr'm his pocket an' took out a small pill. 'What's that?' says I. ''Tis what I take in place iv sugar,' says he. 'Sugar is fattenin', an' this rayjoocees th' weight,' says he. 'An' ar-re ye goin' to match that poor little tablet

against that breakfast?' says I. 'I am,' says he.
' Cow'rd,' says I.

"Th' latest thing that Carney has took up to
make th' fight again' Nature is called Fletching.
Did ye iver hear iv it? Well, they'se a lad be th'
name iv Fletcher who thinks so much iv his stomach
that he won't use it, an' he tells Carney that if he'll
ate on'y wan or two mouthfuls at ivry meal an' thurly
chew thim he will invinchooly be no more thin skin
an' bones an' very handsome to look at. In four
weeks a man who Fletches will lose forty pounds an'
all his frinds. Th' idee is that ye mumble ye'er food
f'r tin minyits with a watch in front iv ye.

"This night Carney was Fletching. It was a fine
supper. Th' table groaned beneath all th' indilicacies
iv th' season. We tucked our napkins undher our
chins an' prepared f'r a jaynial avenin'. Not so
Carney. He laid his goold watch on th' table, took
a mouthful iv mutton pie an' begun to Fletch. At
first Hogan thought he was makin' faces at him, but
I explained that he was crazy. I see be th' look in
Carney's eye that he didn't like th' explanation, but
we wint on with th' supper. Well, 'twas gloryous.
' Jawn, ye'er health. Pass th' beefsteak, Malachi.
Schwartzmeister, ol' boy, can't I help ye to th' part
that wint over th' fence last? What's that story?
Tell it over here, where Carney can't hear. It might
make him laugh an' hurt him with his frind Fletcher.
No? What? Ye don't say? An' didn't Carney
resint it? Haw, haw, haw! This eyesther sauce is th'
best I iver see. Michael, this is like ol' times. Look
at Schwartzmeister. He's Fletching, too. No, be
gorry, he's chokin'. I think Carney's watch has

stopped. No wondher; he's lookin' at it. Haw, haw, haw, haw, haw! A good joke on Carney. Did ye iver see such a face? Carney, me buck, ye look like a kinetoscope. What is a face without a stomach? Carney, ye make me nervous. If that there idol don't stop f'r a minyit I'll throw something at it. Carney, time's up. Ye win ye'er bet, but 'twas a foolish wan. I thought ye were goin' to push Fletcher in a wheel-barrow.'

"I've known Jawn Carney, man an' boy, f'r forty year, but I niver knew ontil that minyit that he was a murdhrer at heart. Th' look he give us whin he snapped his watch was tur-rble; but th' look he give th' dinner was aven worse. He set there f'r two mortal hours miditatin' what form th' assassynations wud take an' Fletchin' each wan iv us in his mind. I walked home with him to see that he came to no harm. Near th' house he wint into a baker's shop an' bought four pies an' a bag iv doughnuts. 'I've promised to take thim home to me wife,' he says. 'I thought she was out iv town,' says I. 'She'll be back in a week,' says he; 'an', annyhow, Misther Dooley, I'll thank ye not to be pryin' into me domestic affairs,' he says.

"An' there ye ar-re. What's th' use iv goin' up again' th' laws iv Nature, says I. If Nature intinded ye to be a little roly-poly, a little roly-poly ye'll be. They ain't annything to do that ye ought to do that 'll make ye thin an' keep ye thin. Th' wan thing in th' wurruld that 'll rayjooce ye surely is lack iv sleep, an' who wants to lose his mind with his flesh. I'll guarantee with th' aid iv an alarm-clock to make anny man a livin' skeliton in thirty days. A lady with a young baby won't niver get no chubbier, nor th' gintleman, its father. Th' on'y ginooine anti-fat threatment is sickness, worry, throuble, an insomnya. Th' scales ain't anny judge iv beauty or health. To be beautiful is to be nachral. Ye have gr-reat nachral skinny beauty, while my good looks is more buxom. Whin I see an ol' fool in a sweater an' two coats sprintin' up th' sthreet an' groanin' at ivry step I want to join with th' little boys that ar-re throwin' bricks at him. If he takes off th' flesh that Nature has wasted on his ongrateful frame his skin won't fit him. They'se nawthin' more hee-jous to look at than a fat man that has rayjooced his weight. He looks as though he had bought his coverin' at an auction. It bags undher th' eyes an' don't fit in th' neck.

" A man is foolish that thries to be too kind to his stomach, annyhow. Fletcher's idee is that th' human stomach is a sort iv little Lord Fauntleroy. If ye give it much to do it will pine away. But Dock Casey tells me 'tis a gr-reat, husky, good-natured pugilist that 'll take on most annything that comes along. It will go to wurruk with grim resolution on a piece iv hard coal. It will get th' worst iv it, but what I mane to say is that it fears no foe, an' doesn't draw th' color-line. I wud put it in th' heavy-weight class, an' it ought to be kept there. It requires plenty iv exercise to be at its best, an' if it doesn't get enough it loses its power until a chocolate eclair might win against it. It musn't be allowed to shirk its jooties. It shud be kept in thrainin', an' says Dock Casey, if its owner is a good matchmaker, an' doesn't back it again' opponents that ar-re out iv its class or too manny at wan time, it will still be doin' well whin th' brain is on'y fit f'r light exercise."

"D'ye expict to go on accumylatin' flesh to th' end iv ye'er days?" asked Mr. Hennessy.

"I do that," said Mr. Dooley. "I expict to make me frinds wurruk f'r me to th' last. They'll be no gayety among th' pallbearers at me obsequies. They'll have no sinycure. Befure they get through with me they'll know they've been to a fun'ral."

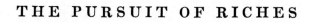

THE PURSUIT OF RICHES

THE PURSUIT OF RICHES

"DEAR me, I wisht I had money," said Mr. Hennessy.

"So do I," said Mr. Dooley. "I need it."

"Ye wudden't get it fr'm me," said Mr. Hennessy.

"If I didn't," said Mr. Dooley, "'twould be because I was poor or tired. But what d'ye want money f'r? Supposin' I lost me head an' handed over all me accumylated wealth? What wud ye do with that gr-reat fortune? Befure ye had spint half iv it ye'd be so sick ye'd come to me an' hand me back th' remainin' eighteen dollars.

"A man has more fun wishin' f'r th' things he hasn't got thin injyin' th' things he has got. Life, Hinnissy, is like a Pullman dinin'-car: a fine bill iv fare but nawthin' to eat. Ye go in fresh an' hungry, tuck ye'er napkin in ye'er collar, an' square away at th' list iv groceries that th' black man hands ye. What 'll ye have first? Ye think ye'd like to be famous, an' ye ordher a dish iv fame an' bid th' waither make it good an' hot. He's gone an age, an' whin he comes back ye'er appytite is departed. Ye taste th' ordher, an' says ye: 'Why, it's cold an' full iv broken glass.' 'That's th' way we always

[35]

sarve Fame on this car,' says th' coon. 'Don't ye think ye'd like money f'r the' second coorse? Misther Rockyfellar over there has had forty-two helpin's,' says he. 'It don't seem to agree with him,' says ye, 'but ye may bring me some,' ye say. Away he goes, an' stays till ye're bald an' ye'er teeth fall out an' ye set dhrummin' on th' table an' lookin' out at th' scenery. By-an'-by he comes back with ye'er ordher, but jus' as he's goin' to hand it to ye Rockyfellar grabs th' plate. 'What kind iv a car is this?' says ye. 'Don't I get annything to eat? Can't ye give me a little happiness?' 'I wudden't ricommend th' happiness,' says th' waither. 'It's canned, an' it kilt th' las' man that thried it.' 'Well, gracious,' says ye. 'I've got to have something. Give me a little good health, an' I'll thry to make a meal out iv that.' 'Sorry, sir,' says th' black man, 'but we're all out iv good health. Besides,' he says, takin' ye gently be th' ar-rm, 'we're comin' into th' deepo an' ye'll have to get out,' he says.

"An' there ye ar-re. Ye'll niver get money onless ye fix th' waither and grab th' dishes away fr'm th' other passengers. An' ye won't do that. So ye'll niver be rich. No poor man iver will be. Wan iv th' sthrangest things about life is that th' poor, who need th' money th' most, ar-re th' very wans that niver have it. A poor man is a poor man, an' a rich man is a rich man. Ye're ayther born poor or rich. It don't make anny diff'rence whether or not ye have money to begin with. If ye're born to be rich ye'll be rich, an' if ye're born to be poor ye'll be poor. Th' buttons on ye'er vest tell th' story. Rich man, poor man, beggar man, rich man, or wurruds to that effect. I always find that I have ayether two buttons or six.

" A poor man is a man that rayfuses to cash in. Ye don't get annything f'r nawthin', an' to gather in a millyon iv thim beautiful green promises ye have to go down ivry day with something undher ye'er ar-rm to th' great pawn-shop. Whin Hogan wants four dollars he takes th' clock down to Moses. Whin Rockyfellar wants tin millyon he puts up his peace iv mind or his health or something akelly valyable. If Hogan wud hock his priceless habit iv sleepin' late in th' mornin' he wud be able to tell th' time iv day whin he got up without goin' to th' corner dhrug-store.

" Look at McMullin. He's rowlin' in it. It bulges his pocket an' inflates his convarsation. Whin he looks at me I always feel that he's wondhrin' how much I'd bring at a forced sale. Well, McMullin an' I had th' same start, about forty yards behind scratch an' Vanderbilt to beat. They always put th' best man in anny race behind th' line. Befure McMullin gets through he'll pass Vanderbilt, carry away th' tape on his shoulders, an' run two or three times around th' thrack. But me an' him started th' same way. Th' on'y diff-rence was that he wud cash in an' I wudden't. Th' on'y thing I iver ixpicted to get money on was me dhream iv avarice. I always had that. I cud dhream iv money as hard as anny man ye iver see, an' can still. But I niver thought iv wurrukin' f'r it. I've always looked on it as dishon'rable to wurruk f'r money. I wurruk f'r exercise, an' I get what th' lawyers call an honorary-ium be dilutin' th' spirits. Th' on'y way I iver expict

to make a cint is to have it left to me be a rich re-
lation, an' I'm th' pluthycrat iv me fam'ly, or to stub
me toe on a gambler's roll or stop a runaway horse
f'r Pierpont Morgan. An' th' horse mustn't be runnin' too fast. He must be jus' goin' to stop, on'y
Morgan don't know it, havin' fainted. Whin he
comes to he finds me at th' bridle, modestly waitin'
f'r him to weep on me bosom. But as f'r scramblin'
down-town arly in th' mornin' an' buyin' chattel
morgedges, I niver thought iv it. I get up at siven
o'clock. I wudden't get up at a quarther to siven
f'r all th' money I dhream about.

"I have a lot iv things ar-round here I cud cash
in if I cared f'r money. I have th' priceless gift iv
laziness. It's made me what I am, an' that's th' very
first thing ivry rich man cashes in. Th' millyionaires
ye r-read about thryin' to give th' rest iv th' wurruld
a good time be runnin' over thim in autymobills all
started with a large stock iv indolence, which they
cashed in. Now, whin they cud enjoy it they can't
buy it back. Thin I have me good health. Ye can
always get money on that. An' I have me frinds;
I refuse to cash thim in. I don't know that I cud
get much on thim, but if I wanted to be a millyionaire
I'd tuck you an' Hogan an' Donahue undher me
ar-rm an' carry ye down to Mose.

"McMullin did cash. He had no more laziness
thin me, but he cashed it in befure he was twinty-
wan. He cashed in his good health, a large stock iv
fam'ly ties, th' affection iv his wife, th' comforts iv
home, an' wan frind afther another. Wanst in a
while, late in life, he'd thry to redeem a pledge, but
he niver cud. They wasn't annything in th' wurruld

that McMullin wudden't change f'r th' money. He cashed in his vote, his pathreetism, his rellijon, his rilitives, and finally his hair. Ye heerd about him, didn't ye? He's lost ivry hair on his head. They ain't a spear iv vigitation left on him. He's as arid as th' desert iv Sahara. His head looks like an iceberg in th' moonlight. He was in here th' other day, bewailin' his fate. ' It's a gr-reat misfortune,' says he. ' What did ye get f'r it?' says I. ' That's th' throuble,' says he. ' Well, don't complain,' says I. ' Think what ye save in barber's bills,' I says, an' he wint away, lookin' much cheered up.

" No, Hinnissy, you and I, me frind, was not cut out be Provydence to be millyionaires. If ye had nawthin' but money ye'd have nawthin' but money. Ye can't ate it, sleep it, dhrink it, or carry it away with ye. Ye've got a lot iv things that McMullin hasn't got. Annybody that goes down to Mose's won't see ye'er peace iv mind hangin' in th' window as an unredeemed pledge. An', annyhow, if ye're really in search iv a fortune perhaps I cud help ye. Wud a dollar an' a half be anny use to ye?"

" Life is full iv disappointments," said Mr. Hennessy.

" It is," said Mr. Dooley, " if ye feel that way. It's thrue that a good manny have thried it, an' none have come back f'r post-gradjate coorse. But still it ain't so bad as a career f'r a young man. Ye niver get what ye ordher, but it's pretty good if ye'er appytite ain't keen an' ye care f'r th' scenery."

SHORT MARRIAGE
CONTRACTS

SHORT MARRIAGE
CONTRACTS

"WHO is George Meredith?" asked Mr.
Hennessy.

"Ye can search me," said Mr. Dooley. "What is th' charge again' him?"

"Nawthin'," said Mr. Hennessy; "but I see he's
in favor iv short-term marredges."

"What d'ye mean?" asked Mr Dooley. "Redu-
cin' th' terms f'r good behavyor?"

"No," said Mr. Hennessy. "He says people
ought to get marrid f'r three or four years at a time.
Thin, if they don't like each other, or if wan gets
tired, they break up housekeepin'."

"Well," said Mr. Dooley, "it mightn't be a bad
thing. Th' throuble about mathrimony, as I have
observed it fr'm me seat in th' gran' stand, is that
afther fifteen or twinty years it settles down to an
endurance thrile. 'Women,' as Hogan says, 'are
creatures iv such beaucheous mien that to be loved
they have but to be seen; but,' he says, 'wanst they're
seen an' made secure,' he says, 'we first embrace, thin
pity, thin endure,' he says. Most iv th' ol' marrid
men I know threat their wives like a rockin'-chair, a
great comfort whin they're tired, but apt to be in
th' way at other times.

"Now, it might be diff'rent if th' ladies, instead

4   [43]

iv bein' secured f'r life, was on'y held on a short-term lease. Whin Archybald, th' pride iv South Wather Sthreet, makes up his mind that it would be well f'r his credit if he enthered th' holy bonds iv mathrimony an' selects th' target iv his mad affections, he thinks that all he has to do is to put a geeranyum in his buttonhole an' inthrajooce himsilf be his first name to be carrid to th' altar. But th' ladies, Gawd bless thim, are be nature skilled in this game, an' befure Archybald has been coortin' two weeks he begins to shift his idees iv his own worth He finds that at best he has on'y an outside chance. He wondhers if he is really worthy iv th' love iv an innocint young girl iv thirty-two. Has he money enough to support her as she shud be supported? He even has doubts f'r th' first time in his life iv his own ravishin' beauty. He detects blemishes that he niver see befure. He discovers that what he used to considher a merry twinkle is a slight cast in th' right eye, an' that th' fillin' shows in his teeth. He consults a manicure an' a hair-dhresser an' buys th' entire stock iv a gents' furnishin'-store. Thin whin he's thurly humble he goes thremblin' to Belinda's house, raysolved that if th' fair wan rayfuses him, as she prob'bly will an' surely ought to, he will walk off th' bridge an' end all.

"It's at this time that th' short-term conthract shud be sprung. I don't know how men propose. I niver thried it but wanst, an' th' hired girl said th' lady was not at home. No wan will iver tell ye. Most marrid men give ye th' impressyon that their wives stole thim fr'm their agonized parents. But, anyhow, we'll suppose that Archybald, layin' a silk

[44]

hankerchief on th' carpet an' pullin' up th' leg iv his pantaloons, to prevint baggin', hurls himsilf impetchoosly at th' feet iv his adored wan an' cries: ' Belinda, I can on'y offer ye th' love iv an honest South Wather Sthreet commission merchant an' mimber iv th' Brotherhood iv Wholesale an' Retail Grocers. Will ye take me f'r life?' Belinda blushes a rosy red an' replies: ' Archybald, ye ask too much. I cannot take ye f'r life, but I'll give ye a five-year lease an' resarve th' right to renew at th' end iv that time,' she says. ' Will that do?' says she. ' I will thry to make ye happy,' says he. An' she falls on his bosom, an' between her sobs cries: ' Thin let us repair at wanst to th' Title Guarantee an' Thrust Comp'ny an' be made man an' wife,' she says.

" Well, after Archybald is safely marrid his good opinyon iv himsilf returns. Belinda does her share to encourage him, an' befure long he begins to wondher how as fine a fellow as him come to throw himsilf away. Not that she ain't a good creature, d'ye mind, an' slavishly devoted to him. He hasn't annything again'-her; still, think iv what he might have done if he had on'y known his thrue worth. Whin a man gets a good repytation he doesn't have to live up to it. So bimeby Archybald, knowin' fr'm what his wife says that he is handsome enough without anny artificyal aid, f'rgets th' mannycure an' th' hair-dhresser. Sometimes he shaves, an' sometimes he doesn't. So far as he is consarned, he thinks th' laundhry bill is too high. He advertises th' fact that he wears a red flannel chest-protictor. His principal convarsation is about his lumbago. He frequently mintions that he likes certain articles iv food, but they

[45]

don't like him. Whin he comes home at night he
plays with th' dog, talks pollyticks with his next-dure
neighbor, puts his hat an' a pair iv cuffs on th'
piannah, sets down in front iv th' fire, kicks off his
boots, and dhraws on a pair iv carpet slippers, and
thin notices that the wife iv his bosom is on th'
premises. ' Hello, ol' woman,' he says. ' How's all
ye'er throubles?' he says.

" Wanst a year Belinda meets him at th' dure with
a flower in her hair. ' Well,' he says, ' what are th'
decorations about?' he says. ' Don't ye know what
day this is?' says she. ' Sure,' says he, ' it's Choosdah.' ' No, but what day?' ' I give it up.   St.
Pathrick's day, Valentine's day, pay day. What's
th' answer?' ' But think.' ' I give it up.' ' It's th'
annyvarsary iv our weddin'.' ' Oh,' says he, ' so it
is. I'd clean f'rgot. That's right. I raymimber it
well, now that ye mintion it. Well, betther luck nex'
time. There, take that,' he says. An' he salutes her
on th' forehead an' goes down in th' cellar to wurruk
on a patent skid that will rivoluchionize th' grocery
business. If he suffers a twinge iv remorse later he
tells her to take two dollars out iv th' housekeepin'
money an' buy herself a suitable prisint.

" He's pleasant in th' avenin'. At supper, havin'
explained his daily maladies at full length, he re-
lapses into a gloomy silence, broken on'y be such
sounds as escape fr'm a man dhrinkin' hot coffee.
Afther supper he figures on th' prob'ble market f'r
rutybagy turnips, while his wife r-reads th' adver-
tisements in th' theaytres. ' Jawn Drew is here this
week,' says she. ' Is he?' says Archybald. ' That's
good,' he says. ' I haven't been to a theaytre since

[46]

Billy Emerson died,' he says. 'I hate th' theaytre. It ain't a bit like rale life as I see it in business hours,' he says. Afther a while, whin Belinda begins to tell him a thrillin' says-she about wan iv the neighbors, he lapses into a pleasant sleep, now an' thin arousin' himsilf to murmur: 'Um-m.' At nine o'clock he winds th' clock, puts th' dog out f'r the night, takes off his collar on th' stairs, an' goes to bed. Belinda sets up a little later an' dhreams Richard Harding Davis wrote a book about her.

"But th' five years ar-re up at last. Wan mornin' Archybald is glarin' fr'm behind a newspaper in his customary jaynial breakfast mood whin his wife says: 'Where will I sind ye'er clothes?' 'What's that?' says he. 'Where d'ye live to-morrah?' 'Don't be foolish, ol' woman. What d'ye mean?' says he. I mean,' says she, 'that th' lease has expired. At tin-thirty to-day it r-runs out. I like ye, Archybald, but I think I'll have to let ye go. Th' property has r-run down. Th' repairs haven't been kept up. Ye haven't allowed enough for wear an' tear. It looks too much like a boardin'-house. I'm goin' into th' market to prospect f'r a husband with all modhren improvements,' says she.

"Well, wudden't that be a jolt f'r Archybald? Ye bet he'd beat th' quarther-mile record to th' joolers. He'd haul out ol' pitchers iv himsilf as he was th' day he won his threasure, an' he'd hurry to a beauty upholsterer an' say: 'Make me as like that there Apollo Belvydere as ye can without tearin' me down altogether.' It wud be fine. He'd get her back, maybe, but it wud be a sthruggle. An' afther that, about a year befure th' conthract expired again,

[47]

ye'd see him pickin' purple ties out iv th' shop window, buyin' theaytre tickets be th' scoor, an' stoppin' ivry avenin' at a flower-shop to gather a bunch iv vilets He'd hire a man to nudge him whin his birthday come around, an' ivry time th' annyvarsary iv th' weddin' occurred he'd have a firewurruks display fr'm th' front stoop. Whin he'd succeeded in convincin' th' objeck iv his affictions that she cud put up with him f'r another five years they cud go on their weddin' journey. Ye'd read in th' pa-apers: ' Misther an' Mrs. Archybald Pullets were marrid again las' night be th' president iv th' First Naytional Bank. They departed on their twelfth weddin' journey, followed be a shower iv rice fr'm their gr-reat grandchildher.' It wud be fine. I hope George What's-his-name puts it through."

" I don't believe wan wurrud ye say," said Mr. Hennessy.

" P'raps not," said Mr. Dooley. " In me heart I think if people marry it ought to be f'r life Th' laws ar-re altogether too lenient with thim." ·

THE BRINGING UP OF
CHILDREN

THE BRINGING UP OF
CHILDREN

"DID ye iver see a man as proud iv annything as Hogan is iv that kid iv his?" said Mr. Dooley.

"Wait till he's had iliven," said Mr. Hennessy.

"Oh, iv coorse," said Mr. Dooley. "Ye have contimpt f'r an amachoor father that has on'y wan off-spring. An ol' profissyonal parent like ye, that's practically done nawthin' all ye'er life but be a father to helpless childher, don't understand th' emotions iv th' author iv a limited edition. But Hogan don't care. So far as I am able to judge fr'm what he says, his is th' on'y perfect an' complete child that has been projooced this cinchry. He looks on you th' way Hinnery James wud look on Mary Jane Holmes.

"I wint around to see this here projidy th' other day. Hogan met me at th' dure. 'Wipe off ye'er feet,' says he 'Why,' says I. 'Baby,' says he. 'Mickrobes,' he says. He thin conducted me to a basin iv water, an' insthructed me to wash me hands in a preparation iv carbolic acid. Whin I was thurly perfumed he inthrajooced me to a toothless ol' gintleman who was settin' up in a cradle atin' his right foot. 'Ain't he fine?' says Hogan. 'Wondherful,' says I. 'Did ye iver see such an expressyon?' says he. 'Niver,' says I, 'as Hiven is me judge, niver.'

[51]

'Look at his hair,' he says. 'I will,' says I. 'Ain't his eyes beautiful?' 'They ar-re,' I says. 'Ar-re they glass or on'y imitation?' says I. 'An' thim cunning little feet,' says he. 'On close inspiction,' says I, 'yes, they ar-re. They ar're feet. Ye'er offspring don't know it, though. He thinks that wan is a doughnut.' 'He's not as old as he looks,' says Hogan. 'He cudden't be,' says I. 'He looks old enough to be a Dimmycratic candydate f'r Vice-Prisidint. Why, he's lost most iv his teeth,' I says. 'Go wan,' says he; 'he's just gettin' thim. He has two uppers an' four lowers,' he says. 'If he had a few more he'd be a sleepin'-car,' says I. 'Does he speak?' says I. 'Sure,' says Hogan 'Say poppa,' he says. "Gah," says young Hogan. 'Hear that?' says Hogan; 'that's poppa. Say momma,' says he. "Gah," says th' projidy. 'That's momma,' says Hogan. "See, here's Misther Dooley, says he. "Blub," says th' phenomynon. 'Look at that,' says Hogan; 'he knows ye,' he says.

"Well, ye know, Hinnissy, wan iv th' things that has made me popylar in th' ward is that I make a bluff at adorin' childher. Between you an' me, I'd as lave salute a dish-rag as a recent infant, but I always do it. So I put on an allurin' smile, an' says I, 'Well, little ol' goozy goo, will he give his Dooleyums a kiss?' At that minyit Hogan seized me be th' collar an' dhragged me away fr'm th' cradle. 'Wud ye kill me child?' says he. 'How?' says I. 'With a kiss,' says he. 'Am I that bad?' says I. 'Don't ye know that there ar-re mickrobes that can be thransmitted to an infant in a kiss?' says he. 'Well,' says I, with indignation, 'I'm not proud iv

[52]

mesilf as an antiseptic American,' I says, ' but in an encounther between me an' that there young canni-bal,' I says, ' I'll lave it to th' board iv health who takes th' biggest chance,' I says, an' we wint out, fol-lowed be a howl fr'm th' projidy. ' He's singin',' says Hogan. ' He has lost his notes,' says I.

" Whin we got down-stairs Hogan give me a lect-ure on th' bringin' up iv childher. As though I needed it, me that's been consulted on bringin' up half th' childher in Archey Road. ' In th' old days,' says he, ' childher was brought up catch-as-catch-can,' he says. ' But it's diff'rent now. They're as carefully watched as a geeranyum in a consarvatory,' he says. ' I have a book here on th' subjick,' he says. ' Here it is. Th' first thing that shud be done f'r a child is to deprive it iv its parents. Th' less th' in-fant sees iv poppa an momma th' betther f'r him. If they ar-re so base as to want to look at th' little darlin' they shud first be examined be a competent physician to see that there is nawthin' wrong with thim that they cud give th' baby. They will thin take a bath iv sulphuric acid, an' havin' carefully attired thimsilves in a sturlized rubber suit, they will approach within eight feet iv th' objeck iv their ignoble affection an' lave at wanst. In no case must they kiss, hug, or fondle their projiny. Manny dis-eases, such as lumbago, pain in th' chest, premachoor baldness, senile decrepitude, which are privalent among adults, can be communicated to a child fr'm th' parent. Besides, it is bad f'r th' moral nature iv th' infant. Affection f'r its parents is wan iv th' mos' dangerous symptoms iv rickets. Th' parents may not be worthy iv th' love iv a

[53]

thurly sturlized child. An infant's first jooty is
to th' docthor, to whom it owes its bein' an'
stayin'. Childher ar-re imitative, an' if they see
much iv their parents they may grow up to look like
thim. That wud be a great misfortune. If parents
see their childher befure they enther Harvard they
ar-re f'rbidden to teach thim foolish wurruds like
" poppa " an' " momma." At two a properly brought
up child shud be able to articulate distinctly th'
wurrud " Docthor Bolt on th' Care an' Feedin' iv
Infants," which is betther thin sayin' " momma," an'
more exact.

" ' Gr-reat care shud be taken iv th' infant's food.
Durin' th' first two years it shud have nawthin' but
milk. At three a little canary-bur-rd seed can be add-
ed. At five an egg ivry other Choosdah. At siven an
orange. At twelve th' child may ate a shredded biscuit.
At forty th' little tot may have stewed prunes. An' so
on. At no time, howiver, shud th' child be stuffed
with greengages, pork an' beans, onions, Boston
baked brown-bread, saleratus biscuit, or other food.

" ' It's wondherful,' says Hogan, ' how they've got
it rayjooced to a science. They can almost make a
short baby long or a blond baby black be addin' to
or rayjoocin' th' amount iv protides an' casens in
th' milk,' he says. ' Haven't ye iver kissed ye'er
young?' says I. ' Wanst in awhile,' he says, ' whin
I'm thurly disinfected I go up an' blow a kiss at him
through th' window,' he says.

" ' Well,' says I, ' it may be all right,' I says, ' but
if I cud have a son an' heir without causin' talk I bet
ye I'd not apply f'r a permit fr'm th' health boord
f'r him an' me to come together. Parents was made

[54]

befure childher, annyhow, an' they have a prire claim
to be considhered. Sure, it may be a good thing to
bring thim up on a sanitary plan, but it seems to
me they got along all right in th' ol' days whin
number two had just larned to fall down-stairs at
th' time number three entered th' wurruld. Maybe
they were sthronger thin they ar-re now. Th'
docthor niver pretinded to see whether th' milk was
properly biled. He cudden't very well. Th' childher
was allowed to set up at th' table an' have a good cup
iv tay an' a pickle at two. If there was more thin
enough to go around, they got what nobody else
wanted. They got plenty iv fresh air playin' in
alleys an' vacant lots, an' ivry wanst in a while they
were allowed to go down an' fall into th' river. No
attintion was paid to their dite. Th' prisint race
iv heroes who are now startlin' th' wurrould in finance,
polytics, th' arts an' sciences, burglary, an' lithrachoor, was brought up on wathermillon rinds, specked
apples, raw onions stolen fr'm th' grocer, an' cocoa-
nut-pie. Their nursery was th' back yard. They
larned to walk as soon as they were able, an' if they
got bow-legged ivrybody said they wud be sthrong
men. As f'r annybody previntin' a fond parent fr'm
comin' home Saturdah night an' wallowin' in his
beaucheous child, th' docthor that suggisted it wud
have to move. No, sir,' says I, ' get as much amusemint as ye can out iv ye'er infant,' says I. ' Teach
him to love ye now,' I says, ' before he knows. Afther
a while he'll get onto ye an' it 'll be too late.' "

" Ye know a lot about it," said Mr. Hennessy.

" I do," said Mr. Dooley " Not bein' an author,
I'm a gr-reat critic."

THE LABOR TROUBLES

THE LABOR TROUBLES

"I SEE th' sthrike has been called off," said Mr. Hennessy.

"Which wan?" asked Mr. Dooley. "I can't keep thrack iv thim. Somebody is sthrikin' all th' time. Wan day th' horseshoers are out, an' another day th' teamsters. Th' Brotherhood iv Molasses Candy Pullers sthrikes, an' th' Amalgymated Union iv Pickle Sorters quits in sympathy. Th' carpinter that has been puttin' up a chicken coop f'r Hogan knocked off wurruk whin he found that Hogan was shavin' himsilf without a card fr'm th' Barbers' Union. Hogan fixed it with th' walkin' dillygate iv th' barbers, an' th' carpinter quit wurruk because he found that Hogan was wearin' a pair iv non-union pants. Hogan wint down-town an' had his pants unionized an' come home to find that th' carpinter had sthruck because Hogan's hens was layin' eggs without th' union label. Hogan injooced th' hens to jine th' union. But wan iv thim laid an egg two days in succission an' th' others sthruck, th' rule iv th' union bein' that no hen shall lay more eggs thin th' most reluctant hen in th' bunch.

"It's th' same ivrywhere. I haven't had a sandwich f'r a year because ivry time I've asked f'r wan ayether th' butchers or th' bakers has been out on sthrike. If I go down in a car in th' mornin' it's

5 [59]

eight to wan I walk back at night. A man I knew
had his uncle in th' house much longer than ayether
iv thim had intinded on account iv a sthrike iv th'
Frindly Brotherhood iv Morchuary Helpers. Afther
they'd got a permit fr'm th' walkin' dillygate an'
th' remains was carrid away undher a profusyon iv
floral imblims with a union label on each iv thim, th'
coortege was stopped at ivry corner be a picket, who
first punched th' mourners an' thin examined their
credintials. Me frind says to me : ' Uncle Bill wud've
been proud. He was very fond iv long fun'rals, an'
this was th' longest I iver attinded. It took eight
hours, an' was much more riochous goin' out thin
comin' back,' he says.

"It was diff'rent whin I was a young man, Hinnissy. In thim days Capital an' Labor were frindly,
or Labor was. Capital was like a father to Labor,
givin' it its boord an' lodgin's. Nayether inther-
fered with th' other. Capital wint on capitalizin', an'
Labor wint on laborin'. In thim goolden days a
wurrukin' man was an honest artisan. That's what he
was proud to be called. Th' week befure iliction he
had his pitcher in th' funny pa-apers. He wore
a square paper cap an' a leather apron, an' he
had his ar-rm ar-round Capital, a rosy binivolint
old guy with a plug-hat an' eye-glasses. They
were goin' to th' polls together to vote f'r simple old
Capital.

"Capital an' Labor walked ar-rm in ar-rm instead
iv havin' both hands free as at prisint. Capital was
contint to be Capital, an' Labor was used to bein'
Labor. Capital come ar-round an' felt th' ar-rm iv
Labor wanst in a while, an' ivry year Mrs. Capital

called on Mrs. Labor an' congratylated her on her
score. Th' pride iv ivry artisan was to wurruk as
long at his task as th' boss cud afford to pay th'
gas bill. In return f'r his fidelity he got a turkey
ivry year. At Chris'mas time Capital gathered his
happy fam'ly around him, an' in th' prisince iv th'
ladies iv th' neighborhood give thim a short oration.
' Me brave la-ads,' says he, ' we've had a good year.
(Cheers.) I have made a millyon dollars. (Sinsation.) I atthribute this to me supeeryor skill, aided be
ye'er arnest efforts at th' bench an' at th' forge.
(Sobs.) Ye have done so well that we won't need so
manny iv us as we did. (Long an' continyous cheerin'.) Those iv us who can do two men's wurruk will
remain, an', if possible, do four. Our other faithful
sarvants,' he says, ' can come back in th' spring,' he
says, ' if alive,' he says. An' th' bold artysans tossed
their paper caps in th' air an' give three cheers f'r
Capital. They wurruked till ol' age crept on thim,
and thin retired to live on th' wish-bones an' kind
wurruds they had accumylated.

" Nowadays 'tis far diff'rent. Th' unions has desthroyed all individjool effort. Year be year th'
hours iv th' misguided wurrukin' man has been cut
down, till now it takes a split-second watch to time
him as he goes through th' day's wurruk. I have a
gintleman plasthrer frind who tells me he hasn't
put in a full day in a year. He goes to his desk ivry
mornin' at tin an' sthrikes punchooly at iliven. ' Th'
wrongs iv th' wurrukin' men mus' be redhressed,' says
he. ' Ar-re ye inthrested in thim?' says I. ' Ye niver
looked betther in ye'er life,' says I. ' I niver felt
betther,' he says. ' It's th' out-iv-dure life,' he says.

[61]

Dissertations by Mr. Dooley

' I haven't missed a baseball game this summer,' he says. ' But,' he says, ' I need exercise. I wish Labor Day wud come around. Th' boys has choose me to carry a life-size model iv th' Masonic Temple in th' parade,' he says.

" If I was a wurrukin' man I'd sigh f'r th' good ol' days, whin Labor an' Capital were frinds. Those who lived through thim did. In thim times th' arrys-tocracy iv labor was th' la-ads who r-run th' railroad injines. They were a proud race. It was a boast to have wan iv thim in a fam'ly. They niver sthruck. 'Twas again' their rules. They conferred with Capi-tal. Capital used to weep over thim. Ivry wanst in a while a railroad prisidint wud grow red in th' face an' burst into song about thim. They were a body that th' nation might well be proud iv. If he had a son who asked f'r no betther fate, he wud ask f'r no betther fate f'r him thin to be a Brotherhood iv Lo-cymotive Ingineers. Ivrybody looked up to thim, an' they looked down on ivrybody, but mostly on th' bricklayers. Th' bricklayers were niver bulwarks iv th' constichoochion. They niver conferred with Capital. Th' polis always arrived just as th' con-ference was beginnin'. Their motto was a long life an' a merry wan; a brick in th' hand is worth two on th' wall. They sthruck ivry time they thought iv it. They sthruck on th' slightest provocation, an' whin they weren't provoked at all. If a band wint by they climbed down th' laddhers an' followed it, carryin' banners with th' wurruds: ' Give us bread or we starve,' an' walked till they were almost hungry. Ivry Saturdah night they held a dance to protest again' their wrongs. In th' summer-time th' wails iv th'

[62]

oppressed bricklayers wint up fr'm countless picnics. They sthruck in sympathy with annybody. Th' union wint out as wan man because they was a rumor that th' superintindent iv th' rollin'-mills was not nice to his wife. Wanst they sthruck because Poland was not free.

"What was th' raysult? Their unraisoning demands fin'lly enraged Capital. To-day ye can go into a bricklayer's house an' niver see a capitalist but th' bricklayer himsilf. Forty years ago a bricklayer was certain iv twelve hours wurruk a day, or two hours more thin a convicted burglar. To-day he has practically nawthin' to do, an' won't do that. They ar-re out iv wurruk nearly all th' time an' at th' seashore. Jus' as often as ye read 'Newport colony fillin' up,' ye read, 'Bricklayers sthrike again.' Ye very sildom see a bricklayer nowadays in th' city. They live mostly in th' counthry, an' on'y come into town to be bribed to go to wurruk. It wud pay anny man who is buildin' a house to sind thim what money he has be mail an' go live in a tent.

"An' all this time, how about th' arrystocracy iv labor, th' knights iv th' throttle? Have they been deprived iv anny hours iv labor? On th' conthry, they have steadily increased, ontil to-day there is not a knight iv th' throttle who hasn't more hours iv wurruk in a day thin he can use in a week. In th' arly mornin', whin he takes his ir'n horse out iv th' stall, he meets th' onforchnit, misguided bricklayer comin' home in a cab fr'm a sthrike meetin'. Hardly a year passes that he can't say to his wife: 'Mother, I've had an increase.' 'In wages?' 'No, in hours.' It's th' old story iv th' ant an' th' grasshopper—th' ant that ye can step on an' th' grasshopper ye can't catch.

"Well, it's too bad that th' goolden days has passed, Hinnissy. Capital still pats Labor on th' back, but on'y with an axe. Labor rayfuses to be threated as a frind. It wants to be threated as an inimy. It thinks it gets more that way. They ar-re still a happy fam'ly, but it's more like an English fam'ly. They don't speak. What do I think iv it all? Ah, sure, I don't know. I belong to th' on-forchnit middle class. I wurruk hard, an' I have no money. They come in here undher me hospital roof, an' I furnish thim with cards, checks, an' refrish-mints. 'Let's play without a limit,' says Labor. 'It's Dooley's money.' 'Go as far as ye like with Dooley's money,' says Capital. 'What have ye got?' 'I've got a straight to Roosevelt,' says Labor. 'I've got ye beat,' says Capital. 'I've got a Supreme Court full of injunctions.' Manetime I've pawned me watch to pay f'r th' game, an' I have to go to th' joolry-store on th' corner to buy a pound iv beef or a scuttle iv coal. No wan iver sthrikes in sympathy with me."

"They ought to get together," said Mr. Hennessy.

"How cud they get anny closer together thin their prisint clinch?" asked Mr. Dooley. "They're so close together now that those that ar-re between thim ar-re crushed to death."

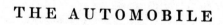

THE AUTOMOBILE

THE AUTOMOBILE

"WELL, sir," said Mr. Hennessy, "it mus' be gran' to be rich an' go r-runnin' around th' counthry in wan iv thim autymobills."

"It must that," said Mr. Dooley. "It's th' gran' spoort entirely. Next to a naygro agitator in Georgia, I don't suppose anny man gets as much excitement out iv a short life as a millyonaire who owns an autymobill. Fr'm all I can larn about it fr'm th' pa-apers, a millyonaire with an autymobill is constantly steerin' between th' county jail an' th' poorhouse. If th' polis don't land him in wan, th' autymobill will in th' other.

"Whin Algernon's father dies, lavin' him th' money iv th' widow an' th' orphan, Algernon brushes a tear fr'm his eye an' hurries over to Paris to get an autymobill. Father used to go down-town in a 'bus, figurin' inthrest on his cuffs, but there is nawthin' f'r Algy but an eighty horse-power red divvle that 'll make th' demon haste-wagon iv his frind nex' dure look like a mud-scow. An' he buys wan, an' with it a Fr-rinch shover. He calls th' shover Franswaw, an' th' shover calls him 'Canal.' He is a haughty fireman, this la-ad, f'r he is a discindint iv Louis Flip, an' th' blood iv kings coorses in his veins. He soon

teaches Algernon his place, which is undher th' autymobill, fixin' up a busted valve, an' afther that
Algernon niver speaks to Franswaw onless he is
spoken to, an' Franswaw niver speaks undher anny
circumstances. Algernon turns over his property to
him to buy tires, an' resigns himsilf to a life iv
pleasure.

"He has it while th' autymobill is in th' masheen
shop havin' a few repairs put into it. But wan day
all is r-ready. Algernon asks Franswaw if he may
go f'r a spin, an' Franswaw motions him into th'
seat iv honor beside th' shover. Now they're off!
Look at thim dash through th' crowded sthreets,
where th' happy childher iv th' tinimints ar-re at
play. How glad th' childher ar-re to see thim. Especially that little boy with th' goolden locks. See, he
has a turnip in his hand. Look, look! he is goin' to
give it to Algy. He gives it to him just back iv th'
ear. See those gintlemen comin' out iv a saloon.
How proud they ar-re to meet Algernon. Look, they
ar-re tearin' up th' sthreets. They ar-re actually
goin' to give Algernon th' r-right iv way. He gets
it in th' small iv th' back. What ar-re those pretty
little girls doin'? They ar-re sthrewin' something
in th' sthreet. Ar-re they sthrewin' roses f'r Algernon? No, they ar-re sthrewin' tacks. What is that
explosion undher th' car, followed be a cry iv ' Get a
hoss '? Algernon's tires have reached th' tacks.
Ar-re th' little girls happy? They ar-re indeed.
They ar-re laughin' an' throwin' coal into Algy's
lap. Who is this who comes r-runnin' out iv a saloon
atin' a clove? It is an officer iv th' law. Why does
he seize Algernon be th' hair an' dhrag him fr'm th'

The Automobile

car? Algy is pinched, Hinnissy. Th' officer has
saved him fr'm a pauper's grave.

"Now, th' sign iv a haughty aristocracy is
dhragged befure th' coort which protects th' liberties iv th' people an' th' freedom iv speech iv th'
magistrates. 'Haynious monsther,' says th' stern
but just judge, ' ye have been caught r-red-handed.
What have ye to say f'r ye'ersilf? Niver mind, it
don't make anny diff'rence, annyhow. Ye cudden't
tell th' thruth. I have no prejudice again' ye, riptile.
I believe th' autymobill has come to stay, in th' barn.
But th' rights iv citizens mus' be pro-ticted. Why,
on'y las' week I was speedin' a two-thirty trotter whin
wan iv these injines iv desthruction come along
through th' crowded thoroughfare an' near frightened me out iv me wits. I stood up on me hind legs,
I dhropped th' rains, I thried to jump over a fence.
If it hadn't been f'r th' ca'mness iv me wife an' th'
horse I wud surely have r-run away an' p'raps have
injured somebody. I tell ye this little anecdote to
show ye, monsther, that I have no prejudices. Swear
th' witnesses.'

"John Coolin, dhruggist's assistant, tistyfied that
he had left his baby-carredge, containin' wan four-
teenth iv all he possessed on arth, on th' sidewalk
while he wint into a saloon to buy a postage-stamp.
Whin he come out th' vehicle rolled down to th'
curb. He wud swear that Algernon's autymobill
was goin' eighty miles an hour. Th' coort: ' How
did ye time him?' ' Th' witness: ' Through th' newspapers.'

"August Schmidt, teamster, tistyfied that while
attimptin' to find a brick to throw at th' masheen

(the coort: ' Good f'r you!') he slipped an' sprained his ankle. (Cries iv ' Shame!')

" Officer Doolittle tistyfied that he followed Algernon f'r two miles on foot. He wud swear that he was goin' between sixty an' wan hundherd an' two miles an hour. ' How did ye time him?' asked th' coort. ' Be me stop-watch.' ' Whin did it stop?' ' Last week.' ' That's all I want to hear,' says th' larned coort. ' Algernon Rox, this coort always timpers justice with mercy, an' timpers mercy with timper. I will not be hard on ye. It is ye'er first offinse. I will merely sintince ye to be hanged. An' let this narrow escape be a warnin' to ye,' he says.

" Such, Hinnissy, is th' happy life an' arly death iv th' millyonaire with th' autymobill. Did I iver r-ride in wan? Almost, wanst. Wan day I hear a cry iv ' Kill him,' followed be a shower iv bricks, an' I knew some millyonaire was out f'r a jaunt or spin or pinch in his autymobill. Who shud th' millyonaire be but Hogan. He has a frind who is a Fr-rinch shover. Th' millyonaire an' his companyon just got to me dure a yard in fr-front iv th' excited popylace. I wint out an' ca'med th' peasanthry with a few well-chosen kicks, an' Hogan asked me to go f'r a spin as far as Brighton Park. But just as I was about to step into me proper place in s'ciety along with Jawn W. Gates, th' autymobill had a convulsion. I heerd a terrific rumblin' in its inteeryor, it groaned an' coughed, an' thried to jump up in th' air. ' Something is wr-rong with ye'er ir-n hourse,' says I. ' He's et something that don't agree with him. Ye ought to take him to a vet.' ' Come along,' says Hogan. ' No,' says I, ' I'll not r-ride no autymobill

The Automobile

with th' epizootic. Ye ought to be took up be th' s'ciety f'r th' previntyon iv croolty to autymobills. Get out an' lead it back to th' barn,' says I. 'Ye're crazy,' says he. 'It's all right,' says he. 'Alley,' says he to th' shover. 'Alley be dam'd,' says th' shover 'Th' biler's leakin'.' Him an' Hogan got down on th' sthreet an' got out a plumber's, a blacksmith's, an' a carpenter's outfit, put on overalls an' wint to wurruk.

"'This is a fine spoort,' says I. 'It's ragal,' I says. 'How happy a blacksmith's helper mus' be to get two dollars a day f'r bein' an autymobilist.' 'Shut up,' says Hogan, fr'm undher th' car. Whin he come out he looked as though he'd been coalin' a liner. 'It's all ready now,' says he. But it wasn't. Th' shover wint to th' front an' turned a crank. A few bars iv Wagner followed, an' thin th' autymobill resigned. Th' shover said something in Fr-rinch be which I recognized that he come fr'm th' same Arondissemint in la belle Roscommon as mesilf, an' turned again. Th' autymobill groaned an' thrembled, and Hogan begun to bounce on his seat, th' shover lept into th' car, pulled five levers, put on th' hard pedal, an' thin th' soft blew his horn an' r-ran into an ice-wagon. 'We're off,' yells Hogan. 'Ye ar-re,' says I, 'an' so is ye'er back tire,' f'r wan iv th' little earnest wurrukers among th' popylace had been busy with a knife. At this minyit a polisman come along. 'Ye're undher arrest,' says he. 'What f'r?' says Hogan. 'F'r exceedin' th' time limit. I timed ye at sixty miles an hour fr'm Halsted Sthreet,' he says. 'An',' says Hogan, 'I timed ye at two hours in Schwartzmeister's saloon,' he says. 'An' I'll have ye

[71]

up befure me uncle Captain Hogan to-morrow f'r exceedin' th' sleep limit, an' I'll make a sthring iv ye'er buttons f'r th' childher,' he says. 'In the mane time,' he says, 'go an' ketch a thief,' he says. Thin he got down out iv th' autymobill. 'Sullivan,' he says to th' shover, 'take that insthrumint iv torture back to th' asylum,' he says. 'I don't want to be a millyonaire,' he says. 'With ye'er permission, Martin, I'll go in, warsh me face, an' raysume me station as a poor but clane citizen,' he says.

"An' there ye ar-re. I don't want anny autymobill, Hinnissy. I don't want to pay tin thousan' dollars to be onpopylar. I'd rather have th' smiles iv th' poor as I walk amongst thim on me two shapely legs thin rayceive th' brickbats iv th' same in a circus-wagon attached to a cook-stove. If I want to be a blacksmith I'll jine th' union an' get me four a day. An' if I'm to be arristed at all, f'r Hivin's sake let it be f'r dhrunkenness.

"Do I think th' autymobill has come to stay? Sure, I'll niver tell ye. I've seen all th' wurruld but me on roller-skates. I've seen ivrybody ridin' a bicycle but me. Tin years ago, whin ye'er son was holdin' on to ye'er ar-rms as ye reeled up th' sthreet on a wheel, sayin' ye'er prayers wan minyit an' th' revarse another, ye tol' me that th' bicycle had come to stay because it was nicissry to get around quick. To-day ye blush as I mintion it. Th' autymobill will stay till it gets cheap enough f'r ivrybody to have wan. Whin th' little, eager messenger-boys is dashin' up th' sthreet in a eighty horse-power Demon Terror th' rich will be flyin' kites or r-runnin' baloons, an' they'll be a parachute foorce iv polismen to

chase thim acrost th' skies. Be that time ivrybody
will have larned to dodge th' autymobill. That's a
good plan f'r poor people, annyhow. Dodge th'
exthravagances iv th' r-rich. They're sure to bust
a tire soon or late."

"I think they ought to be locked up f'r tearin'
through th' sthreets," said Mr. Hennessy.

"Well, maybe," said Mr. Dooley. "But don't
ye think a man that owns an autymobill is punished
enough?"

THE COMFORTS OF TRAVEL

6

THE COMFORTS OF TRAVEL

"**D**'YE know," said Mr. Hennessy, "ye can go fr'm Chicago to New York in twinty hours? It must be like flyin'."

"It's something like flyin'," said Mr. Dooley, "but it's also like fallin' off a roof or bein' clubbed be a polisman."

"It's wondherful how luxuryous modhren thravel is," said Mr. Hennessy.

"Oh, wondherful," said Mr. Dooley. "It's almost a dhream. Ye go to bed at night in Kansas City an' ye ar-re still awake in Chicago in th' mornin'. Ye lave New York to-day an' nex' Thursdah ye ar-re in San Francisco an' can't get back. An' all th' time ye injye such comforts an' iligances as wud make th' Shah iv Persha invious if he heerd iv thim. I haven't thravelled much since I hastily put four thousan' miles iv salt wather an' smilin' land between me an' th' constabulary, but I've always wanted to fly through space on wan iv thim palace cars with th' beautiful names. Th' man that names th' Pullman cars an' th' pa-aper collars iv this counthry is our greatest pote, whoiver he is. I cud see mesilf steppin' aboard a palace on wheels called Obulula or Onarka an' bein' fired fr'm wan union deepo to another. So las' month, whin a towny iv mine in Saint Looey asked me down there, I deter-

mined to make th' plunge. With th' invitation come
a fine consarvitive article be th' gin'ral passenger
agent indivrin', Hinnissy, to give a faint idee iv th'
glories iv th' thrip. There was pitchers in this little
pome showin' how th' thrain looked to th' passenger
agent. Iligantly dhressed ladies an' gintlemen set
in th' handsomely upholstered seats, or sthrolled
through th' broad aisles. Pierpont Morgan was disclosed in a corner dictatin' a letter to Andhrew Carnaygie. In th' barber-shop Jawn D. Rockyfellar
was bein' shaved. In th' smokin'-car ye cud see a
crowd iv jolly men playin' poker; near by sat three
wags tellin' comic stories, while a naygur waither
dashed to an' fro an' pushed mint juleps into th'
fash'nable comp'ny. Says I to mesilf: ' Here is life.
They'll have to dhrag me fr'm that rollin' home iv
bliss feet foremost,' says I.

" An' I wint boundin' down to th' deepo. I slung
four dollars at th' prisidint iv th' road whin he had
con-cluded some important business with his nails,
an' he slung back a yard iv green paper, by which I
surrindered me rights as an American citizen. With
this here deed in me hand I wint through a line iv
haughty gintlemen in unyform, an' wan afther another looked at th' ticket an' punched a hole in it.
Whin I got to th' thrain th' last iv these gr-reat men
says: ' Have ye got a ticket?' ' I had,' says I. ' This
porous plasther was a ticket three minyits ago!' ' Get
aboard,' says he, givin' me a short, frindly kick, an'
in a minyit I found mesilf amid a scene iv Oryental
splendhor an' no place to put me grip-sack.

" I stood dhrinkin' in th' glories iv th' scene until a proud man, who cud qualify on color f'r all his

meals at th' White House, come up an' ordhered me to
bed. Fond as I am iv th' colored man, Hinnissy, I
wud sometimes wish that th' summer styles in Pullman porters was more light an' airy. It is thrue
that th' naygur porter is more durable an' doesn't
show th' dirt, but on th' other hand he shows th' heat
more. 'Where,' says I, 'do I sleep?' 'I don't know
where ye sleep, cap,' says he, 'but ye'er ticket reads
f'r an upper berth.' 'I wud prefer a thrapeze,' says
I, 'but if ye'll call out th' fire department maybe
they can help me in,' I says. At that he projooced
a scalin' laddher, an' th' thrain goin' around a curve
at that minyit I soon found mesilf on me hands an'
knees in wan iv th' cosiest little up-stairs rooms ye
iver saw. He dhrew th' curtains, an' so will I. But
some day whin I am down-town I am goin' to dhrop
in on me frind th' prisidint iv th' Pullman Company
an' ask him to publish a few hints to th' wayfarer.
I wud like to know how a gintleman can take off his
clothes while settin' on thim. It wud help a good deal
to know what to do with th' clothes whin ye have
squirmed out iv thim. Ar-re they to be rolled up in
a ball an' placed undher th' head or dhropped into
th' aisle? Again, in th' mornin' how to get into th'
clothes without throwin' th' thrain off th' thrack? I
will tell ye confidintially, Hinnissy, that not bein' a
contortionist th' on'y thing I took off was me hat.

"Th' thrain sped on an' on. I cud not sleep. Th'
luxury iv thravel kept me wide awake. Who wud
coort slumber in such a cosey little bower? There
were some that did it; I heerd thim coortin'. But not
I. I lay awake while we flew, or, I might say,
bumped through space. It did not seem a minyit

befure we were in Saint Looey. It seemed a year.
On an' iver on we flew past forest, river, an' plain.
Th' lights burned brightly just over me left ear, th'
windows was open an' let in th' hoarse, exultant shriek
iv th' locymotive, th' conversation iv th' baggage-
man to th' heavy thrunk, th' bammy night air, an'
gr-reat purple clouds iv Illinye coal smoke. I took
in enough iv this splindid product iv our prairie soil
to qualify as a coal-yard. Be th' time th' sun peeked,
or, I may say, jumped into me little roost, I wud've
made a cheerful grate-fire an' left a slight deposit
iv r-red ashes.

"Th' mornin' came too soon. I called me illusthrees almost Booker Wash'nton, an' with th' assist-
ance iv th' step-laddher, th' bell-rope, an' th' bald
head iv th' man in th' lower berth, I bounded lightly
out iv me little nook an' rose fr'm th' flure with no
injury worse thin a sprained ankle. I thin walked
th' long an' splindid aisle, flanked be gintlemen who
were writhin' into their clothin', an' soon found mesilf
in th' superbly app'inted washroom.

"What hasn't American ingenuity done f'r th'
wurruld? Here we were fairly flyin' through space,
or stoppin' f'r wather at Polo, Illinye, an' ye cud
wash ye'ersilf as comfortably as ye cud in th' hydrant
back iv th' gas-house. There were three handsome
wash-basins, wan piece iv soap, an' towels galore—
that is, almost enough to go round. In front iv each
wash-basin was a dilicately nurtured child iv luxury
cleansin' himsilf an' th' surroundin' furniture at wan
blow. Havin' injyed a very refreshin' attimpt at a
bath, I sauntered out into th' car. It looked almost
like th' pitchers in th' pamphlet, or wud've if all

The Comforts of Travel

th' boots had been removed. Th' scene was rendered more atthractive be th' prisince iv th' fair sect. A charmin' woman is always charmin', but niver more so thin on a sleepin'-car in th' mornin' afther a hard night's rest an' forty miles fr'm a curlin'-ir'n. With their pretty faces slightly sthreaked be th' right iv way, their eyes dancin' with suppressed fury, an' their hair almost sthraight, they make a pitcher that few can f'rget—an' they're lucky.

"But me eyes were not f'r thim. To tell ye th' thruth, Hinnissy, I was hungry. I thought to find a place among th' coal in me f'r wan iv thim sum-chous meals I had r-read about, an' I summoned th' black prince who was foldin' up th' beddin' with his teeth. 'I wud like a breakfast fr'm ye'er superbly equipped buffay,' says I. 'I got ye,' says he. 'We have canned lobster, canned corn-beef, canned to-matoes, canned asparygus, an' wather fresh fr'm th' company's own spring at th' Chicago wather wurruks,' he says. 'Have ye annything to eat?' says I. 'Sind me th' cook,' I says. 'I'm th' cook,' says he, wipin' a pair iv shoes with his sleeve. 'What do ye do ye'er cookin' with?' says I. 'With a can-opener,' says he, givin' a hearty laugh.

"An so we whiled th' time away till Saint Looey was reached. O'Brien an' his wife nursed me back to life; I rayturned on th' canal-boat, an' here I am, almost as well as befure I made me pleasure jaunt. I'm not goin' to do it again. Let thim that will bask in their comforts. I stay at home. Whiniver I feel th' desire to fly through space I throw four dollars out iv th' window, put a cinder into me eye, an' go to bed on a shelf in th' closet.

[81]

Dissertations by Mr. Dooley

"I guess, Hinnissy, whin ye come to think iv it, they ain't anny such thing as luxury in thravel. We was meant to stay where we found oursilves first, an' thravellin' is conthry to nature. I can go fr'm Chicago to New York in twenty hours, but what's th' matther with Chicago? I can injye places betther be not goin' to thim. I think iv Italy as th' home iv th' Pope, but Hogan, who has been there, thinks iv it as th' home iv th' flea. I can see th' dome iv St. Pethers risin' again' th' sky, but he can on'y see th' cabman that charged him eighty liars, or thirty cents iv our money, to carry him around th' block. I think iv New York as a place where people set shinin' their dimonds with satin napkins at th' Waldorf an' dhrinkin' champagne out iv goold coalscuttles with Jawn W. Gates, but I know a man down there that dhrives a dhray. I've always wanted to see th' Rocky Mountains, but they don't look as tall near by as they do far away.

"They ain't anny easy way iv thravellin'. Our ancesthors didn't have anny fast thrains, but they didn't want thim. They looked on a man thravellin' as a man dead, an' so he is. Comfort is in havin' things where ye can reach thim. A man is as comfortable on a camel as on a private car, an' a man who cud injye bouncin' over steel rails at sixty miles an hour cud go to sleep on top iv a donky-injine. Th' good Lord didn't intind us to be gaddin' around th' wurruld. Th' more we thry to do it th' harder 'tis made f'r us. A man is supposed to take his meals an' his sleep in an attichood iv repose. It ain't nachral to begin on a biled egg at Galesburg an' end on it at Bloomington. We weren't expected to spread

[82]

The Comforts of Travel

a meal over two hundred miles, an' our snores over a thousand. If th' Lord had wanted San Francisco to be near New York he'd have put it there. Th' railroads haven't made it anny nearer. It's still tin thousan' miles, or whativer it is, an' ye'd be more tired if ye reached it in wan day thin ye wud if ye did it in two months in a covered wagon an' stopped f'r sleep an' meals. Th' faster a thrain goes th' nearer th' jints iv th' rails ar-re together. Man was meant to stay where he is or walk. If Nature had intinded us to fly she wud've fixed us with wings an' taught us to ate chicken-feed."

"But th' railroads assist Nature," said Mr. Hennessy.

"They do," said Mr. Dooley. "They make it hard to thravel."

OUR REPRESENTATIVES
ABROAD

OUR REPRESENTATIVES
ABROAD

"I'D like to be an ambassadure," said Mr. Hennessy.

"An' why?" said Mr. Dooley.

"It mus' be a gran' job," said Mr. Hennessy.

"'Tis an aisy job," said Mr. Dooley, "an' 'tis a gran' job if ye care f'r it. But it ain't th' job it used to be. Th' time was, Hinnissy, whin a man that was an ambassadure was th' whole thing, d'ye mind. He wint off to a foreign counthry, an' they was no cables an' no fast ships, an' he done as he pleased, an' th' first thing anny iv us heerd iv him he'd hit th' king in th' eye, an' we had a war on our hands. Thim was th' days whin ye'd have a good time as an ambassadure. I can see ye now mixin' in a little proosic acid with th' soup iv ye'er frind th' Eyetalian ambassadure, rayceivin' spies on th' doings iv th' prime ministher's wife, an' sindin' a letter to th' king: 'I have th' honor to inform ye'er majesty that if ye don't do so-an'-so befure six o'clock this av'nin' I will be obliged to bump ye. Accept th' assurances iv me mos' distinguished considheration, an' hurry up.' An ambassadure, d'ye mind, was a kind iv a Prisidint iv th' United States, livin' abroad, an' he done what he thought th' Prisidint would do

[87]

if he was in th' same place, an' th' Prisidint had to
make good f'r him.

"But nowadays we don't need an ambassadure
anny more thin we need a stage-coach to go down to
Mitchigan City. The requiremints has changed with
th' time. If me frind Prisidint Tiddy wants to know
what's goin' on annywhere, all he has to do is to subscribe to th' pa-apers. If he wants to do annything
about it he can dhrop into a tillygraft office an' sind
a cable message to th' king iv Boolgahrya or whoiver it is that's makin' th' throuble. To be an ambassadure all a man needs is to have his wife want to
live in Europe; to be a first sicrety he must be a good
waltzer; to be a sicond sicrety he must know how to
press clothes an' take care iv childher. Ye don't see
annybody nowadays that stands a chanct to be ilicted
sheriff thryin' to be ambassadure annywhere. An
ambassadure is a man that is no more use abroad thin
he wud be at home. A vice-prisidint iv a company
that's bein' took in be a thrust, a lawyer that th'
juries is onto, a Congressman that can't be reilicted,
a milishy gin'ral whose fam'ly wants to larn Fr-rinch
without th' aid iv a teacher, thim's th' kind that lands.
Ye cudden't blindfold me an' back me into th' job.
No, sir. If me frind in Wash'nton iver offered to
sind me to reside at or near th' Coort iv Saint James
I'd ask him: ' Ar-re all th' gaugers' jobs took?' No
wan that loves his fellow-counthrymen as I do, an'
knows thim, wud accipt th' honor an' lave his property an' good name in their care f'r four years.
While I have me vigor I'll remain here with me hand
on th' gun. I bet ye I cud put an adver-tisement
in th' pa-apers to-morroh: ' Wanted—An ambassa-

dure exthrordin'ry; middle-aged Protestant gintleman iv good figure, kind disposition, an' used to
s-ciety; salary, $3 a week,' an' Ar-rchey Road 'd be
blocked with applicants, an' they'd all be good
enough.

"No, sir, it ain't th' job it was. I used to think
I'd like to be wan an' go over to Rooshya, an' whin
some good la-ad fr'm this counthry got into throuble
over hurlin' remarks iv an unkind nature at the Czar
to wrap him up in an American flag an' dhrive him
through town in an express wagon while th' Roosyan
gin'ral that was goin' to shoot him bit holes in his
whiskers an' muttered: ' Curse that American dog-
sky. He's foiled me befure me ar-rmy!' An' if th'
American citizen was pinched I'd dhrive up to th'
palace in a furyous rage, push th' guards aside, an'
march into th' chamber where th' Czar sat on his
throne, an' say: ' Sign an order to release this man
in tin minyits or I'll blow up th' flat.' ' Ar-re ye
aware,' says th' Czar, with blanched face, ' that
ye're addhressin' a king?' ' I am,' says I, with me
hand on th' breast iv th' uniform iv th' Hibernian
Rifles, iv which I was ilicted (in me mind) th' colonel
befure I sailed. ' I am, dishpot,' says I. ' An',' I
says, ' ar-re ye aware,' I says, ' that ye ar-re addhressin',' I says, ' Martin Dooley, Ministher Pleni-
pootootchinary an' Ambassadure Exthrordin'ry iv th'
United States iv America, County iv Cook, s.s., huroo,' says I, pullin' a little American flag fr'm me
vest pocket an' wavin' it over me head. ' Great
Hivins,' says th' Czar, signin' th' ordher with thremblin' hands, an' I hurry off to th' dungeon an' release
Eben Perkins, an' he gives me a goold watch, an'

his good-lookin' wife throws her arms around me neck an' calls me their presarver. 'Twas wan iv th' dhreams iv me youth. I'm oldher now.

"Gin'rally whin ye see in th' pa-apers that a man's been app'inted an ambassadure ye know it ought to r-read that his wife has been app'inted ambassadhress. His wife wants him to lave th' counthry, an' th' counthry is resigned, an' th' place he's goin' to don't raise no objections. Whin he reads in th' pa-apers all th' things he's called he begins to think th' job is almost as high as a place in th' custom house, an' th' good woman sees hersilf an' th' queen rompin' together, an' maybe she won't give th' cold eye to th' wife iv th' rich undhertaker up th' sthreet whin she comes to Boodypest an' sees her an' th' rile fam'ly rowlin' by in th' rile coach dhrawn be camels. Th' ambassadure lands at th' coort, where he's goin' to avinge th' insults to his native land f'r four years, an' the sicrety iv th' legation, who used to be a good tennis-player befure he lost his mind, meets him at th' deepo an' hurries him into a closed hack. 'What's this f'r?' says th' ambassadure, who's had th' coat iv arms iv Noo Jersey painted on th' soles iv his boots, an' would like to put thim out th' window. 'Why am I threated like a pris'ner?' he says. 'Hush,' says Alonzo, th' first sicrety. 'Ye can't be seen until ye've been gone over be th' tailor,' he says. 'If anny wan got onto that blue Prince Albert it'd be ye to th' Basteel,' he says. 'I'll take ye home an' keep ye locked up till th' harness-maker has got through with ye,' he says. 'But,' says th' ambassadure, 'whin do I begin th' important jooties iv me exalted station?' he says. 'Thank

Hivin,' says th' sicrety iv legation,' there ain't a
ball f'r a week,' he says. ' Please keep ye'er face
away fr'm th' window, an' do throw away that pocket
comb,' he says.

" The first sicrety has th' divvle's own time f'r a
week or two. Ivry mornin' he spinds in tachin' th'
ambassadure an' his lady th' two-step an' th' wurruds
iv th' counthry indicatin' ' How d'ye do.' ' I'm
plazed to meet ye.' ' It's a fine, big house ye have.'
' I'll take a little more iv th' spinach,' an' so on.
Fin'lly he has it all right, an' th' first sicrety takes
him up to see th' king. As he enthers with a martial
sthride th' speech he prepared in Jersey City slips
his mind, he falls aisily on a rug into a settin' or
kneelin' posture, an' th' king mutters a few kindly
wurruds in th' language that th' ambassadure used
to shoot at whin he was in th' milishy, an' all is
over. Th' first sicrety carries him out, an' he goes
home an' finds his wife in hysterics fr'm thryin' to
explain her position in Cedar Rapids to a Rooshyn
princess through a Danish maid iv honor that wanst
lived in Scotland.

" Afther a while he begins to apprecyate th' honors
iv his place. Th' king sinds him an invitation to peek
into th' rile gardens on public holidays, to speak at a
dinner iv th' Bus Dhrivers' Assocyation, an' to attind
anny fun'rals iv th' rile fam'ly. Th' first sicrety
gets him so he can weep ivry time th' name iv Shakespeare is mintioned. Th' first sicrety tells him that
he oughtn't to know too manny Americans, but that's
because th' first sicrety don't understhand his fellow-
counthrymen. Ivry mornin', whin th' ambassadure
opens his mail, expictin' a letther fr'm th' Prisidint

tellin' him to run right over to th' palace an' ask
th' king about th' Pannyma Canal, he gets a few
lines fr'm an American stoppin' at th' Stars an'
Sthripes Hotel, sayin': 'Dear Ambassadure, I have a
letther fr'm Joe Cannon tellin' ye to give me th'
best rooms in ye'er house, or lose ye'er job. I will
move in to-morroh. Manewhile plaze sind me th'
name iv a good store in this accursed hole where an
American can buy a pair iv suspinders.' If he's a
wise ambassadure he does it. A man that riprisinted
this counthry abroad soon larns how to match silks
an' where to buy rockin'-chairs. If he don't, he's no
good. An' on th' Fourth iv July he stands at home
an' grasps manny a wet an' frindly hand.

"All this I larned fr'm Dargan, who was over
there las' year. He met an ambassadure that used
to run f'r Congress ivry time he had a mind to. Dargan got his money eight times befure th' good man
larned that Dargan didn't live in th' disthrict. He
says that th' ambassadure tol' him what I'm tellin' ye,
an' wept on his shouldher. 'How long ar-re ye in
for?' says Dargan. 'Three years more,' says th'
ambassadure. 'Three years more,' he says, 'an'
thin I'll give th' first sicrety a punch in th' nose an'
rayturn to th' land iv th' free,' he says. 'Have ye
anny fine-cut?' he says. At this minyit a young man
come around th' corner an' grabbed th' ambassadure
be th' collar. 'Didn't I tell ye niver to come out iv
th' park in thim pants?' he says. 'Here comes Lord
Gimlets,' he says. It was th' first sicrety. An' Dargan niver see th' ambassadure again. He thinks they
have him locked up in th' coal cellar.

"So I don't want to be anny ambassadure, Hin-
[92]

nissy. Th' cable is quicker, th' newspaper rayporther is more important, an' theyse more diplomatic business done be Jew men fr'm Wall Sthreet thin be all th' diplomats fr'm Constantinople to Copenhagen, bedad."

"But supposin' Ireland was free," said Mr. Hennessy.

"Ah," said Mr. Dooley, "thin 'twud be ye I'd like to see get th' job. I cudden't have too manny iv me ol' frinds presintin' their cridintials to me."

DIPLOMATIC UNIFORMS

DIPLOMATIC UNIFORMS

"WELL, sir," said Mr. Dooley, "I see be th' pa-apers that th' American ambassadure to Rooshya has invinted a unyform f'r himsilf. It's a plain unyform, but nate. A chapeau, with a long, graceful feather in it; a broadcloth coat, very full in th' basque, an' thrimmed with American eagles in goold; vest iv th' same mateeryal; pantaloons iv pale blue, with a dillycate goold sthripe, four inches wide an th' outside seam; wan hip an' two side pockets; thirty-eight chest, forty-five waist. Th' ambassadure will carry a hankerchief iv th' star-spangled banner, with th' rile ar-rms in a corner, an' will wear upon his shirt-front th' device: 'E plooribus unum, American ambassadure. Use no hooks.'"

"What does he want with a unyform, annyhow?" asked Mr. Hennessy.

"Well, it's a long an' a sad story," said Mr. Dooley. "Bear with me while I tell it ye, or do not, as ye please. I'll tell it, annyhow. Ye see, in th' arly days iv this raypublic no wan cared what an ambassadure wore, so long as it had pockets enough to carry away what he got f'r his beloved counthry fr'm th' effeet monarchies iv th' ol' wurruld. I've seen pitchers iv Binjamin Franklin, who was that thick with Looey, King iv France, that he cud call on him anny hour iv th' day or night, an' Binjamin Franklin's unyform was a fur cap an' a pair iv specs.

"In thim simple days, whin th' fathers iv th' raypublic wanted to sind a man abroad to skin a king, they put their heads together an' picked out a good, active, thravellin' salesman kind iv a man. Th' fathers iv th' raypublic was mos'ly in th' fish-ile business, an' knew th' cap'ble men in thrade. 'Who'll we sind to Fr-rance?' says Thomas Jefferson. 'This here matther iv th' Loosyany purchase has got to be delicately handled or we won't get all th' best iv it,' he says. 'I suggest Obadiah Perkins iv Newburypoort,' says Jawn Adams. 'Has he had anny diplomatic expeeryence?' says Pathrick Hinnery. 'I wanst see him sell a bar'l iv tin-pinny nails to a lady that come to th' store to buy a pound iv sody-crackers,' says Jawn Adams. 'He's our man,' says all th' others, an' Obadiah Perkins got th' job.

"He packed a collar an' an exthry pair iv socks in a bag, took along a copy iv th' Westminsther Confissyon an' an inthrest table f'r riference, provisioned himsilf with atin' tobacco, an' started out. At eight o'clock he landed in Paree; at eight-eight he knocked down a coort chamberlain an' a jawnnydarm, an' landed in th' lap iv Looey th' Magnificent-but-Tired. At nine o'clock th' monarch had given him a goold watch, a jooled snuff-case, a finger-ring, an' a soord, had signed a deed thransferrin' th' Change All Aisy to th' American people, who have owned it to this day, an' was in fits iv laughter over a story about Silas Cooper iv Salem, which Ambassadure Obadiah told him in th' perfect Fr-rinch he had picked up fr'm th' cook iv th' ship goin' over. Afther that

Diplomatic Uniforms

Obadiah was all right. He had his feet undher th'
king's mahogany ivry day at dinner, an' on th'
mahogany most iv th' rest iv th' time. He inthrajooced rockin'-chairs in th' rile palace, an' taught
th' Fr-rinch nobility how to rock without fallin' out.
No wan cared how he dhressed. He attinded th'
coort rayciptions in a jumper an' leather breeches
wan day, an' th' nex' day all th' nobility, includin'
th' king, come in jumpers an' leather breeches. He
blowed in his tay to make it cool, an' afther that all
th' Fr-rinch arrystocracy cud be seen blowin' into
their tay. He wore a hat that had shtud him in good
stead through tin hard winters on th' road, an' th'
gr-reatest nobles in France took to sittin' on their
hats befure goin' out to make thim look like th'
' Chapeau Obadiah,' which had become th' style. An'
whin he wint away, which he did not because he was
not succissful, but because he didn't like th' cookin',
he was followed to th' boat be th' king an' all th' rile
fam'ly.

" Thim was th' modest days iv th' raypublic, Hinnissy. It's diff-rent now that we've become a wurruld
power. Th' sufferin's iv some iv our ambassadures
on account iv their clothes has been turr'ble. I was
r-readin' th' sad case iv th' ambassadure to Rooshya,
th' Hon'rable Charleymayne Tower, iv Phillydelphy,
Pa. If I had that name, divvle a czar wud scare me.
I'd ask f'r no unyform. Th' name itsilf is unyform
enough. Some names sounds like overalls; some
sounds like a long coat an' a high hat, but Charleymayne Tower sounds like th' clothes a boss knights
timplar wears ivry three years. It has forty pounds
iv epaulets on its shoulders. It's th' kind iv a name

[99]

Gin'ral Miles wud like to wear f'r a unyform. If
I had that name I'd go to th' palace in a sheet an'
ixpict th' guards to fall down on their faces. But
all th' time he was in Saint Petersburg, Charleymayne
Tower suffered th' gr-reatest torture on account iv
th' clothes he had on an' th' clothes he didn't have on.
He had no unyform. At coort rayciptions he looked
like a detective at a fancy ball. He was onable
to perform anny iv th' gr-reat jooties iv an
ambassadure. Ivry step was blocked be his mis'rable
attire. He was double-crossed be th' lowliest iv
diplomats who were entitled to put on glad, bright
things whin they wint to see th' Czar. Wan day he
come rollin' up to th' palace carryin' in th' tail
iv his simple black coat a most important threaty.
He had made many attimpts to have this threaty
signed be the Czar, but th' Czar had always spurned
him, owin' to th' machinations iv Lord Ronald, th'
English ambassadure, an' Veecont Boulbaze, th'
Fr-rinch ambassadure. Both these haughty ambassadures had a window-dhresser fr'm a gints' furnishin' store f'r a valley, an' whin th' American ambassadure stood alongside iv thim I tell ye he looked
cheap.

" But this day Charleymayne Tower was prepared
to brave th' Czar in his very throne. He rolled up in
his carredge, and' th' sintry cried: ' Who goes there?'
' Th' ambassadure iv th' United States iv America,
huroo!' says th' coachman. ' That man?' says th'
sintry. ' To th' kitchen dure with ye, waiter,' he says.
Well, th' ambassadure stifled his rage, an' attimpted
to explain about himsilf, an' th' sintry run him in.
Yes, sir, he run in th' ambassadure iv these United

Diplomatic Uniforms

States, an' they was just about to take his photoy-graft an' sind him off in th' Black Maria to Sibeerya whin a gran'-jook come along an' identified him, an' they let him go. He hurried to th' throne-room, where Nicholas, Czar iv Rooshya, was settin' on his rile throne, an' took his place in line. Th' ambassa-dure iv England wore th' gorjous unyform iv his sta-tion; th' ambassadure iv France jingled with medals; th' ambassadure iv Chiny wore a pink-an'-green tea-gown. Wan be wan they were prisinted, an' th' Czar complimented thim on their clothes. 'Very tasty, Lord Ronald.' 'Handsome pants ye're wearin' this day, Veecont.' 'Ling Ching, me wife, th' Czaretta, wants me to ask ye th' name iv ye'er dhressmaker.' But whin th' ambassadure iv th' United States bent his proud knee befure th' Czar th' haughty monarch said, with an evil smile: 'Garson, bring th' check. Oh,' he wint on, pretindin' to jus' recognize Charley-mayne Tower, 'I didn't know ye at first. I thought ye was th' waiter,' he says. Loud an' long was th' laughter provoked be this kingly sally. Th' jest flew like wildfire through th' crowd. Fair ladies smiled behind their fans. 'Bring me a cup iv tay an' some spare-ribs,' says th' Princess Olgoinskia, with a maddenin' smile. 'What is th' title iv th' king iv ye'er counthry, Misther Tower,' drawled Lord Ronald, in his most supercilyous tones. 'Is it head waiter?' he says. 'Mong doo,' said th' Veecont; 'America, it is a lar-rge resthrant, ain't it?' he says. Th' air was filled with cries iv 'Waiter.' 'Here you.' 'S-s-st.' 'Boy, th' bill.' 'Ain't I niver goin' to get that pie?' An' so on.

"Charleymayne Tower hurrid fr'm th' room.

While he was standin' at th' dure iv th' palace an'
lookin' down with horror on his broadcloth pantaloons, a gran'-jook came behind him, tapped him on
th' shoulder, an' said: 'Call Gran'-Jook Oscaroff-
ski's hack, an' be quick about it.' Charleymayne
Tower cud hear no more. He leaped fr'm th' scene
iv his disaster, an' callin' a drofsky, bade th' dhriver
haste at wanst to a tailor-man's. There he ordhered
th' suit I tell ye about.

" Wan week later a tall, magnificently attired man
sthrode into th' rile chamber. It was th' American
ambassadure. As he marched along a buzz iv excitemint ran acrost that splindid room. Th' English
ambassadure turned with an oath an' left th' rile
prisince. 'Malydiction,' says th' Veecont Boulbaze.
'Le stuff is off.' Th' Gran'-Duchess Olgarina give
a passionate cry an' fainted. Th' American ambassadure sthrode on, unmindful iv th' excitemint. Th'
Czar, who is a prudent husband, sint his wife fr'm
th' room. Thin steppin' fr'm th' throne, he advanced
to meet th' riprisintative iv a gr-reat people. Th'
ambassadure was preparin' to kneel whin th' monarch
said: 'Nay, Charleymayne, kneel not to me in thim
pants on this flure. Rather shud I kneel to thee, f'r
niver since king an' tailor jined together to rule th'
wurruld, has human legs been encased in so happy a
pair iv bloomers. At last America takes its thrue station among th' nations iv th' earth.' That night th'
threaty was signed be which th' Czar agreed to sind
three millyon Rooshyan Jews to this counthry befure
th' first iv May, an' Lord Ronald hurled himsilf fr'm
th' great Popolapotcheff bridge into th' Neva afther
shootin' his tailor. Now they have promoted Charley-

mayne Tower, but his unyform remains upon th'
banks iv th' frozen Neva, an' against it nayether
arrystocratic inthrigue nor dispotic whim will pre-
vail.

"I think it's a good thing, Hinnissy. It's goin'
to save us a lot iv throuble in pickin' out diplomats.
It will no longer be nicissry to find some wan who
wudden't wurruk at home, an' whose rilitives wud like
to sind him out iv th' counthry to uphold th' dignity
an' honor iv our fair land abroad. All we have to
do is to get th' unyform an' thrust anny kind iv a
man into it. 'Th' Prisidint has disignated a pair
iv olive-green pantaloons an' a ecroo coat to be ambassadure exthraordhinry an' ministher plinipoo-
tinchry iv th' United States at th' coort iv Saint
Jeems.' 'Th' Hon'rable Caliphas Snivvy has been
promoted fr'm th' Hussars unyform at Lisbon to
th' more important suit at Madhrid.' 'Th' demands
iv th' United States govermint on th' Impror iv Chiny
was prisinted yisterdah be a bear-skin cap, a blue-
an'-silver coat, an' a pair iv yellow pantaloons. Th'
Impror was much imprissed.' It 'll be grand. Whin
th' Prisidint wants to find an imissary f'r an important missyon he'll call on a tailor. They'll be
signs in th' windies iv th' clothing stores: 'Plymouth
Rock diplomats; they niver tear.' 'Nobby styles in
American ambassadures, fifteen dollars.' An' there
ye ar-re."

"Well, it must be thryin' f'r an ambassadure to
be took f'r a waiter," said Mr. Hennessy.

"It is," said Mr. Dooley. "It is exthremely
annoyin' to a proud soul to be mistook f'r a waiter.
But I shud like to hear what th' waiters think about

it. Annyhow, I bet no wan iver took Binjamin Franklin f'r a waiter."

"I wondher why?" asked Mr. Hennessy.

"I don't know," said Mr. Dooley, " onless it was that even in th' prisince iv a king Binjamin Franklin niver felt like a waiter."

THE INTELLECTUAL LIFE

THE INTELLECTUAL LIFE

"WELL, sir," said Mr. Dooley, "it must be a grand thing to be a colledge pro-fissor."

"Not much to do," said Mr. Hennessy.

"But a gr-reat deal to say," said Mr. Dooley. "Ivry day th' minyit I pick up me pa-aper afther I've read th' criminal an' other pollytical news, th' spoortin' news, th' rale-estate advertisemints, th' in-vytation fr'm th' cultured foreign gent to meet an American lady iv some means, th' spoortin' news over again, thin th' iditoryals, I hasten to find out what th' colledge pro-fissor had to say yisterdah. I wish th' iditor wud put it in th' same column iv the pa-aper ivry day. Thin he wudden't have to collect anny other funny column. 'Humorous: Pro-fissor Wind-haul iv Harvard makes a savidge attack on Abraham Lincoln.' As it is, I sometimes have to hunt through th' pa-aper fr'm th' Newport scandal on page wan to th' relligious notes on page two hundherd an' four be-fure I come acrost me fav'rite funny sayin's iv funny fellows.

"I've been collictin' these wurruds iv wisdom f'r a long time, Hinnissy, an' I'm now prepared to deliver ye a sample colledge lecture on all subjicks fr'm th' creation iv th' wurruld: 'Young gintlemen: I will begin be sayin' that I have me doubts about th'

8   [107]

varyous stories consarnin' th' creation iv th' wurruld. In th' first place, I dismiss with a loud laugh th' theery that it was created in six days. I cud make such a poor wurruld as this in two days with a scroll-saw. Akelly preposterous is th' idee that it wasn't made at all, but grew up out iv nawthin'. Me idee is that th' wurruld is a chunk iv th' sun that was chipped off be a collisyon with th' moon, cooled down, an' advertised f'r roomers. As to its age, I differ with th' Bible. Me own opinyon iv th' age iv th' arth is that it is about twinty-eight years old. That is as far as I go back.

" ' Speakin' iv th' Bible, it is an inthrestin' wurruk, but th' English is poor. I advise all iv ye not to injure ye'er style be readin' th' prisint editions, but if ye want rale good English ye will read th' Bible thranslated into Hoosier d'lect be Pro-fissor Lumsum Jiggs iv th' Univarsity iv Barry's Corner, wan iv our gr-reatest lithrachoors, whose loss to th' sody-wather business was a gloryous gain to relligion an' letthers. If ye want to make a comparison to show ye how lithrachoor has improved, compare th' wurruks iv Homer an' Jiggs. Homer nodded. He niver nodded to me, but he nodded. But has Jiggs nodded? Niver. He hasn't time. He is on his four thousandth book now, an' has larned to wurruk a second typewriter with his feet. Read Jiggs an' f'rget about Homer. As f'r Shakespeare, he is a dead wan. Th' opinyon I have iv Shakespeare is so low that I will not express it befure ladies. I ain't sayin' that his wurruks have not been pop'lar among th' vulgar. An' he might have amounted to something if he had been ijjacated, but his language is base, an' he had no imagination. Th' gr-reatest potes th' wurruld has projooced are Ransom Stiggs an' J. B. Mulcoon iv Keokuk. Th' Keokuk school iv pothry has all others badly stung. J. B. Mulcoon has discovered more rhymes f'r dear thin Al Tinnyson iver heerd iv.

" ' Me opinyon iv pollyticks, if ye shud ask me f'r it, is that we might as well give up th' experimint. A govermint founded be an ol' farmer like George Wash'nton an' a job-printer like Bin Franklin was bound to go down in roon. It has abandoned all their ideels—which was a good thing—an' made worse wans. Look at Lincoln. There's a fellow ivrybody is always crackin' up. But what did he amount to? What did he do but carry on a war, free th' slaves, an' run this mis'rable counthry? But who asked him to free th' slaves? I didn't. A man utterly lackin' in principle an' sinse iv humor, he led a mob an' was conthrolled be it. An' who ar-re th' mob that direct this counthry? A lot iv coarse, rough people, who ar-re sawin' up lumber an' picklin' pork, an' who niver had a thought iv th' Higher Life that makes men aspire to betther things an' indijestion. They ar-re ye'er fathers an' mine, young gintlemen. Can I say worse thin that? An' to think iv th' likes iv thim runnin' this govermint! By Jove, if I had raymimbered las' Choosdah that it was iliction day I'd have larned fr'm me milkman how to vote an' gone down to th' polls an' dhriven thim fr'm power. Well, there's wan consolation about it all: th' counthry won't last long. I noticed th' other day it had begun to crack. Whin it sinks ye'ers thruly will be near th' edge, ready to jump off. Annyhow, it don't matther much. Th' American people ar-re all gettin' to be Indyans again. Walkin' down to-day, I obsarved twenty-two people who looked to me like Indyans. Next week I intind to verify me conclusyons be buyin' a picture iv an Indyan. But I'm intirely convinced that in three or four years at laste we'll all be livin' in wickey-ups an' scalpin' each other. With these few remarks, let us inquirers f'r knowledge go out an' commit suicide on th' futball field. Ruh-ruh-ruh-ruh! Bazzybazoo!"

"I like it, Hinnissy. What I like most about it is that a colledge pro-fissor niver speaks fr'm impulse. He thinks ivrything out thurly befure announcin' his opinyon. Th' theery iv me larned frind down in Rockyfellar's colledge that very soon ye'd seen me r-rushin' down Archey Road with a tommyhawk in me hand, thryin' to thrade off a pony f'r a wife an' a wife f'r a bottle iv wood alcohol, didn't leap out iv his gr-reat brain in a scandalous hurry. He pondered it long an' carefully. Th' idee sthruck him at breakfast while he was eatin' his prunes, an' did not machure till he was half through with th' ham an' eggs. So with Pro-fissor Windhaul. He didn't land on Lincoln till he was sure iv his ground. He first made inquiries, an' found out that there was such a man. Thin he looked f'r his name among th' gradjates iv Harvard. Thin he bumped him. It's a good thing Lincoln was dead befure he was assaulted. He niver wud have survived th' attack.

"It's a fine thing f'r th' young men who set at th' feet iv these larned ducks. A little boy is chased away

fr'm home an' enthers wan iv these here siminaries.
He was licked yisterdah f'r neglectin' to scrub below
the chin, but to-morroh he will be cheerin' wildly
while Pro-fissor Bumpus tells him universal suffrage
was a bad break. If he has a weak chest, an' can't
play futball, he goes on imbibin' wisdom ontil he
arrives at th' dew pint, whin his alma mather hurls
him at th' onforchnit wurruld. He knows fifty thousan' things, but th' on'y wan iv thim that he cud
prove is that Heffelfinger was a gr-reat futball
player. Thin begins his rale colledge career. Th'
post-gradjate coorse is th' best in th' wurruld. Th'
enthrance fee is all he has. Th' wurruld takes it
away fr'm him th' minyit he thries to apply his colledge pro-fissor's idee that undher th' doctrine iv
probabilities two pair ought to beat three iv a kind.
He hasn't on'y wan new pro-fissor, but twinty millyon, old an' young, rich an' poor, men an' women,
especyally women. He can't shirk his lessons. He
has to be up in th' mornin' bright an' arly larnin'
an' passin' examinations. He's on'y told annything
wanst. If he don't raymimber it th' next time he is
asked, some pro-fissor gives him a thump on th' head.
Anny time he don't like his dear ol' alma mather he
can quit. Th' wurruld ain't advertisin' f'r anny
students. It has no competitors, an' th' lists are
always full. Th' coorse lasts fr'm wan to sixty years,
an' it gets harder to'rd th' commincemint day. If
he's a good scholar, an' behaves himsilf, an' listens to
th' pro-fissors, and wurruks hard, he can gradjate
with honors. In anny case, he is allowed to write out
his own diploma. He knows best what he is entitled to."

Dissertations by Mr. Dooley

" If ye had a boy wud ye sind him to colledge?"
asked Mr. Hennessy.

" Well," said Mr. Dooley, " at th' age whin a boy
is fit to be in colledge I wudden't have him around th'
house."

THE VICE-PRESIDENT

THE VICE-PRESIDENT

"IT'S sthrange about th' vice-prisidincy," said Mr. Dooley. "Th' prisidincy is th' highest office in th' gift iv th' people. Th' vice-prisidincy is th' next highest an' th' lowest. It isn't a crime exactly. Ye can't be sint to jail f'r it, but it's a kind iv a disgrace. It's like writin' anonymous letters. At a convintion nearly all th' dillygates lave as soon as they've nommynated th' prisidint f'r fear wan iv thim will be nommynated f'r vice-prisidint. They offered it to me frind Joe Cannon, and th' language he used brought th' blush iv shame to th' cheeks iv a naygur dillygate fr'm Allybamy. They thried to hand it to Hinnery Cabin Lodge, an' he wept bitterly. They found a man fr'm Wisconsin, who was in dhrink, an' had almost nommynated him whin his wife came in an' dhragged him away fr'm timptation. Th' way they got Sinitor Fairbanks to accipt was be showin' him a pitcher iv our gr-reat an' noble prisidint thryin' to jump a horse over a six-foot fence. An' they on'y prevailed upon Hinnery Davis to take this almost onequalled honor be tellin' him that th' raison th' Sage iv Esoopus didn't speak earlier was because he has weak lungs.

"Why is it, I wondher, that ivrybody runs away fr'm a nommynation f'r vice-prisidint as if it was an indictment be th' gran' jury? It usen't to be so.

Dissertations by Mr. Dooley

I've hollered mesilf black in th' face f'r ol' man
Thurman an' Hendricks iv Injyanny. In th' ol'
days, whin th' boys had nommynated some unknown
man fr'm New York f'r prisidint, they turned in an'
nommynated a gr-reat an' well-known man fr'm th'
West f'r vice-prisidint. Th' candydate f'r vice-
prisidint was all iv th' ticket we iver see durin' a
campaign. Th' la-ad they put up f'r prisidint stayed
down East an' was niver allowed to open his mouth
except in writin' befure witnesses, but th' candydate
f'r vice-prisidint wint fr'm wan end iv th' counthry to
th' other howlin' again' th' tariff an' other immortal
issues, now dead. I niver voted f'r Grover Cleveland.
I wudden't vote f'r him anny more thin he'd vote f'r
me. I voted f'r old man Thurman an' Tom Hendricks an' Adly Stevenson befure he became a profissional vice-prisidint. They thought it was an
honor, but if ye'd read their bio-graphies to-day ye'd
find at th' end: ' Th' writer will pass over th' closin'
years iv Mr. Thurman's career hurriedly. It is
enough to say iv this painful peryod that afther a
lifetime iv devoted sarvice to his counthry th' statesman's declinin' days was clouded be a gr-reat sorrow.
He become vice-prisidint iv th' United States. Oh,
how much betther 'twere that we shud be sawed off
arly be th' gr-reat reaper Death thin that a life iv
honor shud end in ignomy.' It's a turr'ble thing.
  " If ye say about a man that he's good prisidintial
timber he'll buy ye a dhrink. If ye say he's good vice-
prisidintial timber ye mane that he isn't good enough
to be cut up into shingles, an' ye'd betther be careful.
  " It's sthrange, too, because it's a good job. I
think a man cud put in four years comfortably in

[116]

th' place if he was a sound sleeper. What ar-re his
jooties, says ye? Well, durin' th' campaign he has
to do a good deal iv th' rough outside wurruk. Th'
candydate f'r prisidint is at home pickin' out th' big
wurruds in th' ditchnry an' firin' thim at us fr'm
time to time. Th' candydate f'r th' vice-prisidincy
is out in Ioway yellin' fr'm th' back iv a car or a
dhray. He goes to all th' church fairs an' wakes an'
appears at public meetin's between a cornet solo an'
a glee club. He ought to be a man good at repartee.
Our now honored (be some) prisidint had to retort
with th' very hands that since have signed th' Pannyma Canal bill to a Colorado gintleman who accosted
him with a scantling. An' I well raymimber another
candydate, an' a gr-reat man, too, who replied to a
gintleman in Shelbyville who made a rude remark be
threatin' him as though he was an open fireplace.
It was what Hogan calls a fine-cut an' incisive reply.
Yes, sir, th' candydate f'r vice-prisidint has a busy
time iv it durin' th' campaign, hoppin' fr'm town
to town, speakin', shakin' hands with th' popylace
who call him Hal or Charlie, dodgin' bricks, fightin'
with his audjeence, an' diggin' up f'r th' fi-nance
comity. He has to be an all-round man. He must
be a good speaker, a pleasant man with th' ladies, a
fair boxer an' rassler, something iv a liar, an' if
he's a Raypublican campaignin' in Texas, an active
sprinter. If he has all thim qualities, he may or
may not rayceive a majority at th' polls, an' no wan
will know whether they voted f'r him or not.

" Well, he's ilicted. Th' ilictors call on th' candydate f'r prisidint an' hand him th' office. They noti-
fy th' candydate f'r vice-prisidint through th' per-

sonal columns iv th' pa-apers: 'If th' tall, dark
gintleman with hazel eyes, black coat an' white vest,
who was nommynated at th' convintion f'r vice-prisidint, will call at headquarters he will hear iv something to his advantage.' So he buys a ticket an'
hops to Wash'nton, where he gets a good room suited
to his station right above th' kitchen an' overlookin'
a wood-yard. Th' prisidint has to live where he is
put, but th' vice-prisidint is free to go annywhere he
likes, where they are not particklar. Th' Constitution
provides that th' prisidint shall have to put up with
darky cookin', but th' vice-prisidint is permitted to
eat out. Ivry mornin' it is his business to call at th'
White House an' inquire afther th' prisidint's health.
Whin told that th' prisidint was niver betther he gives
three cheers, an' departs with a heavy heart.

"Th' feelin' iv th' vice-prisidint about th' prisidint's well-bein' is very deep. On rainy days he calls
at th' White House an' begs th' prisidint not to go out
without his rubbers. He has Mrs. Vice-Prisidint knit
him a shawl to protect his throat again' th' night
air. If th' prisidint has a touch iv fever th' vice-
prisidint gets a touch iv fever himsilf. He has th'
doctor on th' 'phone durin' th' night. 'Doc, I hear
th' prisidint is onwell,' he says. 'Cud I do annything
f'r him,—annything like dhrawin' his salary or ap-
pintin' th' postmasther at Injynnapolis?' It is prin-
cip'lly, Hinnissy, because iv th' vice-prisidint that most
iv our prisidints have enjoyed such rugged health.
Th' vice-prisidint guards th' prisidint, an' th' prisidint, afther sizin' up th' vice-prisidint, con-cludes
that it wud be betther f'r th' counthry if he shud
live yet awhile. 'D'ye know,' says th' prisidint to

th' vice-prisidint, ' ivry time I see you I feel tin years
younger?' ' Ye'er kind wurruds,' says th' vice-prisidint, ' brings tears to me eyes. My wife was sayin'
on'y this mornin' how comfortable we ar-re in our
little flat.' Some vice-prisidints have been so anxious
f'r th' prisidint's safety that they've had to be warn-
ed off th' White House grounds.

"Aside fr'm th' arjoos duties iv lookin' afther th'
prisidint's health, it is th' business iv th' vice-prisidint to preside over th' deliberations iv th' Sinit.
Ivry mornin' between ten an' twelve, he swings his
hammock in th' palachial Sinit chamber an' sinks off
into dhreamless sleep. He may be awakened by
Sinitor Tillman pokin' Sinitor Beveridge in th' eye.
This is wan way th' Sinit has iv deliberatin'. If so,
th' vice-prisidint rises fr'm his hammock an' says:
' Th' Sinitor will come to ordher.' ' He won't,' says
th' Sinitor. ' Oh, very well,' says th' presidin' officer; ' he won't,' an' dhrops off again. It is his jooty
to rigorously enforce th' rules iv th' Sinit. There
ar-re none. Th' Sinit is ruled be courtesy, like th'
longshoreman's union. Th' vice-prisidint is not expected to butt in much. It wud be a breach iv Sinitoryal courtesy f'r him to step down an' part th'
Sinitor fr'm Texas an' th' Sinitor fr'm Injyanny in
th' middle iv a debate undher a desk on whether
Northern gintlemen ar-re more gintlemanly thin
Southern gintlemen. I shuddent wondher if he thried
to do it if he was taught his place with th' leg iv a
chair. He isn't even called upon to give a decision.
All that his grateful counthry demands fr'm th' man
that she has ilivated to this proud position on th'
toe iv her boot is that he shall keep his opinyons to

himsilf. An' so he whiles away th' pleasant hours in th' beautiful city iv Wash'nton, an' whin he wakes up he is ayether in th' White House or in th' sthreet. I'll niver say annything again' th' vice-prisidincy. It is a good job, an' is richly deserved be ayether iv th' candydates. An', be Hivens, I'll go further an' say it richly desarves ayether iv thim."

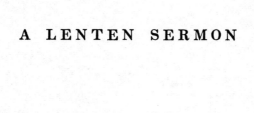

A LENTEN SERMON

A LENTEN SERMON

"O-HO," said Mr. Hennessy, "twinty-wan days to Saint Pathrick's day."

"Ar-re ye keepin' Lent?" asked Mr. Dooley.

"I am," said Mr. Hennessy. "I put th' pipe back iv th' clock day befure yisterdah night. Oh, but th' las' whiff iv th' ol' clay was plisint. Ar-re ye keepin' Lent?"

"I am that," said Mr. Dooley. "I'm on'y smokin' me seegars half through, an' I take no sugar in me tay. Th' Lord give me stren'th to last till Pathrick's day! I'm keepin' Lent, but I'm not goin' up an' down th' sthreet tellin' people about it. I ain't anny prouder iv keepin' Lent thin I am iv keepin' clean. In our fam'ly we've always kept it. I ray-mimber seein' me father tuck away th' pipe, cork up th' bottle an' put it in a thrunk with something between a moan an' a cheer, an' begin to find fault with th' wurruld. F'r us kids Lent was no gr-reat hardship. It on'y meant not enough iv something besides meat. I don't raymimber much about it excipt that on Ash Winsdah ivrybody had a smudge on his forehead; an' afther awhile th' house begun to smell a little iv fish, an' about th' thirtieth day th' eggs had thrown off all disguise an' was just plain, yellow eggs.

" Yes, sir, in our fam'ly we all kept Lent but me Uncle Mike. He started with th' rest, an' f'r a day or two he wint up an' down th' road whippin' butchers. 'Twas with gr-reat difficulty, Hinnissy, that he was previnted fr'm marchin' into th' neighborin' saloons an' poorin' out th' sthrong wathers on th' flure. F'r a short distance me Uncle Mike was th' most pious man I have iver met. At such times he organized th' Uncle Michael th' Good S'ciety, an' wint ar-round inityatin' mimbers. To hear him talk about nine o'clock on Ash Winsdah mornin' ye'd think he was jus' goin' into th' arena to fight a line befure th' onholy Roman popylace. He'd take down *Th' Lives iv th' Saints* an' set r-readin' it with a condescindin' smile on his face like a champeen athleet goin' over th' ol' records. ' Oh, yes,' he seemed to be sayin', ' They were all r-right, very good in their day, no doubt, but where wud they be now? They'se no mintion iv Saint Jerome goin' without his smoke, an' I haven't had a pipe iv tobacky since twelve o'clock last Choosdah night, an' here it's nine o'clock Winsdah mornin'.' Thin he wud look casully to'rd th' back iv th' book to see whether p'raps something mightn't 've been put in about him at th' las' moment, an' thin he wud throw it down an' say to himsilf: ' *Th' Lives iv th' Saints* f'r eighteen hundred an' fifty ain't out yet,' an' march savagely fr'm th' room, kickin' his nieces an' nevvews as he wint. At four o'clock in th' afthernoon he was discovered be me father settin' on a saw-horse in th' woodshed, puffin' away at a pipe with a bowl like a small stove that he'd took away fr'm a German, an' singin' to himsilf.

A Lenten Sermon

" But me Uncle Mike, though a gr-reat warryor in his day an' th' soul iv s'ciety, was not a model f'r a long-distance Christyan champeen. He started with th' others, but he always pulled up lame. Th' throuble with him, an' th' throuble with th' rest iv us, is that we expict to be canonized in time to show th' brief to th' fam'ly at dinner. So I say I don't go ar-round cillybratin' Lent. I don't expict Father Kelly will sind down th' Father Macchew Fife an' Dhrum Corps to serenade me because I left that lump iv sugar out iv me tay an' put in twice as much milk. Whin th' postman comes to th' dure with th' usual line iv bills an' love-letthers fr'm th' tailors, me hands don't thremble, expictin' a note fr'm th' pope tellin' me I've been canonized. No, sir, I con-grathylate mesilf on me sthrong will power, an' ray-flict that sugar makes people fat. I am niver goin' to place anny medals on anny wan f'r bein' varchous, Hinnissy, f'r if varchue ain't always necissity, me boy, its th' next thing to it. I'm tim'prate because too much dhrink doesn't agree with me; modest be-cause I look best that way; gin'rous because I don't want to be thought stingy; honest because iv th' polis force; an' brave whin I can't r-run away.

" Dock Grogan, who's an ol' Pagan, don't agree with Father Kelly on more thin two things, though they're th' frindliest iv inimies; an' wan iv thim is Lent. Father Kelly says 'tis good f'r th' soul, an' Dock Grogan he says 'tis good f'r th' body. It comes at th' r-right time iv th' year, he says, whin ivry-body has had a winther iv stuffin' thimsilves an' floodin' their inteeryors an' settin' up late at night. It's a kind iv a stand off f'r th' Chris'mas holidays.

Dissertations by Mr. Dooley

We quit atin' meat because 'tis Lent—an' we've had too much meat. We quit smokin' because 'tis Lent—an' we have a smokers' heart. We quit dhrink because it's Lent—an' we want to see if th' brakes ar-re wurrukin'. We quit goin' to th' theaytres because it's Lent—an' we're sick iv th' theaytres. If it wasn't f'r Lent in March none iv us wud live till th' Fourth iv July. 'In Lent,' says Father Kelly, 'I get me congregation back.' 'In Lent,' says Dock Grogan, 'I lose mine.' 'Lent,' says Father Kelly, 'brings thim nearer Hiven.' 'An longer away,' says Dock Grogan. 'It's hard wurruk f'r me, but I like it,' says Father Kelly. 'It's my vacation time,' says Dock Grogan, 'but I don't care f'r it.' 'It makes thim think iv th' next wurruld,' says Father Kelly. 'An' gives thim a betther hold on this,' says Dock Grogan. 'It's rellijon,' says Father Kelly. 'It's med'cine,' says Dock Grogan.

"So I say, no medals, plaze, f'r me on account iv that lump iv sugar. I done me jooty an' no more. Whin th' divvle timpted me to put in th' lump I said: 'Get thee behind me, Satan, I'm too fat now.' That was all. I done what was r-right, because it was r-right an' pious an' a good thing f'r me to do. I don't claim no gratichood. I don't ask f'r anny admiration iv me piety. But don't I look betther, Hinnissy? Don't ye see I'm a little thinner?"

"Not an inch," said Mr. Hennessy. "Ye're th' same hippypotymus ye was."

"Well, well," said Mr. Dooley. "That's sthrange. P'raps I'm a betther man, afther all. How long did ye say it was to Pathrick's day?"

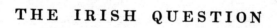

THE IRISH QUESTION

THE IRISH QUESTION

"THEY was gr-reat ructions in th' House iv Commons th' other day," said Mr. Dooley. "What about?" asked Mr. Hennessy. "About our downthrodden land," said Mr. Dooley. "Not this wan, but that little green imrald island iv th' opprissed acrost th' sea. I can't make out what 'twas all about, on'y wan iv th' good lads ast th' Right Hon'rable Arthur James Balfour, a long-legged Scotchman with side whiskers, wud he or wud he not give a day to th' discussion iv th' state iv Ireland. He wud not, says th' Right Hon'rable Arthur James Balfour. Divvle th' day. 'Well, thin,' says th' good fellow with th' fine name iv O'Donnell, 'seein' that I can get no justice f'r me beloved counthry, I will, with th' kind permission iv th' Speaker, an' not angrily, but in a sperit iv parlyminthry propriety, step acrost th' hall, makin' a ginyflixion to th' Speaker on th' way over, shake me fist in ye'er face thus, an' lave th' room,' he says. An' he done it. Th' ol' oak hall iv Westminsther sildom has witnessed such a scene, but manny like it. Th' air was filled with cries iv 'Shame,' 'Splindid,' 'O'Donnell aboo,' while th' Right Hon'rable Arthur James Balfour set in his chair, his face livid, but smilin', th' Speaker tugged narvously at his overskirt an' felt iv his frizzes, an' siveral iv th' more violent mimbers iv th' Irish party took off their hats an' put thim on again in token iv their rage. It was some minyits befure th' House raysumed its nap. Thus was another Irish riv'lution brought to a successful con-clusion.

" 'Twas a g-reat day f'r th' race, Hinnissy. I thought, whin I begun to read th' pa-aper an' see th' name O'Donnell: 'Well, here's where th' Right Hon'rable Arthur James Balfour gets a good smack in th' eye.' They're a fightin' breed, th' O'Donnells, though niver a match f'r us, an' no mimber iv th' fam'ly that I iver knew cud get his fist within an inch iv a man's nose without lavin' it go two inches further. Says I to mesilf: 'Go it, O'Donnell, me boy. Eight to wan on ye.' But no! Ne'er a blow was sthruck. Th' race iv O'Donnells has changed. They're no longer th' burly boys with th' pike an' th' scythe. They're f'r riv'lution, but don't upset th' tay-things. They no more attimpt to catch th' Speaker's eye with th' thumb. They're in favor iv freein' Ireland, but with th' permission iv th' comity on rules. It's right, too, Hinnissy. I'm opposed to vilence in anny form. We must be pathrites, but we must first iv all be gintlemen. Afther ye, me dear Alphonse.

" But whin I come to think iv it, I guess p'raps I'm wrong. Ye can't be a rivolutionist in a silk hat an' a long coat. Riv'lution is wurruk f'r th' shirt-sleeves. A riv'lution can't be bound be th' rules iv th' game because it's again' th' rules iv th' game. Put away th' tall hat, niver mind th' cups an' sau-cers, tell ma to pack up her things, an' take th' girls off to her mother's. Pah an' th' boys ar-re goin' to have a riv'lution.

[130]

The Irish Question

" Th' Irish wud have no throuble with th' English if th' English were Irish. Th' throuble with Englishmen governin' Ireland is that they're English. An Englishman niver gets to know an Irishman. They don't speak th' same language. An Englishman can understand a German, a Turk, a Chinyman, a naygur, or an Indyan, but he don't know anny more what an Irishman is talkin' an' thinkin' about thin what th' angels in Hiven ar-re sayin'. What's th' use iv con-varsin' with him? Give him a belt in th' jaw. That's a language so gin'rally undhershtud that ye niver need a pocket ditchnry to make it out. An Irishman is always dhreamin' dhreams. If ye cud get into th' mind iv a hungry Irishman an' a hungry Englishman ye'd find th' Irishman was thinkin' about a banket iv th' gods with him in seat number wan singin' a song, an' th' Englishman was reflictin' on th' smell iv th' thripe down th' sthreet.

" An Englishman don't know they'se anny such things as wrongs in th' wurruld. He sets down in front iv his dinner an' says he to himsilf : ' What a jolly wurruld this is ! What an awf'lly beastly jolly wurruld ! Ivrybody is happy. Annybody that kicks does it f'r exercise. I can't see a spot where th' wurruld needs improvemint. It's such a complete job I must have done it mesilf. Very civil iv me. What th' doose is that man over there spoutin' pothry about? He's a loonytick. Put him out. Why, he's pintin' a gun at me. Well, p'raps I'd betther listen to him.'

" Mind ye, Hinnissy, I ain't in favor iv dinnymite. Far fr'm it. Even an Englishman was niver im-

proved be bein' blown up. Or I'll put it this way:
I'm in favor iv dinnymite, but not in favor iv its
goin' off. They always ought to be a little iv it
undher an Englishman's chair. Thin we cud go up
to him an' say: 'Things is goin' badly in Ireland, an'
somethin' must be done. Plaze to sign this pa-aper
an' redhress our wrongs.' 'Wrongs?' says he.
'What ar-re wrongs?' he says. 'It wud take too
long to explain,' says me. 'We will on'y say they'se
a bunch iv joynt powdher undher ye'er chair that
may go off anny minyit. Sign here.'

"I ain't a Feenyan, d'ye mind, though I was, an' I
ain't a Clan-na-Gael, though ye can't prove it be me,
but I niver in me life see annything done without
they was a gun-play somewhere concealed in it.
Hiven f'rbid that I shud want annything to happen
to those dear cousins iv ours acrost th' sea. I wudden't bring a tear to th' blue eye iv Whitelaw Reid.
I don't believe in too much foorce, but ye've always
got to flavor th' porridge with it. I'd have a little
constichoochinal agytation an' a little foorce, a
sthreak iv wan an' a sthreak iv th' other, a polite
request an' a punch in th' eye, an argymint an' a
kick, a janial la-ad in parlymint with a mellow voice
an' a good, ginteel accint, an' a boy in corduroys
behind a rock in th' County Sligo to pint th' moral.
I wud shoot off th' mouth wan day an' th' blundher-
buss th' next. I'd have me frind Tay Pay stand up
in parlymint an' say: 'Gintlemen, ye know I'm
sthrongly again' th' use iv foorce. Th' name iv
dinnymite fills me with abhorrence, an' th' explosion
iv a fire-cracker gives me th' jumps. As a rale ol'
English gintleman in a long coat to rale ol' English

gintlemen in long coats, as between fellow-subjicks iv th' king, that dear, good man whom all revere, I plead with ye to do justice to th' fair land iv mine, which I often see on th' maps as I come down to th' House,' he says. 'Go to th' divvle,' says th' Right Hon'rable Arthur James Balfour. 'They ain't enough justice to go around amongst us now, an' why wud we be throwin' it away on a nice, polite people like ye,' he says. 'I f'rgot to add,' says Tay Pay, 'that a frind iv mine is settin' in th' gall'ry with a bag containin' about thirty pounds iv up-with-ye,' he says. 'He has just wrote me a note sayin' that his arm is tired, an' wud I mind if he tossed th' bag down to ye,' he says. 'I'm greatly grieved with th' action iv me fellow-counthryman, but his name is O'Brien, an' I can't conthrol him,' he says. 'So here I go f'r th' fire-escape,' he says; 'an',' he says, 'if ye'll bring th' pa-apers with ye,' he says, 'we might discuss th' terms iv th' settlemint as we climb down,' he says.

"That's my policy, Hinnissy, an' it's been th' policy iv all other gr-reat statesmen. Niver start a riv'lution without a gun. Niver ask a man f'r anny-thing unless ye can make him think ye're li'ble to take it, annyhow. My wrongs ar-re my wrongs, an' it's little ye mind thim until they begin to hurt ye. If I'm sick in me room up-stairs ye don't care, but whin I begin hollerin' an' jumpin' on th' flure an' knockin' th' plastherin' down on ye'er head ye'll sind f'r th' doctor. I'd have all th' mimbers iv parlymint wear black coats, but they ought to be ready to peel thim off at a minyit's notice an' show up ready f'r business in red shirts.

Dissertations by Mr. Dooley

"F'r, Hinnissy, Ireland 'll niver get annything fr'm England but a threaty iv peace."

"I wondher will England iver free Ireland?" asked Mr. Hennessy.

"Niver," said Mr. Dooley. "What talk have ye? No wan wants it that way. England will niver free Ireland, but some day, if we make it inthrestin' enough f'r her she'll have to free England iv Ireland. An' that 'll be all right."

THE AMERICAN FAMILY

THE AMERICAN FAMILY

"IS th' race dyin' out?" asked Mr. Dooley.

"Is it what?" replied Mr. Hennessy.

"Is it dyin' out?" said Mr. Dooley. "Th' ministhers an' me frind Dock Eliot iv Harvard say it is. Dock Eliot wud know diff'rent if he was a rale dock an' wint flying up Halsted Sthreet in a buggy, floggin' a white horse to be there on time. But he ain't, an' he's sure it's dyin' out. Childher ar-re disappearin' fr'm America. He took a squint at th' list iv Harvard gradjates th' other day, an' discovered that they had ivrything to make home happy but kids. Wanst th' wurruld was full iv little Harvards. Th' counthry swarmed with thim. Ye cud tell a Harvard man at wanst be a look at his feet. He had th' unmistakable cradle fut. It was no sthrange thing to see an ol' Harvard man comin' back to his almy mather pushin' a baby-carredge full iv twins an' ladin' a fam'ly that looked like an advertisemint in th' newspapers to show th' percintage iv purity iv bakin'-powdhers. Prisidint Eliot was often disturbed in a discoorse, pintin' out th' dangers iv th' counthry, be th' outcries iv th' progeny iv fair Harvard. Th' campus was full iv baby-carredges on commincemint day, an' specyal accomydations had to be took f'r nurses. In thim happy days some wan was always teethin' in a Harvard fam'ly. It looked as if ivin-

[137]

chooly th' wurruld wud be peopled with Harvard men, an' th' Chinese wud have to pass an Exclusion Act. But something has happened to Harvard. She is projoocin' no little rah-rahs to glad th' wurruld. Th' av'rage fam'ly iv th' Harvard gradjate an' th' jackass is practically th' same. Th' Harvard man iv th' prisint day is th' last iv his race. No artless prattle is heerd in his home.

"An' me frind Prisidint Eliot is sore about it, an' he has communicated th' sad fact to th' clargy. Nawthin' th' clargy likes so much as a sad fact. Lave wan iv me frinds iv th' clargy know that we're goin' to th' divvle in a new way an' he's happy. We used to take th' journey be covetin' our neighbor's ox or his ass or be disobeyin' our parents, but now we have no parents to disobey or they have no childher to disobey thim. Th' American people is becomin' as unfruitful as an ash-heap. We're no betther thin th' Fr-rinch. They say th' pleasin' squawk iv an infant hasn't been heerd in France since th' Franco-Prooshun war. Th' governmint offers prizes f'r families, but no wan claims thim. A Frinch gintleman who wint to Germany wanst has made a good deal iv money lecturin' on 'Wild Babies I have Met,' but ivry wan says he's a faker. Ye can't convince anny wan in France that there ar're anny babies. We're goin' th' same way. Less thin three millyon babies was bor'rn in this counthry las' year. Think iv it, Hinnissy—less thin three millyon, hardly enough to consume wan-tenth iv th' output iv pins! It's a horrible thought. I don't blame ivry wan, fr'm Tiddy Rosenfelt down, f'r worryin' about it.

"What's th' cause, says ye? I don't know. I've

been readin' th' newspapers, an' ivrybody's been tellin' why. Late marredges, arly marredges, no marredges, th' cost iv livin', th' luxuries iv th' day, th' tariff, th' thrusts, th' spots on th' sun, th' difficulty iv obtainin' implyemint, th' growth iv culture, th' pitcher-hat, an' so on. Ivrybody's got a raison, but none iv thim seems to meet th' bill. I've been lookin' at th' argymints pro an' con, an' I come to th' conclusion that th' race is dyin' out on'y in spots. Th' av'rage size iv th' fam'ly in Mitchigan Avnoo is .000001, but th' av'rage size iv th' fam'ly in Ar-rchey R-road is somewhat larger. Afther I r-read what Dock Eliot had to say I ast me frind Dock Grogan what he thought about it. He's a rale dock. He has a horse an' buggy. He's out so much at night that th' polis ar-re always stoppin' him, thinkin' he is a burglar. Th' dock has prepared some statistics f'r me, an' here they ar're: Number iv twins bor-rn in Ar-rchey Road fr'm Halsted Sthreet to Westhern Avnoo, fr'm Janooary wan to Janooary wan, 355 pairs; number iv thrips iv thriplets in th' same fiscal year, nine; number iv individjool voters, eighty-three thousan' nine hundherd an' forty-two; av'rage size iv fam'ly, fourteen; av'rage weight iv parents, wan hundherd an' eighty-five; av'rage size iv rooms, nine be eight; av'rage height iv ceilin', nine feet; av'rage wages, wan dollar sivinty-five; av'rage duration iv doctor's bills, two hundherd years.

"I took th' statistics to Father Kelly. He's an onprejudiced man, an' if th' race was dyin' out he wud have had a soundin'-boord in his pulpit long ago, so that whin he mintioned th' wurrud ' Hell,' ivry wan in th' congregation wud have thought he meant

him or her. ' I think,' says Father Kelly, ' that Dock
Grogan is a little wrong in his figures. He's boast-
in'. In this parrish I allow twelve births to wan
marredge. It varies, iv coorse, bein' sometimes as
low as nine, an' sometimes as high as fifteen. But
twelve is about th' av'rage,' he says. ' If ye see
Dock Eliot,' he says, ' ye can tell him th' race ain't
dyin' out very bad in this here part iv the wurruld.
On th' conthry. It ain't liable to, ayether,' he says,
' onless wages is raised,' he says. ' Th' poor ar-re
becomin' richer in childher, an' th' rich poorer,' he
says. ' 'Tis always th' way,' he says. ' Th' bigger
th' house th' smaller th' fam'ly. Mitchigan Avnoo
is always thinnin' out fr'm itsilf, an' growin' fr'm
th' efforts iv Ar-rchey R-road. 'Tis a way Nature has
iv gettin' even with th' rich an' pow'rful. Wan part
iv town has nawthin' but money, an' another nawthin'
but childher. A man with tin dollars a week will
have tin childher, a man with wan hundherd dollars
will have five, an' a man with a millyon will buy an
autymobill. Ye can tell Schwartzmeister, with his
thirteen little Hanses an' Helenas, that he don't have
to throw no bombs to make room f'r his childher. Th'
people over in Mitchigan Avnoo will do that thimsilves. Nature,' he says, ' is a wild dimmycrat,' he
says.

" I guess he's right. I'm goin' to ask Dock Eliot,
Tiddy Rosenfelt, an' all th' rest iv thim to come up
Ar-rchey R-road some summer's afthernoon an' show
thim th' way th' r-race is dyin' out. Th' front stoops
is full iv childher; they block th' throlley-cars;
they're shyin' bricks at th' polis, pullin' up coal-hole
covers, playin' ring-around-th'-rosy, makin' paper

[140]

dolls, goin' to Sundah - school, hurryin' with th' sprinklin'-pot to th' place at th' corner, an' indulgin' in other spoorts iv childhood. Pah-pah is settin' on th' steps, ma is lanin' out iv th' window gassin' with th' neighbors, an' a squad iv polis ar-re up at th' church, keepin' th' christenin' parties fr'm mobbin' Father Kelly while he inthrajooces wan thousan' little howlin' dimmycrats to Christyan s'ciety. No, sir, th' race, far fr'm dyin' out in Ar-rchey R-road, is runnin' aisy an' comin' sthrong."

" Ye ought to be ashamed to talk about such subjicks, ye, an ol' batch," said Mr. Hennessy. " It's a seeryous question."

" How many childher have ye?" asked Mr. Dooley.

" Lave me see," said Mr. Hennessy. " Wan, two, four, five, eight, siven, eight, tin,—no, that's not right. Lave me see. Ah, yes, I f'rgot Terence. We have fourteen."

" If th' race iv Hinnissys dies out," said Mr. Dooley, " 'twill be fr'm overcrowdin'."

THE CARNEGIE-HOMER
CONTROVERSY

THE CARNEGIE-HOMER
CONTROVERSY

"IT'S turr'ble th' way me frind Andhrew Carnaygie has been jumpin' on Homer," said Mr.
Dooley.

"What Homer?" asked Mr. Hennessy.

"Homer, th' pote," said Mr. Dooley.

"Has Andhrew been roastin' him?" asked Mr.
Hennessy.

"He has," said Mr. Dooley. "He's been givin'
it to him good. It's all up with Homer. No wan will
print his stuff anny more. He'll be goin' round with
a pome undher his ar'rm fr'm newspaper to newspaper, thryin' to sell it. 'They'se a man wants to
see ye,' says th' office boy. 'What's he like?' says
th' iditor. 'He's an ol' bald-headed man, with long
whiskers an' dhressed in a table-cloth. I think he's
blind, f'r he was led in be a dog on a sthring,' says
he. 'Oh, it's on'y ol' Homer,' says th' iditor. 'Tell
him I'm busy,' he says. Carnaygie has busted him.
People will talk about him fr'm now on as th' fellow
that Carnaygie threw into th' fire.

"'Twill be a hard blow to Hogan. I niver r-read
annything that Homer wrote, but Hogan an' th' ol'
fellow was gr-reat frinds. I got an idee that Homer
ain't anny too well off. He niver knew annything

[145]

about mannyfacthrin' pig-ir'n, an' bein' blind he couldn't tell good money fr'm bad. He niver sold canned air to th' govermint f'r armor-plate, an' he didn't know th' Prince iv Wales at all. If ye wint to ol' Homer an' thried to tell him that be handin' a little coin to th' freight agent iv th' Pinnsylvania he cud ship his pothry fr'm Pittsburg to Phillydel-phy cheaper thin Roodyard Kiplin', th' chances ar-re he'd tell ye to go to th' divvle, an' raysume his pome. He had no business head, an' he niver founded a libry buildin', though I've heerd tell he founded a few libries.

"Poor, ol' la-ad! I feel bad about him. An' it's hard on Hogan. He's always blowin' about Homer. Ye'd think this ol' fellow was all th' potes there iver was. It was Homer this an' Homer that. Homer says so-an'-so. D'ye raymimber what Homer said about that? He's as blind as a bat, but he can see more thin mortial man. He is poor, but his head is full iv kings an' princes, an' not fat little kings that are th' same height annyway ye take thim, but long, lean kings that ar-re always chargin' round, soord in hand, an' slayin' each other. Sivin cities claim Homer's birthplace, which is eight more thin claim Andhrew Carnaygie's—Ithaca, Utica, an' five other places in cinthral New York that I don't raymimber. 'I felt,' says Hogan, 'whin I first met Homer, like th' pote that said he felt like somebody or other whin first he looked out upon th' Passyfic fr'm th' City iv Mexico,' he says. Why, th' man's been crazy about that ol' blind fellow. Now it's my turn. Whin he comes round ye'll hear me say: 'How's ye'er frind Homer now?' or 'Have ye heerd fr'm Homer lately?'"

or ' What's Homer doin' in th' pothry line?' I'll make life a burden to Hogan.

"Ye didn't see what Carnaygie said, did ye? I'll tell ye. ' Th' other night,' he says, ' I wint home, tired out with th' complimints I had rayceived fr'm mesilf, an' settled in me cosey libry, full iv th' choicest back-gammon boords,' he says. ' I picked up wan book afther another fr'm th' libry-table. Sthrange to say, they were all be th' wan author—me fav'rite author, th' kindly sowl that is a constant inspiration to me,— mesilf,' he says. ' I craved lighter readin', an' sint out to me butler, who's a grajate iv a Scotch college —which I have made into a first-class intilligence office—f'r anny readin' matther he had on hand. He sint me a copy iv a pote be th' name iv Homer— I don't recklect his full name, but I think 'twas James J. Homer. P'raps some iv ye will know. He's a Greek pote, an' this book was in th' original Greek, thranslated into English,' he says. ' I read it very fluently,' he says. ' Well, I don't know that th' matther is worth talkin' about, excipt to tell ye how I felt about it; but if this is th' way modhren lithra-choor is tindin' I'm goin' to put a blast chimbly into all me libries.

" ' Iv all th' foolish books! Here's a fellow settin' down to write, an' gettin' th' good money iv th' pub-lic, that hasn't anny style, anny polish, an' don't know th' first iliments iv th' Greek language. An' his charackters! I tell ye, boys, I know a few things about kings. I don't go be hearsay about thim. I know thim. I've had thim right in me own house. They've slept undher me roof, an' even fr'm th' barn, where coort etiket prescribes I must lay me bed whin

rielty is in th' house, I've heerd th' kingly snore iv
that charmin' monarch Edward iv illusthrees memory,
who raymimbers me name. I can tell ye all about
kings, an' I will if some wan will lock th' dure. An'
I say to ye that this man Homer don't know a king
fr'm a doose.

" ' He's got wan charackter in th' book, a king be
th' name iv Achills. What kind iv a king does he
make iv him? Is he a small, r-round, haughty king,
with a pinted beard, who says: " Andy, f'r a foolish
little man, ye have a very good house." Not at all;
this Achills is no more an' no less thin a dhrunken
vagabone. He's roysterin' an' cuttin' up fr'm mornin' to night; he's choppin' people open; he's insultin'
his frinds an' bethrayin' his counthry, an' fin'lly he
dies be bein' hit on th' heel. Did ye iver hear th'
like? I know kings, I tell ye, an that's not th' kind
iv men they ar-re at all. They don't carry soords,
but canes. I wear a chip fr'm th' cane iv wan iv thim
who shall be nameless to all but ye, me frinds; but it
was King Edward, I wear a sliver fr'm his walkin'-
stick over me heart at this minyit. They don't get
dhrunk at all. As a rule they ar-re very tim-prate in
their habits, though not teetotal, mind ye. A little
booze at lunch, an' a little more at dinner, an' a short,
hot wan befure goin' to bed. If a king gets a little
pickled be anny chanst, I don't mind tellin' ye, he
don't go an' fight like a cabman. He slaps me on th'
back, offers to race me ar-round Skibo Castle f'r a
dollar, weeps a little because he ain't well threated at
home, an' goes to sleep on a lounge. Far fr'm
dhressin' in a little short ballet-dancer's skirts, with
bare legs, th' way this fellow Homer makes thim out,

kings is very modestly attired in a black coat an'
pearl-colored pants, although I don't mind tellin' ye
that I did wanst have th' good fortune to see a monarch that I won't name, but p'raps ye can guess, in
a pair iv pyjamas—but aven thin ivry inch a king.
Homer don't know th' customs iv good s'ciety. He
writes like a cook. I was so furyous I hurled th'
book into th' fire, an' I'm goin' to direct that anny
future wurruk iv his be excluded fr'm me libries,' he
says.

"An' there's Homer in th' fire. Poor ol' la-ad.
His day is done. He's been caught fakin', an' nobody will thrust him again. If ye go into th' Dope
Lover's Libry an' ask f'r th' pomes iv Homer they'll
say: ' I want ye to undherstand this is a rayspictable
shop. Take a copy iv *Treeumphant Dimocracy*, be
A. Carnaygie. Hol' on there! Don't ye throw that
inkstand!'

"Poor, ol' la-ad. Where'll he turn now? Mind
ye, I think me frind Andhrew Carnaygie is r-right.
Th' book iv Homer's pomes that Hogan brought in
here wan day had pitchers iv th' kings, an' wud ye
believe it, they was all thruckmen. Yes, sir, ivry
king iv thim was dhrivin' a dhray an' fightin' fr'm
it just like ye see thim on th' docks. I suppose th'
poor, ol' man niver see a king in his life. His idee
iv a king is a big fellow on a deliv'ry wagon. But
I'm sorry Carnaygie wint at him that r-rough. He
ought to considered that he was ol' an' blind an'
hasn't got more thin a millyon years longer to live.
If he'd sint him a phottygraft or a short description
or something to wurruk on, an' thin if he didn't put
a cutaway coat on Achills, it wud be time to hammer

him. But th' harm is done. Homer's cooked. It's a gr-reat joke on Hogan."

"I wondher what he'll say," said Mr. Hennessy.

"Maybe," said Mr. Dooley, "he'll say that Homer don't care."

GAMBLING

GAMBLING

"WHAT'S a gamblin' system?" asked Mr. Hennessy.

"A gamblin' system," said Mr. Dooley, "like alyenation iv affictions, is wan way iv makin' a livelihood among th' British arrystocracy. A young jook in New York has th' best wan I iver heerd iv. He's been tellin' about it. ' On Janooary twinty-eighth,' he says, ' I held a meetin' iv me syndicate. Unforchnitely sivral iv th' most enthusyastic an' insurable was absent, it bein' a busy day in th' insane coort, but at nightfall I was able to speed with tin thousan' dollars in th' sweat-band iv me coronet to th' altar where th' Goddess iv Fortune, riprisintin' a syndicate iv binivolent Jews, presides,' he says, ' over th' exercises iv her votaries,' he says. ' In other wurruds, I wint to play th' foolish wheel,' he says. ' I will read fr'm me di'ry: Thursdah: Played on'y th' twinty-siven an' th' three, f'r I'm thirty years ol' to-day, an' three fr'm thirty laves twinty-siven. Th' system wurruks splindidly. I dhropped on'y two thousan', whereas th' man on wan side iv me, that was playin' a dhream his wife had, lost twinty-five hundherd, an' th' man on th' other side iv me, who was asleep, lost three thousan' an' a Masonic imblim. A good day. Fridah: To-day I play th' four, th' siven, an' th' thirteen, twice four bein' siven, an'

[153]

thirteen th' reg'lar Fridah number. Almost won twinty thousan'. Lost six thousan'. Saturdah: Play th' color system. I am detarmined to win. Th' bank is ividintly afraid iv me, f'r th' crooper has just tol' me in a voice croopy with emotion that he will accipt on'y money f'r chips. It is too aisy. I play th' r-red. Th' crooper is white with fear. I can hear him move his feet narvously undher th' table like a man wurrukin' a sewin'-machine. Th' wheel stops suddenly. It is black. How sthrange! Sundah: It is my day. Th' bether th' day th' bether I'll do thim. But they ar-re frightened. They rayfuse to tu-rn f'r a pair iv cuff buttons an' a solid, gun-metal cigareet case. I lave th' room, an' as I go out th' crooper, to concale his fear, whistles: "Ar-re they anny more at home like you?" I will take me system to America, an' have it fi-nanced. Me system,' he says, ' needs nourish-mint,' he says.

"It's a surprise to me, Hinnissy, that th' men r-runnin' gamblin' houses ain't broke. Maybe they ar-re broke. Maybe they're broke, an' just keep up th' game because it's a thradition in th' fam'y, an' they're proud an' they don't want th' ol' folks at home to hear they've quit. But it's a shame to take their money fr'm thim in this undherhanded way. Th' jook iv Roslyn will niver have no luck with that kind iv money. I warn him now. A curse will hang over th' ill-gotten gains, wrenched fr'm th' poor, ign'rant gambler be means iv a lead pencil an' a prim'ry arithmetic. He may die rich, but his conscience will afflict him to th' end, an' his name will be spoken with scorn be future gin'rations to come. Th' law ought to step in an' intherfere. Manny a gambler who has

spint th' best years iv his life dalin' two at a time
an' haulin' in sleepers is in fear iv his life that th'
jook iv Roslyn will dayscind on him, slug him with
his system, an' take th' bread an' butther out iv th'
mouths iv his childher an' th' di'monds out iv th'
ears iv his wife. Wan iv our naytional industhries
is threatened. If this sign iv arrystocracy can come
over here an' roon our gamblers, what's to prevint him
fr'm robbin' Russell Sage or deprivin' Hetty Green
iv th' discomforts iv life?

" I niver was in a gamblin'-house but wanst. Hogan took me there. Besides bein' a pote he's a great
fi-nancier. ' Come up,' he says, ' an' help me woo
th' Goddess iv Chance,' he says. ' I have a system,'
he says. ' I haven't seen th' lady f'r years,' I says,
' but I'll go along an' see ye home whin she turns
loose th' dog on ye,' I says. ' Where does she live
now?' I says. ' Over Dorsey's saloon,' he says. An'
I wint with him. Th' Goddess of Chance certainly
lives well, Hinnissy. They was a naygur at th' dure,
an' th' room was full iv light fr'm chandyleers, an'
they was onyx cuspidors upon th' flure. Business
seemed to be good, but I cudden't see th' goddess
annywhere. ' Where is th' Goddess iv Chance?' I
ast Hogan. ' Here,' says he, settin' down in front
iv th' wheel an' pushin' over his pay envelope. ' She's
a burly lady,' says I, f'r th' goddess had a black
mustache an' wore a sthraw hat with a hole knocked
in it. ' Woo her very gently,' says I. Not lookin'
f'r anny chances, I wint over to th' side-boord an'
dealt mesilf two dollars' worth iv turkey. I was
imptyin' th' pickle-dish whin th' owner iv th' parlor
took me be th' ar-rm an' led me away to a quiet

corner. He was a nice man, an' him an' me soon had our feet in each other's laps.

" 'Ye have a fine business here,' says I. 'It's betther thin it was a few minyits ago,' says he. 'But it's a dull life.' 'I don't see what r-right ye have to complain,' I says. 'Ye have a gran' palatchial place,' I says. 'Ye ought to be happy with these Brussel's carpets, glass chandyleers, an' jooled spittoons,' I says. 'What d'ye want?' I says. 'That's what ivrybody thinks,' says he. 'People invy us who know nawthin' about th' hardships iv th' life. In th' first place, I detest cards. I niver gamble,' he says. 'Befure I left me home in Injianny me father, who was a Methodist ministher in Terry Hut, placed his hand on me head and said: "Ikey, ye ar-re goin' out into th' wurruld. Promise me niver to touch a card." I promised, an I've kept me vow.

" 'I wish he hadn't ast. It's thrue I have made some money, but th' life is a dog's life, afther all. I have established a fine business, although th' hours is long an' they'se a great dale iv wear an' tear fr'm th' polis, an' we're obliged to have th' windows shut to keep in th' noise iv th' chips an' th' suckers an' th' smell, he says. 'I have a reli'ble staff. That salesman behind th' faro-box is an excellent clerk. I pay him eight dollars a night, an' he arns it. Th' wheelwright who is just now handin' ye'er frind with th' specs a stack iv bone in exchange f'r a pitcher iv Salmon P. Chase, is cap'ble an' thrustworthy. Th' bright-lookin' fellow at th' chuck-a-luck table I took out iv a broker's office an' made a man iv him. He was a con-firmed gambler, but to-day he is thurly reli'ble. All this, iv coorse, is satisfactory to a business man. But what I complain iv is th' occypation is so teejous. It's th' same thing night afther night. They'se no excitemint. Th' same dull routine in th' same overheated air, th' same chin-to-chin chat with th' young, dhrunk, an' affictionate, childher iv th' rich.

I don't gamble. Does J. Pierpont Morgan buy his own bonds? It's th' same thing. I wisht I did. In ivry other business in life th' ilimint iv chance enthers in. But not in mine. Th' banker, th' dhry-goods merchant, th' lawyer, th' money-lender takes risks. His days are enlivened be excitemint. But there ar-re no risks in this business. It's wan dull, monotonous grind, th' same ol' percintage, th' same dhreary gatherin' in iv th' mazuma, till me heart sickens within me, an' I'm almost timpted to thry some risky pursoot like pawnbrokin'. Wanst in a while th' dead waste iv monotony is enlivened be an incident. Wan iv me op'ratives sprained his wrist las' week takin' th' money fr'm an expert accountant, who had a system that no wan cud bate. Sometimes a man comes in here without a system at all. They was wan such las' week. We cud on'y take half what he got, an' I had to go out an' wait f'r him in a muddy alley to get th' r-rest. But these cases ar-re rare. I on'y mintion thim to show ye how excited we become with th' smallest pleasures. It's a dhreary, dhreary life. Jawn, go over to th' hotel an' see what ails th' jook iv Roslyn. He's late.'

"I took th' poor man be th' hand, Hinnissy, an' says I: 'But, me poor frind, is there no way to enliven ye'er pursoot?' I says. 'Is there no way iv increasin' th' chances again' ye?' I says. 'None,' says he, 'while there ar-re so manny people with pear-shaped heads,' he says. An' a tear was in his eye as he felt f'r me watch. I looked acrost at Hogan. Th' Goddess iv Chance was settin' back in his chair twirlin' her mustache. Hogan was standin' up, an' his face wore a bright green flush fr'm th' passion iv play. He felt in his vest-pocket, an' projooced a collar button an' a pinch iv smokin' tobacco. 'How is th' system?' says I. 'The system is all right,' says he. 'An' how ar-re ye?' says I. 'It's a fine, star-light night,' says he. 'Lave us walk home,' he says.

"Don't ye suppose they'se anny system iv gettin' their money?" asked Mr. Hennessy.

"They'se on'y wan," said Mr. Dooley.

"What's that?" asked Mr. Hennessy.

"It's called th' polis system," said Mr. Dooley.

AN INTERNATIONAL POLICE FORCE

AN INTERNATIONAL POLICE FORCE

"I THOUGHT," said Mr. Dooley, "that whin me young frind th' Czar iv Rooshya got up that there Dutch polis coort f'r to settle th' backyard quarr'ls among th' nations iv th' earth, 'twud be th' end iv war f'r good an' all. It looked all right to me. Why not? If be anny chanst I get mesilf full iv misconduck an' go ar-round thryin' to collect me debts with a gun, an' camp out in some-body's house an' won't lave, th' polis take me down to Deerin' Sthreet station an' throw me in among th' little playmates iv th' criminal, an' in th' mornin' I'm befure me cousin th' chief justice, an' he con-fiscates th' gun an' sinds me up th' bullyvard f'r thirty days. Why not th' same thing f'r th' powers whin they go off on a tear? I thought I'd be readin' in th' pa-apers: ' Judge Oolenboff, at th' Hague coort, had a large docket yisterdah mornin'. Thirty mimbers iv th' notoryous Hapsburg fam'ly was sint up f'r varyous terms, an' th' polis think they have completely broke up th' gang. Th' King iv Spain was charged with non-support, but was dismissed with a warnin'. Th' Impror iv Chiny was let off with a fine f'r maintainin' a dope jint, an' warrants was issued f'r th' owners iv th' primises, the King of England an' th' Czar iv Rooshya. Th' Sultan iv

[161]

Turkey, alias Hamid th' Hick, alias th' Turrible Turk, was charged with poly-gamy. Th' coort give him th' alternative iv five more wives or thirty days. Whin these cases had been cleared away th' bailiff led into th' dock three notoryous charackters. Th' first was a large, heavy-set German, who proved to be Bill th' Bite, less known by his thrue name iv Willum H. J. E. I. K. L. M. N. O. P. Q. R. S. T., etc., Hohenzollern. By his side was an undhersized, little dark man, th' notoryous Emilio Casthro, a pro-fiss-yonal deat-beat an' embizzler, an' a stout party be th' name iv Albert Edward or Edwards, who is said be th' internaytional polis to be behind some iv th' biggest grafts that have been run through f'r th' last twinty years, though niver so far caught with th' goods on. Hohenzollern was accused iv assault with intint to kill, robbery, blackmail, carryin' concealed weepins, an' raysistin' an officer. Edward or Edwards was charged with maintainin' a fence f'r rayceivin' stolen property an' carryin' concealed weepins. Casthro was charged with vagrancy, maintainin' a disordherly house, an' fraud.

"'Th' attorney f'r th' pro-secution made out a sthrong case again' th' pris'ners. He said that Hohenzollern was a desprit charackter, who was constantly a menace to th' peace iv th' wurruld. He had no sympathy f'r Casthro, who was an idle, dangerous ruffyan, an' he hoped th' coort wud dale severely with him. He niver paid his debts, an' none iv th' neighbors' chickens was safe fr'm him. He was a low-down, worthless, mischief-makin' loafer. But Casthro's bad charackter did not excuse th' other pris'ners. It seems that Casthro, who niver paid

annybody annything, owed a bill with th' well-known
grocery firm iv Schwartzheim an' Hicks, which he
rayfused to settle. Hearin' iv this, Hohenzollern an'
Edward or Edwards con-spired together to go to
Casthro's place undher pretinse iv collectin' th' bill
an' throw Casthro out an' take possission iv his
property. Hohenzollern was th' more vilent iv th'
pair. He appeared, carryin' loaded revolvers, which
he fired into th' windows iv Casthro's shop, smashed
in th' dure, an' endangered th' lives iv manny innocint people. He was ar-rested afther a sthruggle,
in which he severely injured wan iv th' internaytional
polis foorce, an' was carried off in a hurry-up wagon.
Edward or Edwards was caught in th' neighborhood.
He pretinded to be an innocint spectator, but whin
sarched was found to have loaded revolvers in his
pocket, as well as an addhress to th' Christian nations iv th' wurruld justifyin' his conduck an' de-
nouncin' his accomplice. Casthro was taken into cus-
tody on gin'ral principles. Th' prosecution asked
that an example be made iv th' pris'ners.

"'Afther tistymony had been inthrojooced showin' th' bad charackter iv th' men in th' dock, Hohenzollern was put on th' stand to testify in his own
definse. He swore that he had no inmity again'
Casthro, but Schwartzheim iv Schwartzheim an'
Hicks, was a German frind iv his, an' he wint down to
see that no injustice was done him. "Did he ask ye
to go?" ast th' coort. "No," says th' pris'ner, "but
me pristige as a slugger wud be in danger if I
didn't go over an' punch this here little naygur," he
says. "Niver, niver shud it be said that a German
citizen sha'n't be able to collect his debts annywhere

but in Germany," he says. "Th' mailed fist," he says, "is iver raised f'r th' protiction—" "No more iv that," says th' judge. "This is a coort iv law. Hohenzollern, ye're a dangerous man. Ye're noisy, ritous, an' offinsive. I'm determined to make an example iv ye, an' I sintince ye to stay in Germany f'r th' rest iv ye'er nachral life, an' may th' Lord have mercy on ye'er sowl. As f'r ye, Edwards, ye'er even worse. I will hold ye without bail ontil th' polis can collect all their ividence again' ye. Casthro, ye're discharged. Th' worst thing I cud think iv doin' to ye is to sind ye back to ye'er beautiful Vinzwala." Th' pris'ner Hohenzollern made a dimonsthration while bein' raymoved fr'm th' dock. It is undherstud that Edward or Edwards has offered to tell all he knows, an' promises to implicate siv'ral prominent parties.'

"That's th' way I thought 'twould be. Be Hivins, Hinnissy, I looked forward to th' day whin, if a king, impror, or czar started a rough-house, th' blue 'bus wud come clangin' through th' sthreets an' they'd be hauled off to Holland f'r thrile. I looked to see th' United States Sinit pulled ivry month or two, an' all th' officers iv th' navy fugitives fr'm justice. I thought th' coort wud have a kind iv a bridewell built, where they'd sind th' internaytional dhrunks an' disordhlies, an' where ye cud go anny day an' see Willum Hohenzollern cooperin' a bar'l, an' me frind Joe Chamberlain peggin' shoes, while gr-reat war iditors, corryspondints, statesmen, an' other disturbers iv th' peace walked around in lock-step, an' th' keeper iv th' jail showed ye a book filled with photygrafts iv th' mos' notoryous iv thim: ' Number

An International Police Force

two thousan' an' wan, Joe Chamberlain, profissional land-grabber, five years '; or ' Willum Hohenzollern, all-round ruffyan, life.'

"That wud be th' fine day whin th' wagon wud be backed up in fr-ront iv th' parlymints iv th' wurruld an' th' bull-pen wud be full iv internaytional grafters, get - rich - quick op'rators, an' sthrong-ar-rm men; whin th' Monroe docthrine wud be condimned as a public nuisance, an' South America wud be burned undher ordhers iv th' coort. But it hasn't come. The coort is there noddin' over th' docket jus' like a coort, while outside th' rowdies ar-re shootin' at each other, holdin' up Chinymen an' naygurs, pickin' pockets, blowin' safes, an' endangerin' th' lives iv dacint people. They'se a warrant out f'r Bill Hohenzollern, but they'se no wan to sarve it. He's on th' rampage, breakin' windows an' chasin' people over th' roofs, while Edward or Edwards stands around th' corner waitin' f'r th' goods to be delivered an' savin' his ammunytion to use it on his pal if they quarrel over th' divide. There's th' internaytional coort, ye say, but I say where ar-re th' polis? A coort's all r-right enough, but no coort's anny good onless it is backed up be a continted constabulary, its counthry's pride, as th' pote says. Th' Czar iv Rooshya didn't go far enough. Wan good copper with a hickory club is worth all th' judges between Amsterdam an' Rotterdam. I want to see th' day whin just as Bill Hohenzollern an' Edward or Edwards meets on th' corner an' prepares a raid on a laundry a big polisman will step out iv a dure an' say: ' I want ye, Bill, an' ye might as well come along

[165]

quiet.' But I suppose it wud be just th' same thing as it is now in rale life"

" How's that?" asked Mr. Hennessy.

" All th' biggest crooks wud get on th' polis foorce," said Mr. Dooley.

OATS AS A FOOD

OATS AS A FOOD

"WHAT'S a breakfast food?" asked Mr. Hennessy.

"It depinds on who ye ar-re," said Mr. Dooley. "In ye're case it's annything to ate that ye're not goin' to have f'r dinner or supper. But in th' case iv th' rest iv this impeeryal raypublic, 'tis th' on'y amusement they have. 'Tis most iv th' advertisin' in th' pa-apers. 'Tis what ye see on th' bill-boords. 'Tis th' inspi-ration iv pothry an' art. In a wurrd, it's oats.

"I wint over to have breakfast New Year's mornin' at Joyce's. Th' air was sharp, an' though I'm not much given to reflectin' on vittles, regardin' thim more as a meedjum f'r what dhrink I take with thim thin annything else, be th' time I got to th' dure I was runnin' over in me mind a bill iv fare an' kind iv wondhrin' whether I wud have ham an' eggs or liver an' bacon, an' hopin' I cud have both. Well, we set down at the table, an' I tucked me napkin into me collar so that I wudden't have to chase it down in me shoe if I got laughin' at annything funny durin' an egg, an' squared away. 'Ar-re ye hungry?' says Joyce. 'Not now,' says I. 'I've on'y been up two hours, an' I don't think I cud ate more thin a couple iv kerosene-lamps an' a bur-rd-cage,' says I. 'But I'm li'ble to be hungry in a few minyits, an', says I,

[169]

' p'raps 'twud be just as well to lock up th' small childher,' I says, ' where they'll be safe,' I says, thinkin' to start th' breakfast with a flow iv spirits, though th' rosy Gawd iv Day sildom finds me much betther natured thin a mustard plasther.

" ' What's ye'er fav'rite breakfast dish?' says Joyce. ' My what?' says I. ' Ye'er fav'rite breakfast dish?' says he. ' Whativer ye've got,' says I, not to be thrapped into givin' me suffrage to annything he didn't have in th' house. ' Anny kind iv food, so long as it's hot an' hurrid. Thank Hiven I have a mind above vittles, an' don't know half th' time what I'm atin',' says I. ' But I mane prepared food,' says he. ' I like it fried,' says I; ' but I don't mind it broiled, roasted, stewed, or fricasseed. In a minyit or two I'll waive th' cookin' an' ate it off th' hoof,' I says. ' Well,' says he, ' me fav'rite is Guff,' he says. ' P'raps ye've seen th' advertisemint: " Out iv th' house wint Luck Joe; Guff was th' food that made him go." Mother prefers Almostfood, a scientific preparation iv burlaps. I used to take Sawd Ust, which I found too rich, an' later I had a peeroyd iv Hungareen, a chimically pure dish, made iv th' exterryor iv bath towels. We all have our little tastes an' enthusyasms in th' matther iv breakfast foods, depindin' on what pa-apers we read an' what billboords we've seen iv late. I believe Sunny Jim cud jump higher on Guff thin on Almostfood, but mother says she see a sign down on Halsted Sthreet that convinces her she has th' most stimylatin' tuck-in. Annyhow,' he says, ' I take gr-reat pains to see that nawthin' is sarved f'r breakfast that ain't well advertised an' guaranteed pure fr'm th' facthry, an' put

Oats as a Food

up in blue or green pa-aper boxes,' he says. 'Well,'
says I, ' give me a tub iv Guff,' I says. 'I'll close
me eyes an' think iv an egg.'

"What d'ye suppose they give me, Hinnissy?
Mush! Mush, be Hivens! 'What kind iv mush is
this?' says I, takin' a mouthful. ' It ain't mush,' says
Joyce. 'It's a kind iv scientific oatmeal,' says he.
'Science,' says I, ' has exthracted th' meal. Pass th'
ink,' says I. 'What d'ye want ink f'r?' says he.
'Who iver heerd iv atin' blottin' pa-aper without
ink?' says I. 'Ate it,' says he. 'Give me me hat,'
I says. 'Where ar-re ye goin'?' he says. 'I f'rgot
me nose-bag,' I says. ' I can't ate this off a plate.
Give it to me an' I'll harness mesilf up in Cavin's
buggy, have mesilf hitched to a post in front iv th'
city hall, an' injye me breakfast,' I says. 'Ye have
a delightful home here,' says I. ' Some day I'm
goin' to ask ye to take me up in th' kitchen an' lave
me fork down some hay f'r th' childher. But now I
must lave ye to ye'er prepared oats,' I says. An' I
wint out to Mulligan's resthrant an' wrapped mesilf
around buckwheat cakes an' sausages till th' cook
got buckwheat cake-makers'-paralysis.

" I don't know how people come to have this mad
passion f'r oats. Whin I was a boy they was on'y
et be horses, an' good horses rayfused thim. But
some wan discovered that th' more ye did to oats th'
less they tasted, an' that th' less annything tastes th'
betther food it is f'r th' race. So all over th' counthry countless machines is at wurruk removin' th'
flavor fr'm oats an' turnin' thim into breakfast food.
Breakfast food is all ye see in th' cars an' on th' bill-
boords. In th' small cities it's th' principal spoort iv th'

people. Where childher wanst looked on th' boords to
see whin th' minsthrel show was comin' to town, they
now watch f'r th' announcement iv th' new breakfast
food. Hogan tol' me he was out in Decatur th' other
day an' they was eighty-siven kinds iv oats on th'
bill iv fare. ' Is they annything goin' on in this
town?' he ast a dhrummer. ' Nawthing' ontil th'
eighth, whin Oatoono opens,' says th' man. People
talk about breakfast food as they used to talk about
bicycles. They compare an' they thrade. A man
with th' 1906 model iv high-gear oats is th' invy iv
th' neighborhood. All th' saw-mills has been turned
into breakfast-food facthries, an' th' rip-saw has
took th' place iv th' miller.

" Does it do anny harm, says ye? Ne'er a bit. A
counthry that's goin' to be kilt be food is on its last
legs, annyhow. Ivry race has its pecoolyarity.
With th' Rooshyans it's ' Pass th' tallow candles ';
with th' Chinese a plate iv rice an' a shark's fin. Th'
German sets down to a breakfast iv viggytable soup,
Hungaryan goolash, an' beer. Th' Frinchman is
satisfied with a rose in his buttonhole an' tin minyits
at th' pianny. An Irishman gets sthrong on potatoes, an' an Englishman dilicate on a sound breakfast iv roast beef, ham, mutton pie, eggs, bacon, an'
'alf-an'-'alf. Th' docthors bothers us too much about
what we put into that mighty tough ol' man-iv-all-
wurruk, th' human stomach. Hiven sint most iv us
good digistions, but th' doctors won't let thim
wurruk. Th' sthrongest race iv rough-an'-tumble
Americans that iver robbed a neighbor was raised
on pie. I'm f'r pie mesilf at anny time an' at all
meals. If food makes anny diff'rence to people, how

do I know that all our boasted prosperity ain't based on pie? Says I, lave well enough alone. It may be that if we sarched f'r th' corner-stone iv American liberty an' pro-gress, we'd find it was apple-pie with a piece iv toasted cheese.

"People don't have anny throuble with their digistions fr'm atin'. 'Tis thinkin' makes dyspepsy; worryin' about th' rent is twinty times worse f'r a man's stomach thin plum-puddin'. What's worse still, is worryin' about digistion. Whin a man gets to doin' that all th' oats between here an' Council Bluffs won't save him."

"Joyce tells me his breakfast food has made him as sthrong as a horse," said Mr. Hennessy.

"It ought to," said Mr. Dooley. "Him an' a horse have th' same food."

THE CARNEGIE LIBRARIES

THE CARNEGIE LIBRARIES

"HAS Andhrew Carnaygie given ye a libry yet?" asked Mr. Dooley. "Not that I know iv," said Mr. Hennessy.

"He will," said Mr. Dooley. "Ye'll not escape him. Befure he dies he hopes to crowd a libry on ivry man, woman, an' child in th' counthry. He's given thim to cities, towns, villages, an' whistlin' stations. They're tearin' down gas-houses an' poor-houses to put up libries. Befure another year, ivry house in Pittsburg that ain't a blast-furnace will be a Carnaygie libry. In some places all th' buildin's is libries. If ye write him f'r an autygraft he sinds ye a libry. No beggar is iver turned impty-handed fr'm th' dure. Th' pan-handler knocks an' asts f'r a glass iv milk an' a roll. 'No, sir,' says Andhrew Carnaygie. 'I will not pauperize this onworthy man. Nawthin' is worse f'r a beggar-man thin to make a pauper iv him. Yet it shall not be said iv me that I give nawthin' to th' poor. Saunders, give him a libry, an' if he still insists on a roll tell him to roll th' libry. F'r I'm humorous as well as wise,' he says."

"Does he give th' books that go with it?" asked Mr. Hennessy.

"Books?" said Mr. Dooley. "What ar-re ye talkin' about? D'ye know what a libry is? I sup-

[177]

pose ye think it's a place where a man can go, haul down wan iv his fav'rite authors fr'm th' shelf, an' take a nap in it. That's not a Carnaygie libry. A Carnaygie libry is a large, brown-stone, impenethrible buildin' with th' name iv th' maker blown on th' dure. Libry, fr'm th' Greek wurruds, libus, a book, an' ary, sildom,—sildom a book. A Carnaygie libry is archytechoor, not lithrachoor. Lithrachoor will be riprisinted. Th' most cillybrated dead authors will be honored be havin' their names painted on th' wall in distinguished comp'ny, as thus: Andhrew Carnaygie, Shakespeare; Andhrew Carnaygie, Byron; Andhrew Carnaygie, Bobby Burns; Andhrew Carnaygie, an' so on. Ivry author is guaranteed a place next to pure readin' matther like a bakin'-powdher advertisemint, so that whin a man comes along that niver heerd iv Shakespeare he'll know he was somebody, because there he is on th' wall. That's th' dead authors. Th' live authors will stand outside an' wish they were dead.

"He's havin' gr-reat spoort with it. I r-read his speech th' other day, whin he laid th' corner-stone iv th' libry at Pianola, Ioway. Th' entire popylation iv this lithry cinter gathered to see an' hear him. There was th' postmaster an' his wife, th' blacksmith an' his fam'ly, the station agent, mine host iv th' Farmers' Exchange, an' some sthray live stock. 'Ladies an' gintlemen,' says he. 'Modesty compels me to say nawthin' on this occasion, but I am not to be bulldozed,' he says. 'I can't tell ye how much pleasure I take in disthributin' monymints to th' humble name around which has gathered so manny hon'rable associations with mesilf. I have been a

very busy little man all me life, but I like hard
wurruk, an' givin' away me money is th' hardest
wurruk I iver did. It fairly makes me teeth ache to
part with it. But there's wan consolation. I cheer
mesilf with th' thought that no matther how much
money I give it don't do anny particular person anny
good. Th' worst thing ye can do f'r anny man is to do
him good. I pass by th' organ-grinder on th' corner
with a savage glare. I bate th' monkey on th' head
whin he comes up smilin' to me window, an' hurl him
down on his impecyoonyous owner. None iv me money
goes into th' little tin cup. I cud kick a hospital, an' I
lave Wall Sthreet to look afther th' widow an' th'
orphan. Th' submerged tenth, thim that can't get
hold iv a good chunk iv th' goods, I wud cut off fr'm
th' rest iv th' wurruld an' prevint fr'm bearin' th'
haughty name iv papa or th' still lovelier name iv
ma. So far I've got on'y half me wish in this
matther.

"'I don't want poverty an' crime to go on. I intind to stop it. But how? It's been holdin' its own
f'r cinchries. Some iv th' gr-reatest iv former minds
has undertook to prevint it an' has failed. They
didn't know how. Modesty wud prevint me agin fr'm
sayin' that I know how, but that's nayether here
nor there. I do. Th' way to abolish poverty an'
bust crime is to put up a brown-stone buildin' in ivry
town in th' counthry with me name over it. That's
th' way. I suppose th' raison it wasn't thried befure
was that no man iver had such a name. 'Tis thrue
me efforts is not apprecyated ivrywhere. I offer a
city a libry, an' oftentimes it replies an' asks me f'r
something to pay off th' school debt. I rayceive de-

graded pettyshuns fr'm so-called proud methropolises f'r a gas-house in place iv a libry. I pass thim by with scorn. All I ask iv a city in rayturn f'r a fifty-thousan'-dollar libry is that it shall raise wan millyon dollars to maintain th' buildin' an' keep me name shiny, an' if it won't do that much f'r lithrachoor, th' divvle take it, it's onworthy iv th' name iv an American city. What ivry community needs is taxes an' lithrachoor. I give thim both. Three cheers f'r a libry an' a bonded debt! Lithrachoor, taxation, an' Andhrew Carnaygie, wan an' insiprable, now an' foriver! They'se nawthin' so good as a good book. It's betther thin food; it's betther thin money. I have made money an' books, an' I like me books betther thin me money. Others don't, but I do. With these few wurruds I will con-clude. Modesty wud prevint me fr'm sayin' more, but I have to catch a thrain, an' cannot go on. I stake ye to this libry, which ye will have as soon as ye raise th' money to keep it goin'. Stock it with useful readin', an' some day ye're otherwise pauper an' criminal childher will come to know me name whin I am gone an' there's no wan left to tell it thim.'

"Whin th' historyan comes to write th' histhry iv th' West he'll say: ' Pianola, Ioway, was a prosperous town till th' failure iv th' corn crop in nineteen hundherd an' wan, an' th' Carnaygie libry in nineteen hundherd an' two. Th' govermint ast f'r thirty dollars to pave Main Sthreet with wooden blocks, but th' gr-reat philanthropist was firm, an' the libry was sawed off on th' town. Th' public schools, th' wurruk-house, th' wather wurruks, an' th' other penal instichoochions was at wanst closed, an' th' people begun

[180]

to wurruk to support th' libry. In five years th'
popylation had deserted th' town to escape taxation,
an' now, as Mr. Carnaygie promised, poverty an'
crime has been abolished in th' place, th' janitor iv
th' buildin' bein' honest an' well paid.'

" Isn't it good f'r lithrachoor, says ye? Sure, I
think not, Hinnissy. Libries niver encouraged lithrachoor anny more thin tombstones encourage livin'.
No wan iver wrote annythin' because he was tol' that
a hundherd years fr'm now his books might be taken
down fr'm a shelf in a granite sepulcher an' some wan
wud write ' Good ' or ' This man is crazy ' in th'
margin. What lithrachoor needs is fillin' food. If
Andhrew wud put a kitchen in th' libries an' build
some bunks or even swing a few hammocks where
livin' authors cud crawl in at night an' sleep while
waitin' f'r this enlightened nation to wake up an'
discover th' Shakespeares now on th' turf, he wud
be givin' a rale boost to lithrachoor. With th'
smoke curlin' fr'm th' chimbley, an' hundherds iv
potes settin' aroun' a table loaded down with pan-
cakes an' talkin' pothry an' prize-fightin', with hundherds iv other potes stacked up nately in th' sleepin'-rooms an' snorin' in wan gran' chorus, with their
wives holdin' down good-payin' jobs as libraryans or
cooks, an' their happy little childher playin' through
th' marble corrydors, Andhrew Carnaygie wud not
have lived in vain. Maybe that's th' on'y way he
knows how to live. I don't believe in libries. They
pauperize lithrachoor. I'm f'r helpin' th' boys that's
now on th' job. I know a pote in Halsted Sthreet
that wanst wrote a pome beginnin', ' All th' wealth
iv Ind,' that he sold to a magazine f'r two dollars,

payable on publycation. Lithrachoor don't need advancin'. What it needs is advances f'r th' lithrachoors. Ye can't shake down posterity f'r th' price.

"All th' same, I like Andhrew Carnaygie. Him an' me ar-re agreed on that point. I like him because he ain't shamed to give publicly. Ye don't find him puttin' on false whiskers an' turnin' up his coat-collar whin he goes out to be benivolent. No, sir. Ivry time he dhrops a dollar it makes a noise like a waith'er fallin' down-stairs with a tray iv dishes. He's givin' th' way we'd all like to give. I niver put annything in th' poor-box, but I wud if Father Kelly wud rig up like wan iv thim slot-machines,so that whin I stuck in a nickel me name wud appear over th' altar in red letthers. But whin I put a dollar in th' plate I get back about two yards an' hurl it so hard that th' good man turns around to see who done it. Do good be stealth, says I, but see that th' burglar-alarm is set. Anny benivolent money I hand out I want to talk about me. Him that giveth to th' poor, they say, lindeth to th' Lord; but in these days we look f'r quick returns on our invistmints. I like Andhrew Carnaygie, an', as he says, he puts his whole soul into th' wurruk."

"What's he mane be that?" asked Mr. Hennessy.

"He manes," said Mr. Dooley, "that he's gin'rous. Ivry time he gives a libry he gives himsilf away in a speech."

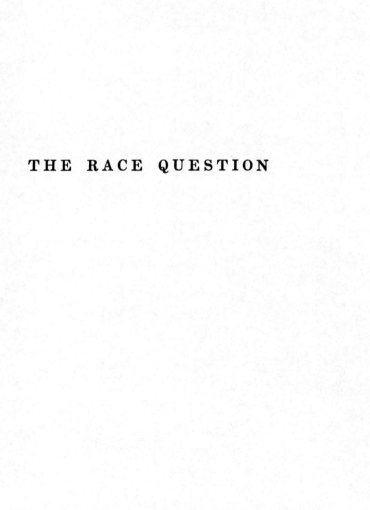

THE RACE QUESTION

THE RACE QUESTION

"WHAT ar-re we goin' to do about th' coons?" asked Mr. Dooley.

"What ought we to do about thim?" asked Mr. Hennessy.

"We've got to do somethin'," said Mr. Dooley. "Somethin's got to be done. Whin I was a young man I raymimber hearin' people talk iv boostin' th' naygur up fr'm his lowly place as an unforchnit slave an' humorist an' makin' him as good as annybody an' betther thin a German be givin' him a vote. I didn't believe it, because I was a Dimmycrat an' didn't believe annything but Stephen A. Douglas. But they used to say it jus' th' same, an' if ye didn't say it, too, it was down to Camp Douglas with ye be th' back iv th' neck as a pris'ner iv war. Th' Dimmycrats knew that a naygur with a vote wudden't be a Willum Shakespeare. It wudden't take anny iv th' dusk out iv his cheeks to sind him down to th' liv'ry stable an' lave him stick an impeeryal ballot that he cudden't r-read into a box with a false bottom. Can th' camel change his hump? as Hogan wud say. A naygur with a vote is a naygur with a vote, an' that's all he is. Th' Dimmycrats knew that forty years ago. Histhry always vindicates th' Dimmycrats, but niver in their lifetime. They see th' thruth first, but th' throuble is that nawthin' is iver officially thrue till a Raypublican sees it.

"Th' naygur ain't anny bether off thin he was. Nobody is. But nearly ivrybody ixpicted, afther th' war, that his locks wud become goolden at wanst an' that he wud soon get a Roman nose. But here he is to-day, lookin' just as he did forty year ago. He ain't got anny more money, he ain't anny lighter in complexion, an' I sometimes doubt whether he's anny happyer thin he was whin they was takin' his darlin' Nelly Grey away fr'm him, an' he'd niver see her more till they met in th' Jim Crow siction iv hiven. Down in th' merry, chivalrous Southland no basket picnic is complete onless a naygur is depindin' fr'm th' shrubbery. Up here, in this free North iv ours, where th' wurruds iv Windell Phillips is still soundin' in th' air, we don't see anny naygurs marryin' into our ladin' fam'lies. We welcome him as our akel in all rayspicts, but none iv our consarvative prize-fighters will put on th' gloves with him.

"So I say somethin's got to be done f'r him, but what it is I dinnaw. Tiddy Rosenfelt's idee is to glad-hand him up to a higher plane. All ye've got to do to make him th' akel iv his white brother is to give him a job an' have him up to th' White House f'r dinner. 'Preparations is bein' made f'r th' dinner to th' Royal Knights iv th' Ordher iv Oryental Splendher iv Pazazas, whose prisidint is th' Hon'rable Egregious Cass, iv Allybama. A wagon-load iv pullets an' hams was delivered yisterdah at th' White House. Th' dinner will be followed be a musical, at which th' Prisidint an' Sinitor Lodge will sing a duet. Both statesmen will black up in honor iv th'

[186]

comp'ny.' 'Th' Prisidint has appinted Hon'rable Lucullus Buffins, th' well-known naygur orator, to be marshal at Pianola, Miss. Frinds iv th' fam'ly ar-re kindly rayquisted to omit flowers.' 'Immejately on rayceivin' his commission as postmasther iv Ozaloo, Louisyany, th' Hon'rable Napolyon Bliggs, th' cillybrated naygur aggytator, took th' night thrain to th' North. In spite iv th' lateness iv th' hour, a large number iv Misther Bliggs's fellow-citizens escorted him to th' thrain. They wud not permit him to walk, but insisted on carryin' him on a two-be-four restin' on their shouldhers. Misther Bliggs expics to spind some time in th' North, when he will consult a prom'nent surgeon an' have th' feathers exthracted.'

"But th' throuble with this here plan is that th' higher ye boost th' naygur be askin' him up to th' White House, th' farther he has to fall whin he gets about two blocks south iv th' White House. Wan iv our dusky fellow-citizens comes out fr'm a meal with th' Prisidint an' cake-walks to a car. He is not puffed up with th' rayciption. Not at all. Th' av'rage chest measuremint iv a colored gintleman who has had three or four fish-balls with th' Prisidint is rarely over wan hundherd an' eighty inches. So he modestly sthruts over to a car, takes a seat, puts his feet in th' lap iv th' lady acrost fr'm him, an' says in a diferinchal yell to a Confidrate colonel nex' to him: 'White pusson, give this here frind iv th' Prisidint a light fr'm ye'er see-gar.' An' whin he comes to his leg is on fire.

"Me frinds down South don't believe in this way iv ilivatin' th' coon. They have ways iv their own.

They think a naygur ought to be improved slowly.
Th' slower th' betther. I was r-readin' a speech be
wan iv thim th' other day. He was consarvative on
th' question. Like all Southern men, he admitted
that something was to be said on both sides. He did
not boast iv his siction iv th' counthry. A thrue
Southerner niver does. It wud ill become him to suggest that th' South is annything more thin th' fair-
est spot on Gawd's footstool, inhabited be th' bravest
men, th' loveliest an' mos' varchous women, th' mos'
toothsome an' encouragin' booze, an' th' fastest
ponies in th' wurruld. Let others tell iv th' beauties
iv th' South. Ye will not dhraw th' tale fr'm th' lips
iv a Southern man. Even in his cups he scorns to
give more thin three cheers a minyit f'r th' gloryous
State iv Mississippi. A Matsachoosetts man will hit
ye over th' head with a codfish if ye don't say that
Matsachoosetts is th' mos' noble jool in th' bright
girdle on th' brow iv Columbia. Ye can't go into a
barroom without seein' a man sthandin' on a table an'
yellin' f'r New Hampshire. Eight or nine bartinders
was shot las' year f'r rayfusin' to sing: ' I was bor-rn
in ol' Ohio, where th' dhrinkin'-wather's blue.' But a
Southern man is rayluctant to speak iv his home.
He laves it speak f'r itself, an' if ye don't listen he
merely nudges ye in th' ribs familyarly with a knife.

" So this here repristintive iv th' culture an' civvy-
lization iv th' South begun his speech with a cautious
allusion to th' well-known fact that th' South is th'
bravest, th' freest, th' sunniest, th' mos' intellechool
region iv th' counthry, peopled be th' most chivalrous
men an' th' sweetest women that th' green light iv
hiven iver shown down upon, where th' latch-sthring

is always out to welcome sthrangers to a hospital cheer, an' no wan is touchy about his r-rights.

" He wint on fr'm this here bald statemint iv fact to say: ' Th' thruth iv th' matther is there is no race question. Th' toast iv th' evenin' is th' Day we Cillybrate, or Th' Ladies, Gawd Bless Thim, or th' Pen is Mightier thin th' Soord, but I feel bound at this moment to addhress a few wurruds to th' race question, iv which there is none, but it is th' wan question that confronts th' nation to-day. We have in th' White House a man who, if he iver comes South iv Mason and Dixon's line, will be subjicted to indignity worthy iv his office. I yield to no man in admiration iv th' office iv prisidint iv this united counthry —united, but ye can see where th' seam was. But I will say that if this rag-time prisidint iver ventures into Ogalochee County, th' finest county in th' noblest State iv th' fair diadem iv th' raypublic, he wants to look out or some wan will insult him.

" ' Th' race question upon which I did not mean to speak, but will, can niver be settled until it is settled r-right. Th' r-right way to settle it is to lave it where it is. We give th' naygur ivry r-right guaranteed be th' Constichoochion. We permit him to vote, only demandin' that he shall prove that his father an' mother were white. We let him perform th' arjoos manyul labor iv our fair land. We bury him or gather him as soovenirs. What more can be asked? But we insist that though this happy fellow-citizen may pass us our vittles, he shall not fork out our stamps. To this ivry intilligence iv th' South that can be seen sunnin' itsilf on th' deepo platform stands committed. In th' sunny Southland we bow to public opinyon, be it iver so noisy. Th' naygur question with us is a burnin' question, an' so it will always be. Th' Prisidint iv these United States mus' know that we will defind white supreemacy to th' last dhrop iv their blood. I wish to discuss this question dispashnately, an' I say that I am in favor iv lavin' it to th' cold light iv raison. An' I thurly endorse th' proposition to fire a few eggs at th' Prisidint whin he comes South, an' approve iv th' round-robin sint be those blue-blooded Southern ladies who ar-re graftin' f'r a church fair in Texas, to tell th' ladies iv th' White House that they ar-re no ladies.'

"An' there ye ar-re, Hinnissy. There's th' naygur, with his vote an' a meal tickit to th' White House in his hand, an' he's no betther off thin he was whin I was opposin' his ilivation on constichoochual groun's, an' because I niver liked a naygur, annyhow."

"What's th' throuble?" asked Mr. Hennessy.

"Th' throuble is," said Mr. Dooley, "that th' naygurs iv th' North have lived too long among th' white people, an' th' white people iv th' South have lived too long among th' naygurs."

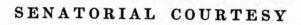

SENATORIAL COURTESY

SENATORIAL COURTESY

" IT'S a question iv Sinitoryal courtesy. What's
that? Well, Hinnissy, ye see, there ain't anny
rules in th' Sinit. Ivrybody gets up whin he
wants to, an' hollers about annything that comes into
his head. Whin Dorgan was in Wash'nton he wint
to hear th' debate on th' naval bill, an' a Sinitor was
r-readin' the *Life iv Napolyon* to another Sinitor who
was asleep.

" Sinitoryal courtesy rules th' body. If ye let
me talk I'll let ye sleep. Th' presidin' officer
can't come down with his hammer an' bid wan iv thim
vin'rable men, grim with thraditions, to chase himsilf
fr'm th' flure. In such a case it wud be parlyminthry f'r th' grim Sinitor to heave an ink-well at th'
presidin' officer. Undher Sinitoryal courtesy it is
proper an' even affable to call a fellow-Sinitor a
liar. It is th' hith iv courtesy to rush over an' push
his cigar down his throat, to take him be th' hair an'
dhrag him around th' room, or to slap him in th' eye
on account iv a diff'rence iv opinyon about collectors
iv intarnal rivinue. Southern Sinitors have been
known to use a small case-knife in a conthrovarsy.
It is etiket to take off ye'er boots in th' heat iv debate.
It is courteous f'r a Sinitor to go to sleep an' swal-
low his teeth while another Sinitor is makin' a speech.
But wanst a Sinitor is on his feet it is th' hith iv

misbehavior to stop him excipt f'r th' purpose iv givin' him a poke in th' nose. Afther a rough-an'-tumble fight, th' Sinitor who previously had the flure can get up fr'm it if able an' raysume his spectacles, his wig, an' his speech. But while he has wan syllable left in his face he is th' monarch iv all he surveys.

" No rules f'r thim ol' boys. Ye can say annything again' thim, but if ye attack that palajeem iv our liberties, th' sacred right to drool, they rally at wanst. Me frind Sinitor Morgan knew this, an' says he: ' Gintlemen, they'se a bill here I don't want to see passed. It's a mischeevous, foul, criminal bill. I didn't inthrajooce it. I don't wish to obsthruct it. If anny wan says I do, Sinitoryal courtesy will compel me to jam th' libel down his throat with a stove-lifter. I will on'y make a speech about it. In th' year fourteen hundherd an' two—' An' so he goes on. He's been talkin' iver since, an' he's on'y got down to th' sixteenth cinchry, where th' question broadens out. No wan can stop him. Th' air is full iv his wurruds. Sinitors lave Wash'nton an' go home an' spind a week with th' fam'ly an' come back, an' that grim ol' vethran is still there, poorin' out moist an' numerous language. They'se no raison why he shouldn't talk f'river. I hope he will. I don't care whether he does or not. I haven't a frind in th' Sinit. As f'r th' Pannyma Canal, 'tis thirty to wan I'll niver take a ride on it. But that's Sinitoryal courtesy."

" What's to be done about it?" asked Mr. Hennessy.

" What do I do whin ye an' ye'er aged frinds

stay here whin ye ought to be home?" asked Mr. Dooley.

"Ye tur-rn out th' gas," said Mr. Hennessy.

"An' that's what I'd do with th' Sinit," said Mr. Dooley.

THE CANDIDATE

THE CANDIDATE

"I SEE," said Mr. Hennessy, "that the Dimmy-crats have gr-reat confidence."

"They have," said Mr. Dooley. "Th' Dimmycrats have gr-reat confidence, th' Raypublicans ar-re sure, th' Popylists are hopeful, th' Prohybition-ists look f'r a landslide or a flood, or whativer you may call a Prohybition victhry, an' th' Socylists think this may be their year. That's what makes pollytics th' gr-reat game an' th' on'y wan to dhrive dull care away. It's a game iv hope, iv jolly-ye'er-neighbor, a confidence game. If ye get a bad hand at poker ye lay it down. But if ye get a bad hand at pollytics ye bet ye'er pair iv deuces as blithe as an English-man who has jus' larned th' game out iv th' spoortin' columns iv' th' London *Times*. If ye don't win fair ye may win foul. If ye don't win ye may tie an' get th' money in th' confusion. If it wasn't such a game wud there be Dimmycrats in Vermont, Raypublicans in Texas, an' Prohybitionists in the stock-yards ward? Ivry year men crawl out iv th' hospitals, where they've been since last iliction day, to vote th' Ray-publican ticket in Mississippi. There's no record iv it, but it's a fact. To-day th' Dimmycrats will on'y concede Vermont, Maine, an' Pennsylvania to th' Ray-publicans, an' th' Raypublicans concede Texas, Ally-bammy, an' Mississippi to th' Dimmycrats. But it's arly yet. Wait awhile. Th' wurruk iv th' campaign has not begun. Both sides is inclined to be pessimistic. Th' consarvative business man who thinks that if a little money cud be placed in Yazoo City th' prejudice again' th' Raypublicans, which is on'y skin-deep annyhow, cud be removed, hasn't turned up at headquarters. About th' middle iv October th' Raypublican who concedes Texas to th' Dimmycrats will be dhrummed out iv th' party as a thraitor, an' ye'll hear that th' Dimmycratic party in Maine is so cheered be th' prospects that his frinds can't keep him sober.

" Th' life iv a candydate is th' happiest there is. If I want annythin' pleasant said about me I have to say it mesilf. There's a hundherd thousan' freemen ready to say it to a candydate, an' say it sthrong. They ask nawthin' in rayturn that will require a civil-service examination. He starts in with a pretty good opinyon iv himsilf, based on what his mother said iv him as a baby, but be th' time he's heerd th' first speech iv congratulation he begins to think he had a cold an' indiff'rent parent. Ninety per cint. iv th' people who come to see him tell him he's th' mos' pop'lar thing that iver was, an' will carry th' counthry like a tidal wave. He don't let th' others in. If annybody says annything about him less frindly thin Jacob Riis he know's he either a sorehead or is in th' pay iv th' other campaign comity. Childher an' dogs ar-re named afther him, pretty women an' some iv th' other kind thry to kiss him, an' th' newspapers publish pitchers iv him as he sets in his libry, with his brow wrinkled in thought iv how fine a man he is. Th' opposition pa-apers don't get up

to th' house, an' he niver sees himsilf with a face like
Sharkey or reads that th' reason he takes a bath in
th' Hudson is because he is too stingy to buy a bath-
tub f'r th' house an' prefers to sponge on th' gr-reat
highway belongin' to th' people.

" If he hasn't done much to speak iv, his frinds
rayport his small but handsome varchues. He niver
punched his wife, he sinds his boys to school, he loves
his counthry, he shaves with a safety razor. A man
expicts to be ilicted Prisidint iv th' United States,
Hinnissy, f'r th' fine qualities that th' r-rest iv us
use on'y to keep out iv th' pinitinchry. All th' time
th' rayports fr'm th' counthry become more an' more
glowin'. Th' tidal wave is risin', an' soon will amount
to a landslide. Victhry is perched upon our banners,
and has sint f'r th' family. F'r th' Dimmycrat candydate th' most glowin' rayports iv gains come fr'm
New England, where there is always most room f'r
Dimmycratic gains. F'r th' Raypublicans, th' news
fr'm th' Southwest is so cheerin' as to be almost incredible, or quite so. But iliction day comes at last.
Th' people iv this gr-reat counthry gather at th'
varyous temples iv liberty in barber-shops an' liv'ry
stables an' indicate their choice iv evils. A gr-reat
hush falls on th' land as th' public pours out iv th'
side dure iv th' saloons an' reverently gathers at th'
newspaper offices to await with bated breath th'
thrillin' news fr'm th' first precinct iv the foorth
ward iv Sheboygan, Wis. An' thin again we hear
th' old but niver tiresome story: Texas give a Dimmycrat majority iv five hundred thousan', but will re-
open th' polls if more is nicessry; th' Dimmycrats
hope, if th' prisint ratio is maintained, th' Raypubli-

can victhry in Pinnsylvanya will not be unanimous.
An' wan candydate rayceives six million votes an' is
overwhelmingly defeated, an' th' other rayceives five
millyon nine hundherd thousan' and is triumphantly
ilicted. An' there ye ar-re.

"Why, Hinnissy, wanst whin I was in pollytics,
me an' Willum O'Brien put up a German be th' name
iv Smeerkase, or some such name, f'r alderman f'r
th' fun iv th' thing. It was a gr-reat joke, an' even
th' Dutchman knew it. But befure he'd been nommynated two weeks he begun to take it seeryous.
'They'se a good dale iv dissatisfaction in th' ward
with th' prisint aldherman,' says he, 'an' ye know
I've lived here a long time, an' I'm popylar with th'
boys. Sthranger things have happened thin if this
joke was to turn out thrue.' 'Well,' says I, 'if ye're
ilicted I want ye to make me uncle Mike chief iv
polis. He's licked thim all, an' he raaly holds th'
job ex-propria vigore, as th' Supreme Coort wud
say,' says I. 'Sure I will,' says Smeerkase. Well,
he come into me place ivry day to tell me how his
campaign was gettin' on. He had assurances fr'm
more people thin there were in th' ward that they'd
vote f'r him. He had his pitcher took an' hung on
th' tillygraft poles. He hired a man to write his
obichury fr'm th' time he took his first glass iv beer
as a baby to th' moment whin th' indignant citizens
iv th' sixth ward arose an' demanded that they shud
crowd their suffrage on him. That meant me an'
O'Brien, d'ye mind? He got up a mass-meeting, with
bands an' calceem-lights, an' th' hall was crowded
while he talked not on'y broken but, be Hivins, pool-
verized English on th' issues iv th' day.

The Candidate

"Well, Hinnissy, ye know 'tis not on'y th' candydate himsilf that's confident, it's ivrybody around him. An' befure th' iliction come I begun to think that maybe me frind did have a chance, so I wint around to see him. He was disthributin' th' spendin' money f'r th' polls, an' I had to fight me way in. 'Glad to see ye, Misther Dooley,' says he. 'I wanted to tell ye that I'm sorry I can't appint ye'er uncle chief iv polis. I've inquired into his charackter,' says he, 'an' 'tis not up to th' standard. Besides,' he says, 'I've promised th' job to th' Amalgamated Union iv Can Openers, who ar-re with me to a man.' 'Ar-re ye that sure ye're goin' to be ilicted that ye've already broken ye'er ante-iliction promises?' says I. 'My, but it's you that ar-re th' hurried statesman.' 'It's over,' says he. 'I've ordhered th' flowers f'r me desk in th' council.' 'Make mine a gates-ajar,' says I, an' wint my way.

"How manny votes did he get? Eight. That was th' amount. 'Where did he get thim?' says I to O'Brien. 'They were some we cudden't use,' says he. 'They belonged to a Bohaymian in th' fourth precint, but I give thim to Smeerkase. He's a good fellow,' says he.

WAR

WAR

"WAR is a fine thing. Or, perhaps I'm wrong. Annyhow, it's a sthrange thing. Here's th' Czar iv Rooshya, an' here's th' Imp'ror iv Japan. They have a diff'rence iv opinyon. All right, says I, lave thim fight it out. It's a good, healthful exercise. I'll arrange th' preliminaries, fix th' polis, an' be Hivens, I'll ref'ree th' fight. I make th' offer now. Anny time anny two high-spirited monarchs feel that their rile blood threatens to blow up I'll arrange ivrything down to th' photygrafts. Whiniver th' boys are ready I'll find th' barn. An' th' offer also goes f'r sicrities iv state.

"But what happens? A couple iv stout, middle-aged gintlemen get into a conthrovarsy. Instead iv layin' their stove-pipe hats on th' table an' mixin' it up, they hurry home an' invite ivrybody in th' house to go out an' do their war-makin' f'r thim. They set up on th' roof an' encourage th' scrap. 'Go in there, Olaf!' 'Banzai, Hip Lung, ye're doin' well f'r me!' 'There goes wan iv me brave fellows. I'd almost send somethin' to his widow if I cud larn her name!'

"An' so it goes. Bill Ivanovitch is settin' at home with his wife an' forty small childher. He has done a good day's wurruk, an' his salary iv nine cents is jinglin' in his pocket. He sets at th'

head iv th' table carvin' th' candle, an' just as he has
disthributed th' portions among th' fam'ly an' kep'
th' wick f'r himsilf, there's a knock at th' dure an' a
man in a fur cap calls him away to thravel eight
thousan' versts—a verst bein' Schwartzmeister's way
iv describin' a mile on a Rooshyan railroad—an' fight
f'r Gawd an' his czar.

"It's th' ol' firm. Whiniver I'm called on
to fight f'r Gawd an' me counthry I'd like to
be sure that th' senyor partner had been consulted. But Bill Ivanovitch puts on his coat, kisses
th' fam'ly good-by, an' th' next his wife sees iv him is
a pitcher iv th' old man an' a Jap he niver met befure
locked in an endurin' embrace, an' both iv thim as
dead as anny Mikado or Czar cud wish their most lile
subjick. Th' Jap don't know what it's all about.
In Japan he was a horse. There ar-re no rale horses
in Japan. If there were th' people wud have more to
eat. So th' citizens iv th' counthry harness thimsilves
up an' haul th' wagons. All ye have to say to a Jap
is 'Get ap,' an' he moves. So th' Mikado says, 'Get
ap,' an' th' little fellow laves his fireside an' his
wives an' fam'lies an' niver comes home no more. Th'
best he gets whin he is kilt is a remark in th' news
fr'm Tokyo that Gin'ral Odzoo's plans is wurrukin'
fav'rably. That ought to make him feel good.

"Now, if I had me way, Hinnissy, I wudden't let
th' common people fight at all. That's th' way it
used to be. Whin wan iv th' old kings in Brian
Boru's day had a spat with a neighbor both of thim
ordhered hats at th' hardware store an' wint out an'
pounded thim till their head ached. That's th' way
it ought to be. Supposin' th' Czar iv Rooshya an'

th' Mikado iv Japan fell out. What wud be da-
cinter f'r thim thin to have a gintlemanly mix-up?
Nick Romanoff, th' Rooshyan champeen, an' Mike
Adoo, th' cillybrated Jap'nese jiu-jitsu bantam, come
together las' night befure a crowd iv riprisintative
spoorts in a barn on th' outskirts iv th' city. Th'
Rooshyan was seconded be Faure, th' Frinch light-
weight, an' Bill Honezollern, th' Prooshyan whirlwind. In th' Jap's corner was Al Guelph, who bate
th' Llama iv Thibet las' week, an' Rosenfelt, th'
American champeen, who has issued a defi to th'
wurruld. Befure th' gong sounded th' Jap rushed
over an' sthruck th' Rooshyan a heavy blow beneath
th' belt. A claim iv foul was enthered but not allowed. At th' tap iv th' gong both boys wint at it
hammer an' tongs, but it was soon apparent that th'
Rooshyan, though heavier, was not in as good condition as his opponent. It was Walcott an' Choynski
all over, on'y th' Rooshyan hung on with gr-reat
courage. At th' end iv th' twentieth round, whin both
boys were on th' ropes, th' ref'ree, th' well-known
fight promotor, Misther Rothschild, declared th' bout
a dhraw. Considherable bad blood was aroused be a
claim be th' fighters that durin' th' battle they were
robbed iv their clothes be their seconds. As a finan-
cial entherprise, th' fight was a frost. Th' box-office
receipts did not akel th' rent iv th' barn an' thrainin'
expinses, an' th' ref'ree decided that as th' fight was
a dhraw he was entitled to th' stakes.

"Wudden't it be fine? Who wudden't walk to
Bloomington, Illinye, to see that sturdy but prudent
warryor, th' King iv England, mixin' it up with th'
Llama iv Thibet, or our own invincible champeen tak-

in' on th' Imp'ror iv Germany? If they didn't like th'
weepins they'd have me permission to use axes. I'd
go further. I wudden't bar annybody fr'm fightin'
who wanted to fight. If annybody felt th' martial
spirit in time he wud have a chance to use it up. I'd
have armies composed on'y iv officers. It wud be
gr-reat. D'ye s'pose they'd iver get near enough to
each other to hurt? They'd complain that th'
throuble with th' long-distance guns was that they
cudden't be made distant enough. Supposin' Gin'ral
Kurypotkin had to do all th' fightin' f'r himsilf. It
wud be betther f'r him, because thin he cud ordher
an advance without bein' so crowded comin' back.
Supposin', to gratify his heeryoic spirit, he had to
ordher himsilf to carry a thrunk, a cook-stove, a
shovel, a pickaxe, an ikon, an' a wurrud iv good cheer
fr'm th' czar two hundherd miles over a clay road,
an' if he did it successfully an' didn't spill annything
he might hope to be punctured be a bayonet. An'
s'pose Gin'ral Oyama had to walk barefooted acrost
Manchuria an' subsist f'r four months be whettin' his
beak on a cuttle-fish bone. How soon, d'ye think,
there wud be a battle? War wud be wan continyous
manoover, with wan iv thim manooverin' west an' th'
other manooverin' east. They'd niver meet till years
afther th' gloryous sthruggle"

"They'll niver do it," said Mr. Hennessy. "There
have always been wars."

"An' fools," said Mr. Dooley.

"But wudden't ye defind ye'er own fireside?"

"I don't need to," said Mr. Dooley. "If I keep
on coal enough, me fireside will make it too hot f'r
anny wan that invades it."

THE "ANGLO-SAXON" TRIUMPH

THE "ANGLO-SAXON"
TRIUMPH

"WELL, sir," said Mr. Dooley, "I'm happy to see how glad ivrybody is about what happened to ye a week ago last Choosdah."

"Much I care what they think," said Mr. Hennessy.

"Well, it's a gr-reat consolation in bereavement," said Mr. Dooley, "to know that ye'er sorrow is a soorce iv joy to others. All th' wurruld is glad ye got it where ye did. Th' czar turned a summersault whin he heerd th' news. Th' King of Italy has not got home since iliction night. Th' Prisidint iv France called on Gin'ral Porther an' kissed him f'r th' Prisidint. Th' Prisidint iv Colombia illuminated th' official palace an' tillygrafted askin' if there was annything Prisidint Rosenfelt cud do to him that hadn't been done. Th' German Imp'ror sat down an' wrote th' followin' cable: 'Congratylations on ye'er iliction as kaiser iv th' well-born American people. May ye'er reign be long an' happy. Toum felix fastumque barazza,' which is Latin f'r 'Why can't we be frinds?'

"But th' most enthusyastic enthusyasm was in England. On hearin' th' glad news on th' Saturdah followin' th' iliction, th' king sint f'r Ambassadure

Choate, who came as fast as his hands an' knees wud carry him. Arrivin' at Buckin'ham Palace, his majesty gracyously extinded his foot an ordhered him to convey his thanks to his lile subjicks acrost th' sea. Th' English pa-apers almost wint crazy with approval. Says wan iv thim: 'Thaydoor Rosenfelt is not a statesman in th' English sinse. He wud not compare with our Chamberlains or aven Markses. He is of more vulgar type. Judged be th' English standards, he is a coorse an' oncultivated man. But in America he stands high f'r good taste an' larnin'. He regards his iliction as a great triumph f'r th' Anglo-Saxon race.'

"So ye see, Hinnissy, 'twas th' Anglo-Saxon vote that did it. I see now what th' Prisidint was up to whin he sint f'r Cassidy iv th' Clan-na-Gael. Th' Clan-na-Gael is wan iv th' sthrongest Anglo-Saxon organyzations we have. It's whole purpose is to improve Anglo-Saxon civilyzation be ilivatin' it. There's on'y wan way to do it, an' that's th' way they do. Th' raison Cassidy an' Kelly an' Murphy an' Burke an' Shea an' all th' boys up an' down th' sthreet voted f'r Rosenfelt was because they ar-re Anglo-Saxons. Th' A. O. H., which, iv coorse, ye know, manes All Ol' H'Englishmen, was f'r Rosenfelt f'r th' same raison. So it was with th' Anglo-Saxon turnvereins an' sangerfests. Me frind Schwartz-meister down th' sthreet voted f'r Rosenfelt because iv his sthrong feelin' in favor iv cimintin' th' alliance between th' two nations. An' he was ilicted, I hear.

"I wondher how he'll threat th' Anglo-Saxon fr'm now on. I'm proud iv bein' a mimber iv that gr-reat race, now that me attintion has been called to it.

The "Anglo-Saxon" Triumph

Gawd bless Anglo-Saxony, says I, with all me heart.
It has made us a free counthry. But in handin'
around th' medals afther th' victhry, I fain wud see
a few pinned to manly coats that were not made in
Bond Sthreet. Give all th' branches iv that noble
herd a chance.

"But this is th' way it usually goes: About a year
befure iliction a man be th' name iv Sheehan or Sullivan or Casey makes up his mind that it's about time
to think iv nommynatin' somebody f'r th' prisidincy.
He looks around him, an' havin' wanst run acrost a
fellow in th' legislachure fr'm down th' State somewhere that niver made a speech, he jumps aboord a
thrain an' tears off f'r th' counthry. Afther some
hours he finds a man that can steer him to th' home
iv th' people's choice, Judge Silas Higgins. Th'
judge rayceives him in th' barn on account iv th'
fam'ly, an' accepts th' call fr'm th' people. He's
surprised he hadn't heerd it befure. Casey says th'
counthry is fairly ringin' with it. Casey comes back
to town, an' takes off his coat an' goes to wurruk.
He argues an' pleads an' palavers an' punches together a majority iv votes, in th' maintime keepin'
Judge Higgins chained down at home an' feedin'
him fr'm time to time with canned principles.

"Th' judge is nommynated, an' makes a whirlwind
campaign. He supplies th' wind an' Casey supplies th'
whirl. Ivrybody takes a kick at Casey. Th' opposition pa-apers ar-re in favor iv hangin' him. Th'
pa-apers iv his own party lament that th' campaign
shud be in th' hands iv such a man whin there are
such pathrites as Perkins an' Sanderson, who ought
to be at headquarthers. They are at headquarthers,

on'y th' pa-apers don't know it. They ar-re at head-quarthers, an' Casey is rehearsin' thim in their speeches an' showin' thim where to mark their ballots.

" On iliction day Casey fixes it up with his frind Mulligan in New York, O'Brien in Saint Looey, Mulcahy in Boston, O'Shay in Hartford, Butler in Buffalo, Doherty in San Francisco, Dorney in New Orleans, Hinnissy in Columbus, Sullivan in Chicago, an McGann in Keokuk, an' Judge Higgins is tri-umphantly ilicted. Th' mornin' afther iliction Casey larns that th' raysult is looked upon as a triumph f'r an Anglo-Saxon policy. He don't shout himsilf hoarse over that because his on'y acquaintance with an Anglo-Saxon policy was whin his fam'y was dhriven out iv th' County Kerry be a bailiff with an Anglo-Saxon bludgeon, but he goes over to see th' judge.

" ' Well, Casey,' says he, ' I done very well,' he says. ' Ye did, f'r a fact,' says Casey. ' It was a gr-reat triumph f'r me,' says th' judge. ' I think what knocked thim was me last speech in Hoboken.' ' It was a gr-reat vote-getter,' says Casey. ' Well,' says th' judge, ' I can't spare ye anny more time to-day, me humble frind,' he says. ' I'm busy makin' up me cab'net,' he says. ' I have decided to appint th' Hon'rable Peabody Perkins, iv th' District iv Colum-bia, sicrity iv state. He is partic'larly fitted f'r th' place, havin' spint all but th' last six weeks iv his life in England. His appintmint is endoorsed be th' London *Times*. I have also,' he says, ' offered th' job iv sicrity iv th' inteeryor to th' Hon'rable Pon-sonby Sanderson. He is th' high chief guy in th' Lile Orange Lodge, an' will know jus' how to handle th' public-school question,' he says. ' Thank ye,' says Casey. 'I have th' names iv a few fellows that have wurruked hard, an' I'd like to find places f'r thim,' he says. 'My man,' says th' judge, 'd'ye realize that ye ar-re talkin' to th' prisidint-elect iv these United States,' he says. 'If I did not feel kindly to'rd ye f'r ye'er arnest, if sometimes misguided, efforts in me behalf, I wud have ye raymoved be th' durekeeper,' he says. 'As it is,' he says, 'ye can sind th' applications iv ye'er frinds to th' clerk iv th' civil service commission, who has charge iv th' day laborers,' he says.

" An' there ye ar-re. Why do boys go to Harvard an' Yale? Is it because iv Eliot an' Hadley, or because iv Hurley an' Hogan? I read th' accounts iv th' futball game. Th' line-up was as follows: Hogan, Rafferty, Murphy, McGuire, Hurley, Cooney, Shevlin, Muldoon, Cassidy, Peabody, Van Renseller. Afther fifteen minyits Peabody retired. At th' end iv twinty minyits Van Renseller was called out be his ma. Flaherty an' Hinnissy in. Hogan through guard. Murphy pushes McGuire through tackle. Cooney slams Saltonstall on th' groun' an' breaks his back. Shevlin throws Witherspoon over th' fence. An' so on till me eyes fill with tears, an' I have dhreams iv invadin' Canada with an ar-rmy iv young Anglo-Saxon futball scholars fr'm Kerry an' th' County Mayo. An' that night Prisidint Hadley or Prisidint Eliot makes an addhress at th' king's birthday dinner, an' rejoices in our inthrest in Anglo-Saxon spoorts, an' congratylates th' wurruld that hereafther if England has a war we will have a chance to do most iv th' fightin' an' pay half th' money.

Dissertations by Mr. Dooley

" I wondher why it is! I suppose it's because we like th' game more thin th' rewards. Wan iv th' Anglo-Saxons who helped ilict Rosenfelt las' Choosdah wud give up his job rather thin be a pollytician, an' I suppose Hogan is thinkin' all through th' game that it's th' Prince iv Wales he has again' him on th' opposin' line."

" Well," said Mr. Hennessy, " if I thought this was an Anglo-Saxon victhry I wud niver have voted th' way I did."

" What!" exclaimed Mr. Dooley. " An' did you, too? Well, be Hivens, if it hadn't been f'r me it wud have been unanimous."

CORPORAL PUNISHMENT

15

CORPORAL PUNISHMENT

"I SEE," said Mr. Dooley, "that th' Prisidint is plannin' an attack on th' good old English custom iv wife-beatin'. He wants to inthra-jooce th' other good old English instichoochion iv a whippin'-post."

"He's all right," said Mr. Hennessy. "I'd like to have th' job."

"So wud I," said Mr. Dooley. "If th' law iver goes through I'll run f'r sheriff an' promise to give back all me salary an' half what I get fr'm th' race-thracks. Not, mind ye, that wife-beatin' is much practised in this counthry. Slug-ye'er-spouse is an internaytional spoort that has niver become pop'lar on our side iv th' wather. An American lady is not th' person that anny man but a thrained athlete wud care to raise his hand again' save be way iv smoothin' her hair. Afther goin' to a school an' larnin' to box, throw th' shot, an' play right-guard on th' futball team, th' gentle crather has what Hogan calls an abundant stock iv repartee. In me life I've known on'y six haitchool wife-beaters. Two iv thim were lucky to beat their wives to th' sidewalk, an' I've rescued th' other four fr'm th' roof iv th' house with a ladder. But now an' thin I suppose an American gintleman, afther losin' three or four fights on his way home, does thry to make a repytation be swingin'

[221]

on th' ex-heavy-weight champeen iv th' Siminary f'r Rayfined Females, an' if she can't put th' baby on th' flure in time to get to wurruk with th' loose parts iv th' stove, 'tis Thaydore's idee that she shud call a polisman an' have father taken down to th' jail an' heartily slapped.

"An' he's right. No gintleman shud wallop his wife, an' no gintleman wud. I'm in favor iv havin' wife-beaters whipped, an' I'll go further an' say that 'twud be a good thing to have ivry marrid man scoorged about wanst a month. As a bachelor man, who rules entirely be love, I've spint fifty years invistigatin' what Hogan calls th' martial state, an' I've come to th' con-clusion that ivry man uses vilence to his wife. He may not beat her with a table-leg, but he coerces her with his mind. He can put a savage remark to th' pint iv th' jaw with more lastin' effect thin a right hook. He may not dhrag her around be th' hair iv her head, but he dhrags her be her sympathies, her fears, an' her anxieties. As a last raycoorse he beats her be doin' things that make her pity him. An' th' ladies, Gawd bless thim, like it. Th' whippin'-post f'r wife-beaters won't be popylar with th' wife-beaters. In her heart ivry woman likes th' sthrong arm. Ye very sildom see th' wife iv an habitchool wife-beater lavin' him. Th' husband that gives his wife a vilet bokay is as apt to lose her as th' husband that gives her a vilet eye. Th' man that breaks th' furniture, tips over th' table, kicks th' dog, an' pegs th' lamp at th' lady iv his choice is seen no more often in our justly popylar divoorce coorts thin th' man who comes home arly to feed th' canary. Manny a skilful mandolin player has been onable to prevint his wife fr'm elopin' with a prize-fighter.

"No, you won't find anny malthreated ladies' names on th' petition f'r th' new govermint departmint. Th' Whippin' Postmasther-Gin'ral will have to look elsewhere f'r applause thin to th' downthrodden wives iv th' counthry. But th' departmint has come to stay; I hope, Hinnissy, to see its mission enlarged. I look forward to th' day whin there will be a govermint whippin'-post, with a large American flag at th' top iv it, in ivry American city. Afther awhile we can attind to th' wants iv th' rural communities. A fourth assistant whippin' postmasther-gin'ral will be sint to th' farmin' counthry, so that Cy an' Alick will get just as good a lammin' as Alphonso an' Augustus. He will carry a red, white an' blue post on his thravels, an' a special cat-o'-nine-tails, with th' arms iv th' United States an' th' motto, 'Love wan another,' engraved on th' handle. Th' whippin'-post will grow up to be wan iv th' foundations iv our govermint, like th' tariff. Whin annybody proposes to abolish it they will be met with th' cry: 'Let th' whippin'-post be rayformed be its frinds.' Th' frinds will build a bigger post an' put a few nails on th' lash. Ivinchooly people will quit goin' to Mt. Vernon an' make pilgrimages to Delaware, where th' whippin'-post has had such a fine moral effect. An' thin Addicks will be ilicted prisidint.

"Won't it be fine? Th' govermint gives us too little amusemint nowadays. Th' fav'rite pastime iv civilized man is croolty to other civilized man. Ye take a Southern gintleman, who has been accustomed to pathronize th' lynchin' iv naygurs. All other

spoorts seem tame to him aftherward. He won't go
to th' theaytre or th' circus, but pines at home till
there's another black man to be burned. A warden iv
a pinitinchry niver has anny fun out iv life afther
he loses his job. Judges in civil coorts sometimes
resign, but niver a hangin' judge in a criminal coort.

" Yes, sir, 'twill be a good thing f'r th' criminal
an' a good thing f'r a spoort-lovin' public, but th'
question that comes up in me mind is, Will it be a
good thing f'r Uncle Sam an' a good thing f'r Sheriff
Dooley. Th' only habit a man or a govermint ought
to pray again' acquirin' is croolty. It's th' gr-reatest
dissypation in th' wurruld. Ye can't swear off bein'
crool wanst ye begin to make a practice iv it. Ye
keep gettin' crooler an' crooler, till ye fin'lly think iv
nawthin' but injurin' ye'er neighbor an' seein' him
suffer. I mind wanst, whin I was a boy at home, a
new school-masther come to th' hedge. He was a nice,
quiet, near-sighted young fellow, an' he began be
larrupin' on'y th' worst iv th' boys. But ye cud see
in a minyit that he was injyin' th' pastime. At th'
end iv th' month he was lickin' somebody all th' time.
He used to get fairly dhrunk switchin' us. Glory be,
it seems to me that I spint all me boyhood days on
another boy's shoulders. He licked us f'r ivrything,
an' annythin' an' nawthin' at all. It wasn't that it
done us anny good, but it gave him pleasure. He's
been dead an' gone these forty years, an' I bear him
no ill-will, but if I iver r-run acrost his ghost I'll put
a head on it.

" So it is with Uncle Sam: If he begins to lick wife-
beaters, befure he's been at it long he won't have anny
time f'r annythin' but th' whippin'-post. He'll be

in his shirt-sleeves all day long, slashin' away at countherfeiters, illicit distillers, postal thieves, an' dimmycrats.

" No, Hinnissy, there ain't a hair's diff'rence between a blackguard who beats his wife an' a govermint that beats its childher. Ye can't cure corp'ral punishmint be makin' th' govermint th' biggest kind iv corp'ral punisher. Ye can't inflict corp'ral punishmint onless ye'er sthronger thin th' fellow ye punish, an' if ye ar-re sthronger ye ought to be ashamed iv ye'ersilf. Whiniver I hear iv a big six-fut school-teacher demandin' that he be allowed to whale a thirty-two-inch child I feel like askin' him up here to put on th' gloves with Jeffreys. Whin a govermint or a man raysorts to blows it shows they're ayether afraid or have lost their timpers. An' there ye ar-re."

" Spare th' rod an' spile th' child," said Mr. Hennessy.

" Yes," said Mr. Dooley, " but don't spare th' rod an' ye spile th' rod, th' child, an' th' child's father."

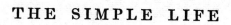

THE SIMPLE LIFE

THE SIMPLE LIFE

"WELL, Chas Wagner has been havin' th' fine old time over here," said Mr. Dooley.

"Is that th' man that wrote th' music?" asked Mr. Hennessy.

"No," said Mr. Dooley; "that was Cal. This is Chas Wagner, an' he's th' author iv th' two hundherd thousandth book that Prisidint Rosenfelt has read since th' first iv Novimber. 'Tis called *Th' Simple Life*. He cudden't find it in France, so he come lookin' f'r it among th' simple an' pasthral people in this counthry.

"He found it. He come over in a large but simple ship iv twenty thousan' simple horse-power, an' landed in th' simple village iv New York, where he was met be a comity iv simple little village lads an' lasses an' escorted to th' simple Waldorf an' installed in a room simply decorated in purple plush. That avenin' he attinded a meetin' iv th' Fifth Avnoo Female Simplicity Club. A lady wearin' a collar iv dimons, whose value was simply fabulous, recited passages fr'm *Th' Simple Life*. Afther this a simple supper iv terrapin an' champagne was sarved. He thin took a simple Pullman thrain to Wash'nton, where he attinded a rayciption at which a lady iv th' diplomatic core—which is all that is left iv diplomacy

[229]

nowadays—poked th' wife iv a Congressman with a lorgnette f'r goin' into supper ahead iv her. Later he was rayceived be th' simple prisidint, who said to him: ' Chas,' he says, ' I've been preachin' ye're book to me counthrymen,' he says. ' Simplicity an' a sthrong navy is th' watchword iv this administhration,' he says.

" Since thin Chas has been whoopin' up th' simple life. They've showed him ivrything simple we have. He's seen th' subway, th' dhrainage canal, th' Stock Exchange, Tom Lawson, Jawn D. Rockefellar, an' Mrs. Chadwick. He's looped th' loops, shot th' shoots, had a ride in a pathrol-wagon, played th' races, an' met Dave Hill. Th' las' seen iv him he was climbin' into a private car in a fur-lined coat an' a plug hat. Whin he goes home to his simple life in Paris he's goin' to have a ticker put in his study. He is undherstood to favor sellin' copper on bulges.

" I haven't read his book, but Hogan says it's a good wan, an' I'm goin' to read it afther I've read th' Bible an' Emerson, which Mike Ahearn ricommended to me th' year iv th' big fire. Th' idee is that no matther what ye ar-re, ye must be simple. If ye're rich, be simply rich; if ye're poor, be simply poor; if ye're nayether, be nayether, but be simple about it. Ye don't have to be gin'rous to be simple. He makes a sthrong pint iv that. It isn't nicissry to open ye'er purse, says Chas. If ye're a miser, be a simple miser. It ain't issintial to be poor to be simple. A poor man walkin' th' sthreet is far less simple thin a rich man lollin' back in his carriage an' figurin' out simple inthrest on his cuff. Th' poor man is envious iv th' rich man, but th' rich man is not envious iv th'

poor man. If ye're a flower, says he, be a flower; if
ye're a bur-rd, be a bur-rd; if a horse, a horse; if
a mule, a mule; if a hummin'-bur-rd, a hummin'-
bur-rd; if a polecat, a polecat; if a man, a man. But
always be simple, be it ever so complex.

" Th' on'y thing Hogan an' I can't make out fr'm
th' book is what is simplicity. I may be a simpleton,
Hinnissy, but I don't know. Father Tom Burke
was forty years writin' a book on ' simplicity,' an' he
niver got beyond th' first sintince, which was: ' It is
simply impossible to define simplicity.' It ain't simple to be poor, it ain't simple to be without clothes,
it ain't simple to be pious or sober. Ye're pretty
simple to believe all I tell ye, but ye may not be as
simple as I think an' hope. A lie may be as simple
as th' thruth. Th' fact iv th' matther is that th'
rale thruth is niver simple. What we call thruth an'
pass around fr'm hand to hand is on'y a kind iv a
currency that we use f'r convenience. There are a
good manny countherfeiters an' a lot iv th' counther-
feits must be in circulation. I haven't anny question
that I take in manny iv thim over me intellechool bar
ivry day, an' pass out not a few. Some iv th coun-
therfeits has as much precious metal in thim as th'
rale goods, on'y they don't bear th' govermint stamp.

" What th' divvle is simplicity, annyhow? Simple
is a foolish wurrud whin ye come to think it over.
Simple, simple, simple. It's a kind iv a mixture iv
silly an' dimple. I don't know how to go about bein'
simple. Th' Lord didn't make me that way. I can
imagine simplicity, but I can't just put me hand on
it. No more can Chas Wagner. Tell me, Chas
how to lead th' simple life. Tell me, Thaydore Ro-

senfelt, simple soul, what I must do. I'll go as far
as ye like. Hand out th' receipt. I'll make mesilf a
simple man if I have to bake in a slow oven to do it.
What 'll I do? Throw away th' superflooties, says
Hogan out iv Chas, his book. But what ar-re th'
superflooties? I'll turn out th' ilicthric light, shut
off th' furnace, an' desthroy th' cash raygister be
which complex macheen I keep mesilf fr'm robbin'
mesilf. But am I anny more simple because I'm
holdin' out on mesilf with frozen fingers be a tallow
dip? Was th' wurruld iver anny more simple thin
it is to-day? I doubt it. I bet ye there was a good
dale iv talk about Adam an' Eve dhressin' ostenta-
tiously an' havin' th' King of Biljum's ancesthor to
supper with thim.

Hogan was readin' me out iv a book th' other day
about th' simple fathers iv th' counthry. It was a
turr'ble shock to me. This fellow says that Robert
Morris, who I supposed sacrificed his fortune f'r
liberty injooced th' govermint to pay good money f'r
bad; Jawn Adams wanted to make a kingdom iv th'
counthry; while as f'r George Wash'nton, he acted
like a coal - oil Jawnny whin he wint to th' White
House, an' his wife put on insuff'rable airs an' had
such bad table manners that this here pathrite was
compelled to lave th' room an' run home to put it
down in his diary.

" An' there ye ar-re. Th' more I think th' less
simple simplicity becomes. Says Wagner *via* Hogan,
a man shud be like a lamp, an' th' more light he sheds
th' betther man he is. That's th' throuble with ivrybody that thries to advise me to be somethin' I ain't.
Whin I run him into a corner an' say: ' Come on now

The Simple Life

an' make good. Show me th' way,' he tells me I'm a lamp, or a three, or a snowflake blown be th' winds, or a bur-rd in a gilded cage, or a paint-brush, or a ship, or something else. But says I: ' I'm none iv these fine things. I'm a kind iv a man, an' I'm not mintioned in th' botany or th' mail ordher list. Tell me what I must do.' An' he looks me in th' eye an' says he: ' Be a man.' An' there ye ar-re. If a man's a lamp it's because he smokes, don't show up well in th' sunlight, an' will wan day be blown out. There ar-re other simple uses f'r lamps besides givin' light, which is wan iv th' poorest things they do nowadays. Rothschild thrades in thim, th' German imp'ror thinks they ar-re on'y useful to throw at his inimies, an' my business is to fill thim with karosene.

" No, sir, they ain't anny simple life. There's on'y life. It's a kind iv an obstacle race. Sinnin', repintin'; sinnin', repintin'. Some can jump high; some can't jump at all. Thim that jump highest have farthest to fall. Those that go farthest are ruled off f'r foulin'. A man's no more thin a man, an' he has as many things in him, anny wan iv thim li'ble to go wrong without a moment's notice, as all th' injines, tools, lamps, an' other hardware figures iv speech in a prize pome. He has to make his clumsy repairs while undher full headway. Lucky man if he staggers into port without havin' caused too manny shipwrecks on th' way over. It isn't th' most succissful passage that has caused th' most ship-wrecks.

" Ye see, Hinnissy, I'm a kind iv a Chas Wagner mesilf, only betther. He gets his out iv a Fr-rinch head, an' I got mine out iv th' *Third Reader* that a

[233]

little boy left in here who come f'r a pint iv simple refreshmint f'r his father's complex thirst."

" I don't think ye know such a lot about it," said Mr. Hennessy.

" I know more about th' sample life," said Mr. Dooley.

HOTELS AND HOTEL LIFE

HOTELS AND HOTEL LIFE

"THAT was a crool thing they done at th'
Waldorf-Astorya to me frind Hagan,"
said Mr. Dooley.

"I don't know him," said Mr. Hennessy. "Who
is he?"

"Ye know him all right, but ye don't reconize th'
name," said Mr. Dooley. "He's more cillybrated
undher what Hogan calls his nom de plume iv Jack
O'Brien—Phillydelphy Jack O'Brien. An, now I see
ye know him. All gr-reat warryors take martial
names whin they enther th' ring, onless they have
thim to start with like Sullivan. I wanst knew a Jew
man be th' name iv Mulkoweski, who fought or run
away or lay down undher th' haughty name iv Ryan.
So this Misther Hagan, whin he took up th' manly
art iv hidin' his fellow-man f'r a percintage iv th'
gate receipts, adopted th' name iv a gallant thribe, a
name, Hinnissy, for-midable enough to make his
opponent jump out iv th' ring without sthrikin' a
blow. He brought much honor be his valor to th'
city iv Willum Penn, an' fin'-ly reached th' top iv his
career be lammin' th' gr-reat Robert Fitzsimmons.
'Twas hardly a fair deal, d'ye mind, f'r Fitzsimmons
is a decrepit, worn-out, decayed, dodderin', senile ol'
man iv past forty. Besides, he was havin' throuble
with his wife, an' all th' time he was fightin' he didn't

see O'Brien at all, but on'y th' beautiful face iv th'
fair but fickle wan, an' thried to punch it. It was
th' vision iv this lovely creature that he swung at, an'
th' result was that he got a good lickin', an' so will
anny wan who fights visions whin a wan-hundherd-
an'-sivinty-pound youth is thryin' to knock his head
off. That is, I thought he got a good lickin', but I
see be th' pa-apers that 'twas not quite so simple.
Th' hero iv a thousan' fights an' a millyon challenges,
intherviews, snap-shots, an' melodhramas bowed his
proud ruby crest in th' anguish iv defeat an' passed
his lorls to th' fair brow iv a youthful conqueror, an'
was gathered to th' gr-reat Valhalla iv pugylism, an'
said he was sick to his stomach an' cudden't go on.
An' O'Brien, iv coorse, jined th' other pro-fession
that its members ar-re so proud iv that they always
change their names whin thy enther it. In other
wurruds, Hinnissy, he become an actor.

"Afther returnin' to his native city, an' bein'
received with more ginooine enthusyasm thin if he
was a reformed mayor, he wint up to New York an'
made sthraight f'r th' centher iv all that is best, an'
says so, in th' life iv our young raypublic. It was
th' avenin' hour, an' th' scene beggared description
an' manny iv' th' guests. All New York had gathered there her beauty an' her chivalry fr'm Aby Hum-
mel's office an' th' Stock Exchange. There was also
some beauty an' a dash iv chivalry fr'm Peotone,
What Cheer, an' Barry's Landing. Th' millyon in-
candescent electhric lights shone upon th' innocint
little childher iv th' cultivated classes, an' was re-
flected in their di'mon' tiaras as they played skip-rope
with ropes iv pearl through th' corrydors, or begged

a frozen absinthe fr'm th' head barkeeper. Their childish prattle about th' prob'ble price iv Amalgamated an' th' latest scandal at Newport give an air iv artless simplicity to th' scene.

"It was th' dinner-time, an' Refined Wealth was at it's avenin' repast, or just goin' to it. Four hundherd bartinders were shootin' cocktails at a sthrugglin' mass iv thirsty but incurable millyonaires in front iv th' bar. A thousan' waiters were dashin' through th' scores iv gilded dinin'-rooms, swingin' plates iv soup wildly over their heads or pourin' thim into th' hair iv favored guests. Th' head waiter was talkin' society gossip with wan iv th' leaders iv th' four hundherd. A gr-reat captain iv industhree was makin' a punch in a coal-scuttle, composed iv akel parts iv champagne an' tobasco sauce. Th' man at th' cigar counter was hammerin' wan iv our most prom'nint speculators f'r gettin' him wrong on copper. A gintleman fr'm Pittsburg was dashin' through th' Palm Room, pursued be th' wife iv his bosom. Two iv what Hogan calls th' jewness dory were mixin' it up on th' flure iv th' billyard-room. Flocks iv process-servers hovered about, ready to deliver summonses in divorce proceedin's. A group iv our most consarvative financeers were locked in their rooms up-stairs an' throwin' empty bottles at officers iv th' law with warrants. Th' hum iv polite convarsation an' th' light laugh was so incessant that it was with difficulty wan cud hear th' fightin' in th' rooms, th' colledge cries iv th' Yale futball team which was rushin' through th' ladies resthrant, th' smashin' iv baggage, th' ringin' iv bells, th' bets, th' music iv th' brass-band, or th' voices iv th' tastefully dhressed pages punchin' their way through th' fam'ly groups an' callin' aloud names that ar-re a household wurrud to all Americans. In short, Hinnissy, 'twas wan iv thim quite hotel avenin's whin American gintlemen an' ladies take their aise afther th' sthrenuse life iv th' day.

"Into this restful home iv elegance th' coorse prize-fighter foorced his way. He was given a room between a promoter iv Hackensack Meadows an' th' well-known ex-puddler who is goin' to marry Miss Flossie Gumdrop iv th' Hot Stuff Exthravaganza Comp'ny, if his wife don't kick up too much iv a fuss. But it was not f'r long. Th' rumor soon spread that th' hospital roof iv th' resort iv aristocratic leisure sheltered a prize-fighter, an' there was th' divvle to pay. Th' home-lover who was makin' th' punch in th' resthrant indignantly demanded his bill an' refused to pay it. Angry mathrons gathered their little wans fr'm th' broker's offices an' th' caffy, put on their pearl an' di'mon' dog-collars, an' prepared to lave. Th' Standard Oil magnates up-stairs telephoned down that they wud give up their rooms an' march out if they weren't afraid of bein' arrested.

"But th' hotel officials were prompt to act. Th' chief detictive, who had been pryin' a cabman off a bank prisidint with deleeryum thremens, brought th' prize-fighter to th' desk. 'You must lave here at wanst,' said th' chief clerk through th' megaphone, that all employees iv th' house use f'r convarsation. 'It shall niver be said that this here fam'ly hotel, consicrated to American domestic life, has been polluted,' he says, 'be a prize-fighter,' he says. 'Prize-fightin' is a lawful occypation,' said the conqueror iv th' gr-reat Fitzsimmons. 'Thin we haven't anny place for ye,' says th' clerk. 'Get out,' he says. An' poor O'Brien had to lave, an' there was no place f'r him to rest his head that night but th' newspaper offices. But th' Waldorf was saved, th' purl was averted, an' be-fure manny hours th' shelter iv wealth resumed th' ordhinry quite an' peace iv a Wild West show.

"An' there ye ar-re, Hinnissy. I see in th' pa-apers th' other day a fellow said we'd soon all be livin' in hotels. I think be all iv us he meant th' rich, f'r th' life is too gay f'r th' poor. I wanst lived in a hotel f'r a night. I was bumped out iv a 'bus at th' dure, an' as I got to me feet th' porter threw me gripsack at me, an' it opened up, an' I was some time findin' me collar. I wint to th' desk, an' afther I'd got th' attintion iv th' clerk, he called a bell-boy about thirty-eight years ol' an' says: 'Take him to room forty thousan' an' eight.' He said it in such a way I thought he wud've been more respictful if he'd put on th' black cap. 'This way,' says th' boy, an' he pushed me into an ilivator filled with ladies an' gintlemen an' th' sparkle iv joolry an' aromy.

"There was plenty iv room f'r me, but hardly enough f'r th' buttons on me vest, which was scraped off as th' ilivator flew on its mad flight. Ivry lady that got off give me a good poke in th' back to remim-ber her by. A heavy ol' gintleman stood on me feet an' thried to pretind he didn't know it be lookin' over me head. Ivry time th' criminal in charge iv th' ilivator stopped th' car he jolted me fr'm me heels up, an' ivry time he started it I had a quare sinsation like a thrickle iv ice-wather run up me spine. But on we wint till we hit th' roof, th' dure swung open, an' I thripped out on me head, just in time to hear th' ilivator man say: 'Look out f'r th' step.' Th' bell-boy led me down a long an' richly darkened hall, through scrubbin' brushes, thrunks, boots an' shoes, an' a sky terrier, opened a secret panel in a wall an' led me into a warm and fragrant recess or room overlookin' th' new chimbley iv a power-house. Th' room was well lighted, but not in a way to blind ye, be a window high up on th' wall, an' be an' electhric light so placed that it was not nicissry to shave be it. Says I to th' boy: 'A very nice place to keep a pair iv suspinders, but where's th' bedroom?' 'What ar-re ye givin' us?' says he. 'This is th' bedroom,' says he. 'But where's th' bed?' says I. 'This is it, ye jasper,' says he, an' he onfolded a bureau again' th' wall an' disclosed a model iv th' bad lands iv Dakota in ossified ticking. 'Am I to sleep in that?' says I. 'Ye ar-re,' says he. 'Well, thin,' says I, 'sind down to th' bar an' get me a quart iv ye'er best ol' vatted chloroform,' says I.

Did I sleep? Almost. Wanst, about iliven o'clock, I almost passed away. I dhreamt I was havin' a plasther cast iv mesilf taken f'r th' Art Museum whin th' tillyphone bell rang an' th' tillyphone lady's voice asked me if I was Jawn W. Grates. I said not yet, an' she says: 'Ring off, thin, I don't want ye,' she says. Thin I thried to sleep again, but it was no use. At midnight th' childher iv th' hotel begun comin' in fr'm th' theaytre, an' had their suppers iv Welsh-rabbits an' jelly-cake befure goin' to bed. At wan o'clock a gintleman who was singin' to himsilf thried to get into me room be mistake an' spint th' nex' hour apologizin' to me an' off'rin' to fight. At two o'clock a lady an' her husband in th' adjinin' room fell out over somethin', an' she cried in th' hall. At three o'clock a poker game on th' flure below broke up in a row. At five o'clock they started holeystonin' th' deck over me head. At half-past five th' carpet-sweeper got to wurruk. At six th' chambermaid begin thryin' th' dure, an' did it ivry five minyits aftherward. Siven o'clock was th' hour f'r th' foldin' bed to resume its original form, an' it did it without lettin' me know. I was rescued, an' I wint home an' slept th' sleep iv th' poor, th' just, an' th' domestic.

"No, sir, hotel life is not f'r th' likes iv us, Hinnissy. It's f'r thim that loves mad gayety, th' merry rattle iv th' tillyphone bell, th' electhric light that ebbs an' flows, th' long an' invigoratin' walk to th' bath, th' ilivator that shoots ye up an' down or passes ye by, th' clink iv th' dark ice in th' pitcher, an' th' mad swirl iv th' food in th' resthrant where th' moist waiter rubs ye'er plate affectionately with th' other man's napkin an' has an attintive ear f'r ivry wurrud iv ye'er private convarsation. All this is f'r th' rich. Gawd bless thim an' keep thim out iv our detached or semi-detached hovels or homes, th' only possessions th' poor have left."

"I've heerd," said Mr. Hennessy, "that this here fellow O'Brien wanst threw a fight."

"I don't believe it," said Mr. Dooley; "if he had he wud've been a welcome guest."

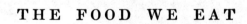

THE FOOD WE EAT

THE FOOD WE EAT

"WHAT have ye undher ye'er arm there?" demanded Mr. Dooley.

"I was takin' home a ham," said Mr. Hennessy.

"Clear out iv here with it," cried Mr. Dooley. "Take that thing outside—an' don't lave it where th' dog might get hold iv it. Th' idee iv ye'er bringin' it in here! Glory be, it makes me faint to think iv it. I'm afraid I'll have to go an' lay down."

"What ails ye?" asked Mr. Hennessy.

"What ails me?" said Mr. Dooley. "Haven't ye r-read about th' invistygation iv th' Stock Yards? It's a good thing f'r ye ye haven't. If ye knew what that ham—oh, th' horrid wurrud—was made iv ye'd go down to Rabbi Hirsch an' be baptized f'r a Jew.

"Ye may think 'tis th' innocint little last left leg iv a porker ye're inthrajoocin' into ye'er innocint fam'ly, but I tell ye, me boy, th' pig that that ham was cut fr'm has as manny legs to-day as iver he had. Why did ye waste ye'er good money on it? Why didn't ye get th' fam'ly into th' dining-room, shut th' windows, an' turn on th' gas? I'll be readin' in th' pa-aper to-morra that wan Hinnissy took an over-dose iv Unblemished Ham with suicidal intint an' died in gr-reat agony. Take it away! It's lible to blow up at anny minyit, scattherin' death an' desthruction in its train.

"Dear, oh dear, I haven't been able to ate annything more nourishin' thin a cucumber in a week. I'm grajally fadin' fr'm life. A little while ago no wan cud square away at a beefsteak with betther grace thin mesilf. To-day th' wurrud resthrant makes me green in th' face. How did it all come about? A young fellow wrote a book. Th' divvle take him f'r writin' it. Hogan says it's a grand book. It's wan iv th' gr-reatest books he iver r-read. It almost made him commit suicide. Th' hero is a Lithuanian, or as ye might say, Pollacky, who left th' barb'rous land iv his birth an' come to this home iv opporchunity where ivry man is th' equal iv ivry other man befure th' law if he isn't careful. Our hero got a fancy job poling food products out iv a catch-basin, an' was promoted to scrapin' pure leaf-lard off th' flure iv th' glue facthry. But th' binifits iv our gloryous civilyzation were wasted on this poor peasant. Instead iv bein' thankful f'r what he got, an' lookin' forward to a day whin his opporchunity wud arrive an', be merely stubbin' his toe, he might become rich an' famous as a pop'lar soup, he grew cross an' unruly, bit his boss, an' was sint to jail. But it all tur-rned out well in th' end. Th' villain fell into a lard-tank an' was not seen again ontil he tur-rned up at a fash'nable resthrant in New York. Our hero got out iv jail an' was rewarded with a pleasant position as a porter iv an arnychist hotel, an' all ended merry as a fun'ral bell.

"Ye'll see be this that 'tis a sweetly sintimintal little volume to be r-read durin' Lent. It's had a

grand success, an' I'm glad iv it. I see be th' publishers' announcemints that 'tis th' gr-reatest lithry
hog-killin' in a peryod iv gin'ral lithry culture. If
ye want to rayjooce ye'er butcher's bills buy *Th'
Jungle*. It shud be taken between meals, an' is
especially ricomminded to maiden ladies contimplatin'
their first ocean voyage.

"Well, sir, it put th' Prisidint in a tur-rble stew.
Oh, Lawd, why did I say that? Think iv—but I
mustn't go on. Annyhow, Tiddy was toying with
a light breakfast an' idly turnin' over th' pages iv
th' new book with both hands. Suddenly he rose
fr'm th' table, an' cryin': ' I'm pizened,' begun
throwin' sausages out iv th' window. Th' ninth wan
sthruck Sinitor Biv'ridge on th' head an' made him
a blond. It bounced off, exploded, an' blew a leg
off a secret-service agent, an' th' scatthred fragmints
desthroyed a handsome row iv ol' oak-trees. Sinitor
Biv'ridge rushed in, thinkin' that th' Prisidint was
bein' assassynated be his devoted followers in th'
Sinit, an' discovered Tiddy engaged in a hand-to-
hand conflict with a potted ham. Th' Sinitor fr'm
Injyanny, with a few well-directed wurruds, put out
th' fuse an' rendered th' missile harmless. Since thin
th' Prisidint, like th' rest iv us, has become a viggy-
taryan, an' th' diet has so changed his disposition that
he is writin' a book called *Suffer in Silence*, didy-
cated to Sinitor Aldrich. But befure doin' annything else, he selected an expert comity fr'm a neighborin' univarsity settlemint to prepare a thorough,
onbiased rayport that day on th' situation an' make
sure it was no betther thin th' book said. Well, what
th' experts discovered I won't tell ye. Suffice it to say,

that whin th' report come in Congress decided to abolish all th' days iv th' week except Friday.

"I have r-read th' report, an' now, whin I'm asked to pass th' corned-beef, I pass. Oh dear, th' things I've consumed in days past. What is lard? Lard is annything that isn't good enough f'r an axle. What is potted ham? It is made in akel parts iv plasther iv Paris, sawdust, rope, an' incautious laborer. To what kingdom does canned chicken belong? It is a mineral. How is soup— Get me th' fan, Hinnissy.

"Thank ye. I'm betther now. Well, sir, th' packers ar-re gettin' r-ready to protect thimsilves again' *The Jungle.* It's on'y lately that these here gin'rous souls have give much attintion to lithrachoor. Th' on'y pens they felt an inthrest in was those that resthrained th' rectic cow. If they had a blind man in th' Health Departmint, a few competint frinds on th' Fedhral bench, an' Farmer Bill Lorimer to protect th' cattle inthrests iv th' Gr-reat West, they cared not who made th' novels iv our counthry. But Hogan says they'll have to add a novel facthry to their plant, an' in a few months ye'll be able to buy wan iv Nels Morris's pop-lar series warranted to be fr'm rale life, like th' pressed cornedbeef.

"Hogan has wrote a sample f'r thim:

"'Dear!' Ivan Ivanovitch was seated in th' consarvatory an' breakfast-room pro-vided be Schwartzchild & Sulsberger f'r all their employees. It was a pleasant scene that sthretched beneath th' broad windows iv his cosey villa. Th' air was redolent with th' aroma iv th' spring rendherin', an' beneath th' smoke

The Food We Eat

iv th' May mornin' th' stately expanse iv Packin'town appeared more lovely than iver befure. On th' lawn a fountain played brine incessantly an' melojously on th' pickled pigs'-feet. A faint odor as iv peach blossoms come fr'm th' embalmin' plant where kine that have perished fr'm joy in th' long journey fr'm th' plains are thransformed into th' delicacies that show how an American sojer can die. Thousan's iv battle-fields are sthrewn with th' labels iv this justly pop'lar firm, an' a millyon heroes have risen fr'm their viands an' gone composedly to their doom. But to rayturn to our story. Th' scene, we say, was more beautiful thin wurruds can describe. Beyond th' hedge a physician was thryin' to make a cow show her tongue, while his assistant wint over th' crather with a stethoscope. Th' air was filled with th' joyous shouts iv dhrivers iv wagons heavily laden with ol' boots an' hats, arsenic, boric acid, bone-dust, sthricknine, sawdust, an' th' other ingreejents iv th' most nourishing food f'r a sturdy people. It was a scene f'r th' eye to dote upon, but it brought no happiness to Ivan Ivanovitch. Yisterdah had been pay-day at th' yards an' little remained iv th' fourteen thousan' dollars that had been his portion. There was a soupcan iv anger in his voice as he laid down a copy iv th' *Ladies' Home Journal* an' said: " Dear!" Th' haughty beauty raised her head an' laid aside th' spoon with which she had been scrapin' th' life-givin' proosic acid fr'm th' Deer Island sausage. " Dear," said Ivanovitch, " if ye use so much iv th' comp'ny's peroxide on ye'er hair there will be none left f'r th' canned turkey." Befure she cud lift th' buttherine dish a cheery voice was heerd at th' dure, an' J. Og-

den Cudahy bounded in. Ivanovitch flushed darkly,
an' thin, as if a sudden determination had sthruck
him, dhrew on his overhalls an' wint out to shampoo
th' pigs. [Th' continyuation iv this thrillin' story
will be found in th' next issue iv *Leaf Lard*. F'r sale
at all dellycatessen-stores.]'

"An' there ye ar-re, Hinnissy. It's a turr'ble
situation. Here am I an' here's all th' wurruld been
stowin' away meat since th' days iv Nebudcud—what-
ye-may-call-him. 'Tis th' pleasant hour iv dinner.
We've been waitin' half an hour, pretindin' we were in
no hurry, makin' convarsation, an' lookin' at th'
clock. There is a commotion in th' back iv th' house,
an' a cheery perfume iv beefsteak an' onions comes
through an open dure. Th' hired girl smilin'
but triumphant flags us fr'm th' dinin'-room. Th'
talk about th' weather stops at wanst. Th' story iv
th' wondherful child on'y four years old that bit his
brother is stowed away f'r future use. Th' comp'ny
dashes out. There is some crowdin' at th' dure.
'Will ye sit there, Mrs. Casey?' 'Mrs. Hinnissy,
squat down next to Mike.' 'Tom, d'ye stow ye'ersilf
at th' end iv th' table, where ye can deal th' potatoes.' 'Ar-re ye all r-ready? Thin go.' There ar-re
twinty good stories flyin' befure th' napkins ar-re
well inside iv th' collar. Th' platter comes in smokin'
like Vesuvyous. I begin to play me fav'rite chune
with a carvin'-knife on a steel whin Molly Donahue
remarks: 'Have ye r-read about th' invistygations
iv th' Stock Yards?' I dhrop me knife. Tom Donahue clutches at his collar. Mrs. Hinnissy says th'
rooms seem close, an' we make a meal off potatoes an'
wathercress. Ivrybody goes home arly without sayin'

good-bye, an' th' next day Father Kelly has to patch
up a row between you an' ye'er wife. We ate no more
together, an' food bein' th' basis iv all frindship,
frindship ceases. Christmas is marked off th' calen-
dar an' Lent lasts f'r three hundherd an' sixty-five
days a year.

" An', be Hivens, I can't stop with thinkin' iv th'
way th' food is got r-ready. Wanst I'm thurly sick
I don't care how much sicker I get, an' I go on
wondherin' what food ra-aly is. An' that way, says
Hogan, starvation lies. Th' idee that a Polish gintleman has danced wan iv his graceful native waltzes
on me beefsteak is horrible to think, but it's on'y a
shade worse thin th' thought that this delicate morsel
that makes me th' man I am was got be th' assassy-
nation iv a gentle animile that niver done me no harm
but look kindly at me. See th' little lamb friskin'
in th' fields. How beautiful an' innocint it is. Whin
ye'er little Packy has been a good boy ye call him
ye'er little lamb, an' take him to see thim skippin' in
th' grass. ' Aren't they cunnin', Packy?' But look!
Who is this gr-reat ruffyanly man comin' acrost th'
fields? An' what is that horrid blade he holds in his
hands? Is he goin' to play with th' lamb? Oh,
dhreadful sight. Take away th' little boy, Hinnissy.
Ye have ordhered a leg iv lamb f'r supper.

" Th' things we eat or used to eat! I'll not mintion anny iv thim, but I'd like some pote to get up
a list iv eatable names that wud sound th' way they
taste. It's askin' too much f'r us to be happy whin
we're stowin' away articles iv food with th' same titles
as our own machinery. ' But why not ate something
else?' says ye. Fish? I can't. I've hooked thim out

iv th' wather. Eggs? What is an egg? Don't answer. Let us go on. Milk? Oh, goodness! Viggytables, thin? Well, if it's bad to take th' life iv a cow or a pig, is it anny betther to cut off a tomato in th' flower iv its youth or murdher a fam'ly iv baby pease in th' cradle? I ate no more iv annything but a few snowballs in winter an' a mouthful iv fresh air in th' summer-time.

"But let's stop thinkin' about it. It's a good thing not to think long about annything—ye'ersilf, ye'er food, or ye'er hereafter. Th' story iv th' nourishmint we take is on'y half written in *Th' Jungle*. If ye followed it fr'm th' cradle to th' grave, as ye might say—fr'm th' day Armour kicked it into a wheelbarrow, through varyous encounters, th' people it met, with their pictures while at wurruk, until it landed in th' care iv th' sthrange lady in th' kitchen—ye'd have a romance that wud make th' butcher haul down his sign. No, sir, I'm goin' to thry to fight it. If th' millyonaire has a gredge again' me he'll land me somehow. If he can't do me with sugar iv lead, he'll run me down with a throlley-car or smash me up in a railroad accident. I'll shut me eyes an' take me chance. Come into th' back room, cut me a slice iv th' ham, an' sind f'r th' priest."

"They ought to make thim ate their own meat," said Mr. Hennessy, warmly.

"I suggested that," said Mr. Dooley, "but Hogan says they'd fall back on th' Constitution. He says th' Constitution f'rbids crool an' unusual punishmints."

NATIONAL HOUSECLEANING

NATIONAL HOUSECLEANING

"IT looks to me," said Mr. Hennessy, "as though this counthry was goin' to th' divvle."

"Put down that magazine," said Mr. Dooley. "Now d'ye feel betther? I thought so. But I can sympathize with ye. I've been readin' thim mesilf. Time was whin I sildom throubled thim. I wanted me fiction th' day it didn't happen, an' I cud buy that f'r a penny fr'm th' newsboy on th' corner. But wanst in a while some homefarin' wandhrer wud jettison wan in me place, an' I'd frequently glance through it an' find it in me lap whin I woke up. Th' magazines in thim days was very ca'ming to th' mind. Angabel an' Alfonso dashin' f'r a marredge license. Prom'nent lady authoressesses makin' pomes at th' moon. Now an' thin a scrap over whether Shakespeare was enthered in his own name or was a ringer, with th' long‑shot players always again Shakespeare. But no wan hurt. Th' idee ye got fr'm these here publications was that life was wan glad, sweet song. If annything, ivrybody was too good to ivrybody else. Ye don't need to lock th' dure at night. Hang ye'er watch on th' knob. Why do polismen carry clubs? Answer, to knock th' roses off th' throlley-poles. They were good readin'. I liked thim th' way I like a bottle iv white pop now an' thin.

"But now whin I pick me fav'rite magazine off
[257]

th' flure, what do I find? Ivrything has gone wrong.
Th' wurruld is little betther thin a convict's camp.
Angabel an' Alfonso ar-re about to get marrid whin
it is discovered that she has a husband in Ioway an'
he has a wife in Wisconsin. All th' pomes be th' lady
authoressesses that used to begin: ' Oh, moon, how
fair!' now begin: ' Oh, Ogden Armour, how awful!'
Shakespeare's on'y mintioned as a crook. Here ye
ar-re. Last edition. Just out. Full account iv th'
Crimes iv Incalculated. Did ye read Larsen last
month on ' Th' use iv Burglars as Burglar Alarums '?
Good, was it? Thin read th' horrible disclosures
about th' way Jawn C. Higgins got th' right to build
a bay-window on his barber-shop at iliven forty-two
Kosciusko Avnoo, South Bennington, Arkansaw.
Read Wash'n'ton Bliffens's dhreadful assault on th'
board iv education iv Baraboo. Read Idarem on
Jawn D.; she's a lady, but she's got th' punch.
Graft ivrywhere. ' Graft in th' Insurance Comp'-
nies,' ' Graft in Congress,' ' Graft in th' Supreem
Coort,' ' Graft be an Old Grafter,' ' Graft in Lith-
rachoor,' be Hinnery James; ' Graft in Its Relations
to th' Higher Life,' be Dock Eliot; ' Th' Homeeric
Legend an' Graft; Its Cause an' Effect; Are They th'
Same? Yes and No,' be Norman Slapgood.

  " An' so it goes, Hinnissy, till I'm that blue, dis-
couraged, an' broken-hearted I cud go to th' edge iv
th' wurruld an' jump off. It's a wicked, wicked, horrible, place, an' this here counthry is about th' tough-
est spot in it. Is there an honest man among us? If
there is throw him out. He's a spy. Is there an
institution that isn't corrupt to its very foundations?
Don't ye believe it. It on'y looks that way because

our graft iditor hasn't got there on his rounds yet. Why, if Canada iver wants to increase her popylation all she has to do is to sind a man in a balloon over th' United States to yell: 'Stop thief!' At th' sound iv th' wurruds sivinty millyon men, women, an' little scoundhrelly childher wud skedaddle f'r th' frontier, an' lave Jerome, Folk, an' Bob La Follette to pull down th' blinds, close th' dure, an' hang out a sign: 'United States to rent.' I don't thrust anny man anny more. I niver did much, but now if I hear th' stealthy step iv me dearest frind at th' dure I lock th' cash dhrawer. I used to be nervous about burglars, but now I'm afraid iv a night call fr'm th' Chief Justice iv th' Supreem Coort or th' prisidint iv th' First National Bank.

"It's slowly killin' me, Hinnissy, or it wud if I thought about it. I'm sorry George Wash'n'ton iver lived. Thomas Jefferson I hate. An' as f'r Adam, well, if that joker iver come into this place I'd— but I mustn't go on.

"Do I think it's all as bad as that? Well, Hinnissy, now that ye ask me, an' seein' that Chris'mas is comin' on, I've got to tell ye that this counthry, while wan iv th' worst in th' wurruld, is about as good as th' next if it ain't a shade betther. But we're wan iv th' gr-reatest people in th' wurruld to clean house, an' th' way we like best to clean th' house is to burn it down. We come home at night an' find that th' dure has been left open an' a few mosquitoes or life-insurance prisidints have got in, an' we say: 'This is turr'ble. We must get rid iv these here pests.' An' we take an axe to thim. We desthroy a lot iv furniture an' kill th' canary bird, th'

cat, th' cuckoo clock, an' a lot iv other harmless in-
sects, but we'll fin'lly land th' mosquitoes. If an
Englishman found mosquitoes in his house he'd first
thry to kill thim, an' whin he didn't succeed he'd say:
' What pleasant little humming-bur-rds they ar-re.
Life wud be very lonesome without thim,' an he'd
domesticate thim, larn thim to sing ' Gawd Save th'
King,' an' call his house Mosquito Lodge. If these
here inthrestin' life-insurance scandals had come up
in Merry ol' England we'd niver hear iv thim, because
all th' boys wud be in th' House iv Lords be this
time, an' Lord Tontine wud sit hard on anny scheme
to have him searched be a lawyer fr'm Brooklyn. But
with this here nation iv ours somebody scents something wrong with th' scales at th' grocery-store an'
whips out his gun, another man turns in a fire alarm,
a third fellow sets fire to th' Presbyterian Church, a
vigilance comity is formed an' hangs ivry foorth
man; an' havin' started with Rockyfellar, who's
tough an' don't mind bein' lynched, they fin'lly wind
up with desthroyin' me because th' steam laundhry
has sint me home somebody else's collars.

" It reminds me, Hinnissy, iv th' time I lived at a
boardin'-house kept be a lady be th' name iv Doherty.
She was a good woman, but her idee iv life was a
combination iv pneumony an' love. She was niver still.
Th' sight iv a spot on th' wall where a gintleman
boorder had laid his head afther dinner would give
her nervous prostration. She was always polishin',
scrubbin', sweepin', airin'. She had a plumber in to
look at th' dhrains twice a week. Fifty-two times a
year there was a rivolution in th' house that wud've
made th' Czar iv Rooshya want to go home to rest.

An' yet th' house was niver really clean. It looked as if it was to us. It was so clean that I always was ashamed to go into it onless I'd shaved. But Mrs. Doherty said no; it was like a pig-pen. ' I don't know what to do,' says she. ' I'm worn out, an' it seems impossible to keep this house clean.' ' What is th' throuble with it?' says he. ' Madam,' says me frind Gallagher, ' wud ye have me tell ye?' he says. ' I wud,' says she. ' Well,' says he, ' th' throuble with this house is that it is occypied entirely be human bein's,' he says. ' If 'twas a vacant house,' he says, ' it cud aisily be kept clean,' he says.

"An' there ye ar-re, Hinnissy. Th' noise ye hear is not th' first gun iv a rivolution. It's on'y th' people iv th' United States batin' a carpet. Ye object to th' smell? That's nawthin'. We use sthrong disinfectants here. A Frinchman or an Englishman cleans house be sprinklin' th' walls with cologne; we chop a hole in th' flure an' pour in a kag iv chloride iv lime. Both are good ways. It depinds on how long ye intind to live in th' house. What were those shots? That's th' housekeeper killin' a couple iv cockroaches with a Hotchkiss gun. Who is that yell-in'? That's our ol' frind High Fi-nance bein' compelled to take his annual bath. Th' housecleanin' season is in full swing, an' there's a good deal iv dust in th' air; but I want to say to thim neighbors iv ours, who're peekin' in an' makin' remarks about th' amount iv rubbish, that over in our part iv th' wurruld we don't sweep things undher th' sofa. Let thim put that in their pipes an' smoke it."

" I think th' counthry is goin' to th' divvle," said Mr. Hinnissy, sadly.

" Hinnissy," said Mr. Dooley, " if that's so I congratylate th' wurruld."

" How's that?" asked Mr. Hennessy.

" Well," said Mr. Dooley, " f'r nearly forty years I've seen this counthry goin' to th' divvle, an' I got aboord late. An' if it's been goin' that long an' at that rate, an' has got no nearer thin it is this pleasant Chris'mas, thin th' divvle is a divvle iv a ways further off thin I feared."

SOCIALISM

SOCIALISM

*Saturday night at Mr. Dooley's—Mr. Dooley in
the chair. Present, Mr. Larkin and Mr. McKenna.
Present, but not voting, Mr. Hennessy and Mr.
Schwartzmeister.*

"SOCIALISM is sweepin' like a wave over
th' counthry," said Mr. Larkin, the radical
blacksmith.

"It hasn't wet my feet yet," said Mr. McKenna
(Rep.).

"But Matthew is right," said Mr. Dooley. "He's
right about it. A few days ago Mulligan wud've
r-run me in because I didn't wear a pitcher iv Hetty
Green in me watch - chain, an' sind me freeman's
sufferage to Pierpont Mulligan to be endorsed befure
I cud use it. To-day Mulligan is prisidint iv th'
Polisman's Binivolent Hammer th' Millyonaires Assocyation, an' he has turned to th' wall th' lithygrafts
iv th' fathers iv his counthry, Addicks Crossin' th'
Delaware, Jakey Schiff sthrikin' th' shekels fr'm th'
slave, an' Grover Cleveland's Farewell to his Life-
insurance agents. These an' other gr-reat names that
wanst us bold but busted peasanthry looked up to
f'r advice that not on'y cost thim nawthin', but was
even what ye might call remooncrative to thim, has
to pay th' same rates as Mrs. Winslow's soothin'

[265]

syrup to have their pathriotic appeals to their fellow-citizens printed in the pa-apers. As Hogan wud say, ye can no longer conjure with thim. Ye can't even con with thim, as I wud say.

" It was diff"rent in the goolden days. A gr-reat chance a Socialist had thin. If annybody undher-stood him he was kilt be infuryated wurrukinmen. It was a good thing f'r him that he on'y spoke Ger-man, which is a language not gin'rally known among cultivated people, Schwartzmeister. They used to hold their meetin's in a cellar in Wintworth Avnoo, an' th' meetin' was most always followed be an outin' in th' pathrol-wagon. 'Twas wan iv th' spoorts to go down to see th' Brotherhood iv Man rushed off in th' on'y Municipal Ownership conveyance we had in thim days, an' havin' their spectacles busted be th' hardy an' loyal polis.

" 'Tis far diff"rent now. No cellars f'r th' Brotherhood iv Man, but Mrs. Vanderhankerbilk give a musical soree f'r th' ladies iv th' Female Billyonaires Arbeiter Verein at her iligant Fifth Avnoo mansion yisterdah afthernoon. Th' futmen were dhressed in th' costume iv th' Fr-rinch Rivo-lution, an' tea was served in imitation bombs. Th' meetin' was addhressed be th' well-known Social-ist leader, J. Clarence Lumley, heir to th' Lumley millyons. This well-known prolytariat said he had become a Socialist through studyin' his father. He cud not believe that a system was right which allowed such a man to accumylate three hundherd millyon dollars. He had frequently thried to inthrest this vin'rable mossback in industhreel questions, an' all he replied was: ' Get th' money.' Th' ladies prisint

cud appreciate how foolish th' captains iv industhree are, because they were marrid to thim an' knew
what they looked like in th' mornin'. Th' time had
come whin a fierce blow must be sthruck f'r human
freedom. In conclusion, he wud sing th' ' Marsel-
laisy,' an' accompany himsilf on a guitar. Th' hostess
followed with a few remarks. She said Socialists were
not dhreamers, but practical men. Socialism was not
a question iv th' hour, but had come to stay as an
afthernoon intertainmint. It was less expinsive thin
bridge, an' no wan cud call ye down f'r ladin' out iv
th' wrong hand. She had made up her mind that
ivrybody must do something f'r th' cause. It was
wrong f'r her to have other people wurrukin' f'r her,
an' she intinded to free or bounce her servants an' go
to live at a hotel. She wud do her share in th'
wurruld's wurruk, too, an' with this in view she was
takin' lessons in minichure paintin'. A lady prisint
asked Mr. Lumley wud large hats be worn undher
Socialism. He answered no, but th' more becomin'
toque; but he wud look th' matther up in a book be
Karl Marx that he undherstood was an authority on
these subjects. Th' meetin' thin adjourned afther
passin' a resolution callin' on th' husband iv th' hostess to go an' jump in th' river.

" An' there ye ar-re, boys. Socialism is no longer
talked to ye in Platt Doitch, but handed to ye fr'm
th' top iv a coach or whispered fr'm behind an ivory
fan. It's betther that way. I prefer to have it in
a goblet all iv goold fr'm fair hands to takin' it out
iv a can. Ye can't make anny new idee too soft f'r
me. If I had me way I'd get thim to put it to music
an' have it danced befure me. It suits me betther

th' way it is thin whin Schulz screened a Schwabian account iv it through his whiskers. ' What d'ye want to do?' says I. 'To make all men akel,' says he. 'Akel to who?' says I. ' If ye mane akel to me, I'm agreeable,' I says. ' I tire iv bein' supeeryor to th' rest iv th' race,' says I. ' But,' says I, ' if ye mane akel to ye,' says I, ' I'll throuble ye to take ye'rsilf off,' says I. ' I shave,' says I."

" But suppose you did get Socialism. What would you do?" asked Mr. McKenna (Rep.).

" Bebel says—" began Mr. Schwartzmeister.

" Shut up, Schwartz," said Mr. Larkin. " Th' first thing we'd do wud be to take all th' money in th' wurruld an' throw it into th' lake."

" Not my money," said Mr. McKenna.

" Yes, ye'er's an' ivrybody else's," said Mr. Larkin.

" Mine wudden't make much iv a splash," said Mr. Hennessy.

" Hush," said Mr. Larkin. " Thin we'd set ivry wan to wurruk at something."

" What wurruk wud ye put us at?" asked Mr. McKenna.

" Liebnicht says—" began Mr. Schwartzmeister.

" Niver mind what he says," said Mr. Larkin. " Ivry man wud wurruk at what plazed him."

" But suppose no wurruk plazed him," said Mr. Dooley and Mr. McKenna at once.

" He'd starve," said Mr. Larkin.

" He wud," said Mr. Dooley.

" Well," said Mr. McKenna, after some thought, " I choose to feed th' swans in Lincoln Park."

" Ye cudden't," said Mr Larkin. " Ye wudden't

Socialism

be let. Whin ye'er case come up I'd be called in as
an expert an' I'd sind th' good woman over to
th' governmint hat-store f'r th' loan iv a stove-pipe,
jump on a governmint sthreet-car r-run be me cousin,
an' go down to th' City Hall or governmint Intillijence
Office. Afther shakin' me warmly be th' hand an'
givin' me a governmint stogy to smoke, th' Mayor
wud say: 'Little Jawnny McKenna is a candydate
f'r feedin' th' swans in Lincoln Park. He has
O'Brien an' a sthrong dillygation behind him, but
what I want to know is, is he fitted f'r th' job?' ' I'm
afraid not,' says I. ' He hasn't got th' requisite
touch. But if ye want an expert hand f'r th' wheel-
barrow at th' governmint rollin'-mills, he's jus' th'
good, sthrong, poor fellow f'r th' sinycure,' says I.
An' th' nex' day at siven o'clock they'd be a polisman
at th' dure an' ye'd be put in handcuffs an' dhragged
off to th' slag pile. An' maybe I wudden't break
ye'er back. F'r I'd be ye'er boss. I'm wan iv th'
original old-line Socialists, an' to th' victor belongs
th' spoils, be Hivens."

"You'd not be my boss then any more than you
are now, me boy," said Mr. McKenna, warmly.

"In Chermany—" began Mr. Schwartzmeister.

"Dhry up," said Mr. Larkin. "Ye mustn't feel
badly, Jawn. Ye wudden't have to wurruk long.
About eight o'clock Martin's shift wud come on, ye'd
make a date to meet me at th' governmint baseball
game, take off ye'er overalls, jump into ye'er autymobill, an' dash over to what used to be Martin's place,
but is now a governmint dispinsary, where an uncle
iv mine wud give ye a much larger glass iv malt free,
d'ye mind."

Dissertations by Mr. Dooley

" Hooray!" said Mr. Hennessy.

" Thin ye'd run over to ye'er iligant brownstone mansion in Mitchigan Avnoo, beautifully furnished be th' govermint; a govermint dhressmaker wud be thryin' a new dhress on ye'er wife, a letther-carrier wud be milkin' a govermint cow on th' back lawn, an' all ye'd have to do f'r th' rest iv th' day wud be to smoke ye'er pipe an' play on th' accorjeen."

" It sounds good," said Mr. McKenna. " But—"

" In Karl Marx—" began Mr. Schwartzmeister.

" Keep quite," said Mr. Dooley. " Ye mustn't monnopolize th' convarsation, Schwartz. It's gettin' to be a habit with ye. I must tell ye f'r ye'er own good. Give somebody else a chance wanst in a while. What were ye goin' to say, Jawn?"

" I wasn't goin' to say annything," said Mr. McKenna. " What's the use arguing against a balloon ascension? The grand old Republican party, under such leaders as—"

" Ye needn't mintion thim," said Mr. Dooley, " until this month's grand jury has adjourned. But ye're right. Th' grand ol' Raypublican party will take care iv this matther. A Raypublican is born ivry minyit, an' they will niver allow money bearin' th' sacred image iv Columbya to be dhrowned in th' lake. It's no use argyin' again' Socialism, an' be th' same token, it's no use argyin' f'r it. Afther listenin' to Larkin an' his talkative German frind here, I don't know anny more about it thin I did befure. Schwartz-meister's idee iv it is that ivry man shall live in a story-an'-a-half house, wear a unyform with a cock's feather in th' hat, an' dhraw his pay in soup tickets fr'm th' German govermint. Larkin is lookin' forward to a chance to get even with his boss. That's his idee iv an industhreel Hiven. Th' Lord knows I'd rejoice to see th' day whin Hinnissy wud be shakin' a throwel fr'm th' top iv a wall an' yellin' 'Mort' at Andhrew Carnaygie scramblin' bare-legged up a ladder, or mesilf lyin' back on a lounge afther a hard day's wurruk writin' pothry f'r th' govermint, ordherin' th' King iv England to bring me a poached egg an' a cup iv tay, an' be quick about it, darn ye.

"But I'm afraid it won't happen in our day. That alone wud make me a Socialist. I'm sthrong f'r anny rivolution that ain't goin' to happen in me day. But th' thruth is, me boy, that naw-thin' happens, annyhow. I see gr-reat changes takin' place ivry day, but no change at all ivry fifty years. What we call this here counthry iv ours pre-tinds to want to thry new experiments, but a sudden change gives it a chill. It's been to th' circus an' bought railroad tickets in a hurry so often that it thinks quick change is short change. Whin I take me mornin' walk an' see little boys an' girls with their dinner-pails on their arms goin' down to th' yards I'm th' hottest Socialist ye iver see. I'd be annything to stop it. I'd be a Raypublican, even. But whin I think how long this foolish old buildin' has stood, an' how manny a good head has busted again' it, I begin to wondher whether 'tis anny use f'r ye or me to thry to bump it off th' map. Larkin here says th' capitalist system is made up iv th' bones iv billions iv people, like wan iv thim coral reefs that I used to think was pethrified sponge. If that is so, maybe th' on'y thing I can do about it is to plant a

few geeranyums, injye thim while I live, an' thin
conthribute me own busted shoulder-blades f'r another
Rockyfellar to walk on."

BUSINESS AND POLITICAL
HONESTY

BUSINESS AND POLITICAL
HONESTY

"IT'S a shame," said Mr. Dooley, laying down
his paper, "that more business men don't go
into pollyticks."

"I thought they did," said Mr. Hennessy.

"No, sir," said Mr. Dooley; "ye don't r-read th'
pa-apers. Ivry year, whin th' public conscience is
aroused as it niver was befure, me frinds on th' pala-
jeems iv our liberties an' records iv our crimes calls
f'r business men to swab out our govermint with business methods. We must turn it over to pathrites who
have made their pile in mercantile pursoots iv money
wheriver they cud find it. We must injooce th' active,
conscientious young usurers fr'm Wall Sthreet to
take an inthrest in public affairs. Th' poolrooms is
open. To thim guilded haunts iv vice th' poor
wurrukinman carries his weekly wage, an' thries to
increase it enough so that he can give it to his wife
without blushin'. Down with th' poolrooms, says I.
But how? says you. Be ilictin' a business man mayor,
says I. But who'll we get? says you. Who betther,
says I, thin th' prisidint iv th' Westhren Union Tillygraft Comp'ny, who knows where th' poolrooms
ar-re.

"Th' wather departmint is badly r-run. Ilict
th' prisidint iv th' gas comp'ny. Th' onforchnit

sthreet railroads have had thimsilves clutched be th' throat be a corrupt city council an' foorced to buy twinty millyon dollars' worth iv sthreets f'r sixty-four wan-hundherd dollar bills. Oh, f'r a Moses to lead us out of th' wilderness an' clane th' Augeenyan stables an' steer us between Silly an' What's-it's-name an' hoist th' snow-white banner iv civic purity an' break th' feathers that bind a free people an' seize th' hellum iv state fr'm th' pi-ratical crew an' restore th' heritage iv our fathers an' cleanse th' stain fr'm th' fair name iv our gr-reat city an' cure th' evils iv th' body pollytick an' cry havic an' let loose th' dogs iv war an' captain th' uprisin' iv honest manhood again th' cohorts iv corruption an' shake off th' collar riveted on our necks be tyrannical bosses an' prim'ry rayform? Where is Moses? Where is this all-around Moses, soldier, sailor, locksmith, doctor, stable-boy, polisman, an' disinfectant? Where else wud such a vallyble Moses be thin in th' bank that owns th' sthreet railroads? If Moses can't serve we'll r-run his lawyer, th' gr-reat pollytickal purist, th' Hon'rable Ephraim Duck, author iv *Duck on Holes in th' Law, Duck on Flaws in th' Constitution, Duck on Ivry Man has His Price, Duck's First Aid to th' Suspicted, Duck's Iliminthry Lessons in Almost Crime, Th' Supreem Coort Made Easy,* or *Ivry Man his Own Allybi* and so on. Where is Judge Duck? He's down at Springfield, doin' a little ligislative law business f'r th' gas comp'ny. Whin he comes up he'll be glad to lead th' gr-reat annyooal battle f'r civic purity. Hurrah f'r Duck an' Freedom, Duck an' Purity, Duck an' th' Protiction iv th' Rights iv Property, Duck an' Fearless Compromise.

Business and Political Honesty

" Befure our most illusthrees life-insurance solic-
itor rose in th' wurruld, whin he was merely prisidint
iv th' United States, th' on'y way we cud dig a job
out iv him f'r a good dimmycrat was to form th'
Sixth Ward Chamber iv Commerce an' indorse th'
candydate.   Whin Cohen first wint to Wash'nton
to have Schmitt appinted counsul at Chefoo, th' chief
ixicutive, as Hogan says, nearly brained him with a
paper-weight marked **J. P. M.**   But whin he wint
down as prisidint iv th' Ar-rchey Road Chamber iv
Commerce th' gr-reat man fell on his neck an' near
broke it.   Th' frindship iv th' gr-reat, Hinnissy, is
worse thin their inmity.   Their hathred sometimes
misses fire, but their frindship always lands in an
unguarded an' vital spot.   This here Chamber iv
Commerce r-run th' pathronage iv th' disthrict f'r a
year.   It used to meet in me back room till th' merchant princes got too noisy over a dice game an' I
put thim into th' sthreet.

" Yes, Hinnissy, me ideel iv a gr-great statesman is
a grocer with elastic bands on his shirt-sleeves, ladlin'
public policies out iv a bar'l with a wooden scoop.
How much betther wud Wash'nton an' Lincoln have
been if they'd known enough to inthrajooce business
methods into pollyticks.   George was a good man,
but he niver thought iv settlin' th' throuble be com-
promisin' on a job as colonyal governor.   He raised
th' divvle with property, so much so, be Hivins, that
no gr-reat financier to this day can tell what belongs
to him an' what belongs to some wan else.   An' there's
Lincoln.   What a little business thrainin' wud've
done f'r him!   Look at th' roon he brought on property be his carelessness.   Millyons iv thim become

worthless except as fuel f'r bonfires in th' Sunny
Southland.

"It's sthrange people can't see it th' way I do.
There's Jawn Cassidy. Ye know him. He's a pollytician or grafter. Th' same thing. His graft is to
walk downtown to th' City Hall at eight o'clock ivry
mornin' an' set on a high stool ontil five in th' afthernoon addin' up figures. Ivry week twinty dollars iv
th' taxpayers' money, twinty dollars wrung fr'm you
an' me, Hinnissy, is handed to this boodler. He used
to get twinty-five in a clothin'-store, but he is a
romantic young fellow, an' he thought 'twud be a
fine thing to be a statesman. Th' diff'rence between
a clothin' clerk an' a statesman clerk is that th'
statesman clerk gets less money, an' has th' privilege
iv wurrukin' out iv office hours. Well, Cassidy come
in wan night with his thumbs stained fr'm his unholy
callin'. 'Well,' says I, 'ye grafters ar-re goin' to
be hurled out,' I says. 'I suppose so,' says he.
'We'll have a business administhration,' says I.
'Well,' says he, 'I wondher what kind iv a business
will it be,' he says. 'Will it be th' insurance business? I tell ye if they iver inthrajooce life-insurance
methods in our little boodle office there'll be a rivolution in this here city. Will it be a railroad administhration, with the' office chargin' ye twice as
much f'r water as Armour pays? Will it be th'
bankin' business, with th' prisidint takin' th' money
out iv th' dhrawer ivry night an' puttin' in a few
kind wurruds on a slip iv paper?

"'What kind iv a business ar-re ye goin' to use
to purify our corrupt govermint? Look here,' says
he. 'I'm goin' out iv pollyticks,' he says. 'Me wife

can't stand th' sthrain iv seein' th' newspapers always referrin' to me be a nickname in quotation marks. I've got me old job back, an' I've quit bein' a states-man,' he says. ' But let me tell ye something. I've been a boodler an' a grafter an' a public leech f'r five years, but I used to be a square business man, an' I'm givin' ye th' thruth whin I say that business ain't got a shade on pollyticks in th' matther iv honesty. Th' bankers was sthrong again' Mulcahy. But I know all about th' banks. Whin I was in th' clothin' business Minzenheimer used to have th' banks over-certify his checks ivry night. That wud mean two years in th' stir-bin f'r a pollytician, but I don't see no bankers doin' th' wan-two in th' iron gall'ries at Joliet. I knew a young fellow that wurruked in a bank, an' he told me th' prisidint sold th' United State Statutes to an ol' book dealer to make room f'r a ticker in his office. We may be a tough gang over at th' City Hall. A foreign name always looks tough whin its printed in a reform iditoryal. But, thank th' Lord, no man iver accused us iv bein' life-insur-ance prisidints. We ain't buncoin' an' scarin' peo-ple with th' fear iv death into morgedgin' their furniture to buy booze an' cigars f'r us,' he says. ' We may take bribes, because we need th' money, but we don't give thim because we want more thin we need. We're grafters, ye say, but there's manny a dollar pushed over th' counter iv a bank that Mul-cahy wud fling in th' eye iv th' man that offered it to him.

" ' Th' pollytician grafts on th' public an' his inimies. It don't seem anny worse to him thin win-nin' money on a horse-race. He doesn't see th' writh-

in' iv th' man he takes th' coin fr'm. But these here
high fi-nanciers grafts on th' public an' their inimies,
but principally on their frinds. Dump ye'er pard-
ner is th' quickest way to th' money. Mulcahy wud
rather die thin skin a frind that had sthrung a bet
with him. But if Mulcahy was a railroad boss instead iv a pollytical boss he wud first wurruk up th'
con-fidence iv his frinds in him, thin he wud sell thim
his stock, thin he wud tell thim th' road was goin'
to th' dogs, an' make thim give it back to him f'r
nawthin'; thin he wud get out a fav'rable report,
an' sell th' stock to thim again. An' he'd go on
doin' this till he'd made enough to be ilicted prisidint
iv a good govermint club. Some iv th' boys down at
our office are owners iv stock. Whin do they first
larn that things ar-re goin' wrong with th' comp'ny?
Afther th' prisidint an' boord iv di-rectors have sold
out.

" ' Don't ye get off anny gas at me about business
men an' pollyticians. I niver knew a pollytician to
go wrong ontil he'd been contaminated be contact
with a business man. I've been five years in th'
wather office, an' in all that time not a postage-stamp
has been missed. An' we're put down as grafters.
What is pollytical graft, annyhow? It ain't stealin'
money out iv a dhrawer. It ain't robbin' th' tax-
payer direct, th' way th' gas comp'ny does. All
there's to it is a business man payin' less money to a
pollytician thin he wud have to pay to th' city if he
bought a sthreet or a dock direct.

" ' Iv coorse, there ar-re petty larceny grabs be polismen. That's so ivrywhere. Wheriver there's polisman there's a shake-down. But in ivry big crooked

job there's a business man at wan end. Th' ligisla-chures is corrupt, but who makes it worth while f'r thim to be corrupt but th' pathrites iv th' life-insur-ance comp'nies? Th' la-ads in th' council ar-re out f'r th' stuff, says ye. But how do they make anny-thing except be sellin' sthreets to th' high fi-nanceers that own th' railroad comp-nies? If business men niver wanted to buy things cheap that don't belong to thim no pollytician that cud carry a precinct wud go into th' council. I'm goin' back to business. Min-zenheimer thinks he will need me to get th' aldher-men to let him add fifty illegal feet to th' front iv his store. I'm goin' back to business, an' I expect to help purify it. What th' business iv this counthry needs,' he says, ' is f'r active young pollyticians to take an inthrest in it an' ilivate it to a higher plane. Me battle-cry is: " Honest pollytical methods in th' administhration iv business," ' he says ' In time,' he says, ' I hope to see th' same honesty, good faith, an' efficiency in th' Life Insurance Comp'nies an' th' Thrusts that we see now,' he says, ' in th' adminis-thration iv Tammany Hall,' he says."

" There's a good deal in that," said Mr. Hennessy. " I knew an aldherman wanst that was honest as th' sun, except whin th' sthreet railroad or th' gas com-p'ny needed something."

" Well, there ye ar-re," said Mr. Dooley. " It seems to me that th' on'y thing to do is to keep polly-ticians an' business men apart. They seem to have a bad infloonce on each other. Whiniver I see an al-dherman an' a banker walkin' down th' sthreet to-gether I know th' Recordin' Angel will have to ordher another bottle iv ink."

SIEGES

19

SIEGES

"THIM poor la-ads in Port Arthur must be havin' a tur-rble time," said Mr. Hennessy.

"Ye niver can tell," said Mr. Dooley. "Iv coorse it looks as though they were. Ivry day or two, whin Port Arthur hasn't fallen no more, or is laid up fr'm th' last fall, I read in th' pa-apers that th' corryspondint iv th' London *Fudge*, a highly onprejudiced obsarver or liar, stationed at Chefoo, has larned fr'm a Chinyman who has jus' arrived fr'm Pekin on a junk that th' conditions is something that wurruds cannot describe.

"Says he: 'Th' conditions at Port Arthur baffle description an' stagger th' imagination. On'y fourteen iv th' original definders survive, an' they ar-re rayjooced to skeletons. They live in undherground caves, an' cook their boots on explodin' bombs dhropped in be th' Jap'nese. Last week Gin'ral Blinkovitch shot an' kilt Gin'ral Bejeeski in a quarrel over a bar iv soap, which th' former was atin' f'r lunch. Gin'ral Stoessel has lost both arms, a leg, an' th' right ear, but he is still cheerful, an' last night had his fur overcoat cooked an' sarved at a dinner to th' officers iv th' Probijienky reg'mint. He proposed a toast to th' imp'ror in kerosene. Th' toast was subsiquintly devoured be th' famished garrison. None iv th' garrison sleep at night much

on account iv th' heejus roar iv th' Jap'nese shells
which are dhropped into th' town at the rate iv wan
millyon a day. Me informant tells me—an' he's a man
whose wurrud I wud accipt as soon as me own—that
th' ships in th' harbor have been convarted into junk,
which must not be confused with th' Chinese boats iv
th' same name. As fast as they ar-re desthroyed they
ar-re eaten be th' crew. It is no uncommon sight to
see a starvin' Rooshyan sailor divin' in th' harbor f'r
a cast-iron bolt or some such toothsome morsel. Th'
intilligent Chinyman who brought me th' news es-
caped just as th' cook f'r Gin'ral Stoessel was about
to put him in th' oven. Th' Chinese are great stick-
lers f'r presarvin' their identity afther death, an' this
man nachrally didn't like to jine his ancesthers in
th' shape iv chop-sooey. Altogether, th' condition
iv' Port Arthur is worse thin ye'er readers cud imagine, an' almost as bad as they cud hope. Th' Port
Arthur *Daily Melojeen*, th' on'y pa-aper now published there, has a long kick in th' last issue about
delinquent subscribers. It is headed " Meanin' You,"
an' goes on to say that th' iditor an' his wife must
live, that they have just moved into a new dug-out,
an' that if th' cash is not forthcomin' he will be
obliged to mintion names.'

"An' that's what I can't undherstand, Hinnissy.
How is it, d'ye suppose, that if Port Arthur is so
bad off, they can have a daily paper? Th' man that
runs it must be a gr-reat journalist. I wudden't like
to give up me pa-aper. It's all I have in life. But
if I was as thin as an empty hen-coop, an' had just
devoured me las' collar, an' if I knew that I wudden't
make even a dacint muss if a Jap'nese shell hit me,

but wud look like a pile iv loose lathes an' shavin's
sthruck be a cyclone, d'ye suppose in thim circumstances I wud be polite to a man who come ar-round
an' offered me an onyx clock an' a hatful iv thradin'-
stamps to subscribe to his pa-aper?

"An' think iv th 'iditor. What a job! He has
aten a pair iv rubber boots an' washed it down with
a pint iv ink, an' he has to go out an' collect th' news
on his hands an' knees. Thin he has to write it up:
'Society jottin's: Oursilves an' wife attinded a mos'
jovyal gatherin' at Gin'ral Pumspinkki's palatchal
quarthers in Bomproof A last night. Th' jaynial
gin'ral had provided a bountiful repast—a beautifully cooked war-map, which he had procured at
gr-reat expinse. Th' Jap'nese advanced positions fell
to our lot, an' we put it away with gr-reat gusto, although, if annything, there was too much red ink on
it. Our host was at his best an' th' mornin' was far
advanced befure we reeled home. Ivrybody agrees
an injyable time was had. There is no war news, as
the London pa-apers ar-re onavoidably late, an' our
corryspondint is at th' front. Th' nex' time we sind
a corryspondint out with a Rooshyan army we'll sind
him to th' rear, where he can get some news.'

"An' while he's gettin' th' pa-aper ready a Jap
shell is lible to come through th' roof iv his office an'
pi both him an' th' form so bad that nayether wan iv
thim can be set up again.

"No, sir, if I ain't far out iv th' way, Port Arthur
ain't sufferin' nearly as bad as I am about it. It wud
prob'bly be th' place to spind th' winther, if ye didnt
mind livin' in a fallen city,—a quiet life, conjaynial
people, comfortable an' safe homes, little wurruk an'

some fightin'. It's always th' same way. I've wept me last weep over th' sufferin' iv th' besieged. I shed manny tears on account iv th' poor Spanyards in Sandago, but whin th' American sojers got into th' town they were almost suffycated be th' smell iv garlic cookin' with omelets. I remimber how pained I was over th' desperate plight iv th' sojers an' diplomats at Pekin. I rushed an army over there. They kilt Chinymen be th' thousan's, an' in th' face iv incredible misstatements fought their way to th' dures iv th' palace, where their starvin' brothers were imprisoned. What did they find? They found th' diplomats in their shirt-sleeves fillin' packin'-cases with th' undherwear iv th' Chinese imp'ror an' th' spoons iv th' Chinese impress. Th' air was filled with cries iv ' Hinnery, won't ye set on this thrunk? I can't get th' lid down since ye put in that hateful idol.' Th' English ambassadure was thryin' on a goold brocaded vest four thousan' years old, th' Frinch ambassadure was cratin' up th' imp'ror's libry, an' th' German embassy an' gallant officers iv th' kaiser were in th' obsarvatory pryin' off th' brass fittin's iv th' tillyscopes.

" So I'll save me tears about Port Arthur till all th' returns are in. I'd like to get hold iv a copy iv th' Port Arthur *Melojeen*. I wondher where I cud subscribe to it. I'd bet ye'd find it cheerful. ' Yisterdah was univintful. Th' Japs threw a few shells befure breakfast an' thin retired. This thing has got to stop. Fridah we had a dog lamed, an' if this occurs again we will appeal to th' authorities. Th' Eschemojensky band give a concert on th' public square, an' manny iv th' townspeople turned out to

hear it. John Smithinski was up befure Judge Ho-
ganenski on th' familyar charge. He was sintinced
to twinty knouts or fifty days. Main Sthreet is torn
up again. How long will this condition last befure
th' people iv our fair city rise in their might again'
th' corruptionists at th' City Hall? Closin' quota-
tions on th' Port Arthur board iv thrade: Caviar,
sixteen asked, fourteen bid; candles quiet an' un-
changed, with a fair demand f'r light upland tallow.

" 'Answers to corryspondints: Mayski: take half
a pound iv tar, a quart iv cookin' sherry, two pints
iv vinegar, an' a pound iv potash an' apply to th'
face with a paint-brush befure retirin. Arthurski
Lumleyvitch: No, Arthur, it is not considered in good
form, whin walkin' with a lady, to run whin a bomb
dhrops in ye'er neighborhood. Seize ye'er fair
companyon be th' elbows an' place her in front iv ye.
Th' rule iv all p'lite circles: " Ladies first." Timothy-
vich K.: Jeffreys in th' sicond round. Anxious: We
don't know.'

" Sure, Hinnissy, it's always th' same way. Wan
iv th' sthrangest things about life is that it will go
on in onfav'rable circumstances an' go out whin ivrything is aisy. A man can live an' have a good time,
no matther what happens to him that don't kill him.
I lived here durin' th' cholery. I didn't like it, but
they was on'y wan other thing to do, an' I didn't
care f'r that. If ye're livin' in a town that's bein'
bombarded ye don't like it at first, but afther awhile
ye begin to accommydate ye'ersilf to it, an' by-an'-
by, whin a shell dhrops while ye're argyin' about
th' tariff, ye step aside, an' if ye're still there afther
th' smoke is cleared away ye resume th' argymint.

Dissertations by Mr. Dooley

Ye have to make new frinds, but so ye do in Chicago. A man iv me age loses more frinds in a year, an' is in more danger thin a definder iv Port Arthur at twenty-wan. Bustin' shells is on'y wan iv th' chances iv life, like pnoomony an' argyin' with a polisman.

"Besides, I bet ye no garrison iver rayfused to surrindher whin it was starvin', onless it was afraid th' inimy wud shoot th' man with th' white flag. A garrison begins to think iv surrindherin' whin it can't get pie at ivry meal. Cut out wan iv its meals, an' it begins to wondher what's th' use iv fightin' a lot iv nice fellows. Rejooce it more, an' some iv th' sojers will say to th' gin'ral: 'If ye haven't got a sheet or a pillow-slip handy f'r a flag ye can use our shirts.' Ye may change th' dite to horse-meat, but horse-meat reminds a European sojer iv what his mother used to call beef. But he's got to have enough. A hungry man won't fight except f'r food, an' he'd follow a beefsteak twice as far as he wud th' flag iv anny imp'ror or czar."

MR. CARNEGIE'S HERO FUND

MR. CARNEGIE'S HERO FUND

"IT'S no use," said Mr. Dooley. "I give it up."

"What's that?" asked Mr. Hennessy.

"I can't get away from him," Mr. Dooley went on. "I can't escape me old frind Andhrew Carnaygie. I've avoided him succissfully f'r manny years. Th' bookless libry an' th' thoughtless univarsity niver touched me. I'm not enough iv a brunette to share annything he done f'r Booker Washin'ton. Up to now he's been onable to land on me annywhere. But he's got me at last. He's r-run me to earth. I throw up me hands. Come on, Andhrew, an' paint ye'er illusthrees name on me. Stencil me with that gloryous name."

"What ar-re ye talkin' about?" asked Mr. Hennessy.

"He has created a hero fund," said Mr. Dooley. "He has put aside five millyon dollars, or it may be fifty, but, annyhow, more thin there is in me sugarbowl, to buy medals f'r heroes in th' daily walks iv life—sojers, polismen, an' invistors barred. Suppose wan day you an' I ar-re walkin' home fr'm a picnic, an' ye thrip ye'ersilf into th' wathers iv th' Illinye an' Mitchigan Canal. I cannot see me frind dhrown, an' besides, Hinnissy, I'd hate to lose ye as a sparrin' partner. A man can on'y talk good to his infeeryors, an' ye're a gr-reat stimylant to convarsation. So I take off me hat an' coat an' vest, hang thim on a three, pull off me Congress gaiters, an' lay thim in th' grass, hang me cravat on th' fence, offer up a short prayer, an' lay down on th' bank an' pull ye out. I grumble at ye f'r ye'er carelessness, an' ye want to fight me f'r bein' so rough in savin' ye'er life whin ye cud have waded out without help, an' I break th' sthrap iv me gaiters pullin' thim on, an' we go home quarrellin' an' jawin' an' ye'er wife thinks I pushed ye in. But th' talk gets ar-round th' neighborhood, an' wan day a comity steps into me place, headed be a little dumplin' iv a man, an' wan iv thim pins me hands while Andhrew Carnaygie nails on me chest a medal all in goold, with this inscription— here it is—that Father Kelly wrote out f'r me:

To Martin Dooley, Hero,

THIS MEDAL IS PRISINTED BY

ANDHREW CARNAYGIE.

DULCY ET DECORUM EST PRO CARNAYGIE

TO SPOIL YE'ER SUNDAY CLOTHES.

" I'll be so mad I'd throw ye in again, but that won't help matthers. I'm a hero f'r good an' all. I'm f'river doomed to be a sandwich man an' parade th' sthreets advartisin' th' gin'rosity an' noble charackter iv Andhrew Carnaygie.

" Iv coorse I won't be good f'r annything else. I'll have to sell out th' liquor-store. What's a hero

doin', pushin' bottles acrost a bar an' mendin' a re-
fracthry beer-pump? I'll quit wurruk f'r good an'
hang ar-round a liv'ry-stable pitchin' horseshoes.
They'se nawthin' a hero with a medal can do f'r a
livin' that ain't beneath him. Wanst a hero always a
hero. Afther awhile I'll be lurkin' in th' corner iv
th' bridge an' pushin' me frinds into th' river an'
haulin' thim out f'r a medal. I'll become an habitchool Carnaygie hero, an' good f'r nawthin' else.
No, me frind, don't iver fall into th' canal whin I'm
ar-round. I might be lookin' th' other way.

"An' think iv th' position ye ar-re in all this time,
th' man who's life I've saved. Nawthin' cud be
lower. Ye're raymimbered f'river as a foolish person that cudden't swim an' was dhragged fr'm a
wathry grave be th' owner iv th' Carnaygie medal.
Ye'er wife despises ye because ye had to have ye'er
life saved. She was always sure that if she iver fell
into th' wather ye'er sthrong aram an' risolute heart
wud rescue her, an' lo an' behold! when ye tumble in
ye'ersilf ye have to be rescued be a stout gintleman
in the liquor business. Ye'er little boys an' girls have
to bring prisints around to me on me birthday. Ye
have to lend me money whin I want it, an' if ye complain people call ye an ingrate. Befure ye die ye'll
wisht ye'd pulled me into th' canal with ye.

"I wanst knowed a la-ad that was more or less
rescued fr'm a wathry grave be a tailor be th' name
iv Muggins. He took th' la-ad be th' ar-rms an'
walked ashore with him. Well, th' ag'nized parents,
not wantin' to appear stingy befure th' neighbors,
prisinted Muggins with a goold watch, an' Muggins
become a hero. Th' la-ad didn't think much iv it.

He'd have done th' same f'r Muggins. But afther
a while he found that Muggins was chained to him
f'r life. As a boy he was spoken iv as th' fellow that
had his life saved be Muggins th' tailor. As he grew
older he was still Muggins' boy. Muggins wasn't
much to look at, bein' a little, bowlegged man, but
afther he become a hero he acted th' part. Me young
frind cudden't get away fr'm him. If he was playin'
baseball in th corner lot Muggins was lanin' over
th' fence with an indulgent smile. Whin he grajated
with honors at th' Brothers' School, Muggins set in
th' front seat, with a look iv fond attintion on his
face. Whin th' Brother Supeeryor handed out th'
first prize he remarked that it gave him gr-reat
pleasure to reward th' ability an' larnin' iv this
young man in th' prisince iv th' hero to whom he
owed his life.

"It was th' same in afther years. He become a
lawyer, an' Muggins niver missed a day in coort.
Th' lawyer f'r th' opposition always managed to appeal to his finer feelin's in th' prisince iv th' man to
whom he owed his life. If it was a suit over a pair iv
pants me frind always lost it. He niver wud take a
case again' a tailor, f'r th' jury wud always vote
again' him. In pollyticks he thried to succeed, but
Muggins hung onto him. Whin th' chairman iv th'
meetin' arose he invaryably began: 'Ladies an' gintlemen: Befure inthrojoocin' th' speaker iv th' evenin', I want to presint to ye th' man to whom he owes
his life an' who is here on th' platform to-night,
Misther Alphonse Muggins.' Me frind was always
supposed to put his handkerchief to his eyes at these
wurrds, an' with falthrin' step escoort him to th' front.

Wan night he tol' me he give Muggins a kick. He said he cudden't help it. Th' timptation was too sthrong f'r human endurance. Muggins didn't mind it. He niver minded annything. He was a hero.

"Afther a while he took to dhrink. Habitchool heroes always do, an' whin in dhrink he was melancholy or quarrelsome, as dhrunk men an' heroes sometimes ar-re. Clancy wud be settin' quitely in a cafe with some frinds whin Muggins wud blow in an' set down with his hat over his eyes. Clancy wud have to inthrajooce him with a catch in his voice an' a tear in his eyes. 'Boys,' he'd say, 'I want to inthrajooce ye to Alphonse Muggins. Gawd bless him, boys, he saved me life.' 'Is that so?' says wan iv his companyons. 'Ye betcher life it is,' says Muggins. 'Did I save his life? Well, ask him. Ye ask him if I din' save his life. Ye just ask him. If he don't lie about it he'll tell ye who saved his life. Din' I leap into th' ragin' flood an' riscue him at th' risk iv me life? Maybe I din'. Maybe it was a man in Milwaukee that done that. Looky here. Look at this clock I got fr'm his folks, if ye don' believe me. An' what's he done f'r me? Tell me that, will ye? Who am I? I'm nothin'. I'm Muggins th' tailor. An' what's he? Look at him, will ye, with his dimon' pin an' his plug hat so gay. An' where'd he be if it wasn't f'r me? But it's all right, boys. It's all right. Life is a cur'ous place, an' gratichood is a thing unknown.' An' he wud weep an' go to sleep.

"Sometimes he wud fight. He punched Clancy two or three times on account iv his ingratichood. Clancy had to support him an' bail him out an' get th' clock out iv th' pawnshop ivry Saturdah night.

Dissertations by Mr. Dooley

But an end comes to all things. Heroes don't live
long. They can't, th' way they live. An' wan day
Muggins wint th' way iv all our kind, proud an'
simple, coward an' brave man, hero an' hero worship-
per. Th' pa-apers had an account iv his fun'ral.
'Among th' mourners none was more affected thin
Congressman Clancy, whose life, near forty years
ago, this humble hero had saved fr'm a wathry doom
in Lake Mitchigan.' Th' rayporthers didn't obsarve
that Clancy tamped th' grave with his fut to make
sure it was solid. He wint home with a light heart,
an' says to his wife: 'Mother, to-day I begin me rale
career. We burrid Muggins.' 'But, Cornelius,'
says th' good woman, 'ye owed him ye'er life.'
'P'raps,' says Clancy; 'but,' he says, 'he took it out
in thrade long ago.'

"No, sir, Hinnissy, if ye see me in disthress kindly call f'r profissyonal help. I'll be riscued be a fireman or a polisman, because it's all in their day's
wurruk, but amachoor heroes is a danger whin they're
riscuin' ye an' a worry iver afther. If I owe me life
to anny wan, let it be to a man who won't thry to collect it. Annyhow, what is heeroism? If a man stops
a runaway team that is dhraggin' an empty milk-
wagon into a ditch he's not a hero. He's a fool. Th'
line is lightly dhrawn, annyhow. A hero is often a
succissful fool, an' a fool is an unsuccissful hero.
I've heerd Andhrew Carnaygie called a hero, but I
don't believe it. If he was he wudden't be givin'
medals f'r heeroism. If he was a profissyonal swim-
mer he wudden't think annything iv savin' people
fr'm dhrownin'. If he was a fireman he'd think
nawthin' iv carryin' a man down th' fire-escape iv a

[298]

burnin' buildin'. If he was a stable-boy he'd find that he'd have to catch runaway horses or lose his job. I wudden't hesitate to go down a laddher on ye'er shouldhers, but if ye thried to save me fr'm dhrownin' I'd scream f'r help. What wud I be doin' thryin' to stop a runaway team? But if ye fell through me coal-hole into me cellar I'd organize a heroic riscue. I know th' way. Heroes ought to know th' way to be safe. If they do they don't need anny medals. If they don't they'd betther turn in an alarm.

" There ar-re heroes an' heroes. We're all heroes, more or less. Ye're a hero ye'ersilf, towin' those tired feet afther ye ivry mornin' whin th' whistle blows. An', be Hivens, if ye'er wife had a medal f'r ivry act iv heeroism she's performed she'd have as manny now as Sousa. Heroes in th' humble walks iv life, says he? Well, there's enough iv thim to break him if he give each wan iv thim th' on'y kind iv medals they need, th' kind th' govermint foundhry makes with an eagle on th' back."

BANKS AND BANKING

BANKS AND BANKING

"WELL, sir," said Mr. Dooley, " I've been doin' th' bankers iv this counthry a gr-reat injustice."

" How's that?" asked Mr. Hennessy.

" I've put thim down all me life as cold, stony-hearted men that wud as soon part with their lives as with their money. I had a pitcher iv a banker in me mind, a stern, hard-featured ol' gintleman, with curly side-whiskers, settin' on th' people's money an' stalin' off both th' borrower who comes be night with a dhrill an' th' more rayfined burglar who calls in th' daytime with a good story. I was afraid iv thim. I wud no more dare to ask a banker to take a dhrink or shoot th' shoots with me thin I wud an archbishop. If I talked to wan iv thim I'd look up all me statements in th' almanack an' all me wurruds in th' ditchnry to see that I got nawthin' wrong. An' I made a mistake about thim. Far fr'm bein' a hard, cynical class, th' bankers iv America is a lot iv jolly dogs, that believes in human nature, takes life as it is, aisy come, aisy go, hurrah boys, we'll be a long time dead. Hard to borrow money fr'm thim? On th' conthry, it's hard to keep thim fr'm crowdin' it on ye. They'll lend ye money on annything ye shove in, on a dhream that ye saw a sojer on horseback, on th' sad story iv ye'er life, or on ye'er wurrud iv honor if ye're ready to go back on it. I niver knew what collateral was ontil this lady fr'm Cleveland come along. Collateral is a misstatement on which bankers lend money. If ye broke into a bank in Ohio to-morrah ye'd prob'ly find th' vaults full iv Louisiana lotthry tickets, bets on th' races, an' rayports iv crystal gazin'.

"Bankin' is a sthrange business, annyhow. I make up me mind that I need more money thin I have, or I want to build a railroad in Omaha or a gas-house in Milwaukee, or Mrs. Chadwick wants an autymobill, or something else happens, an' I start a bank. I build a brick house, put ir'n gratin's on th' window, an' ye an' Donohue fight each other to see who'll get his money first to me. I accept it very reluctantly an' as a gr-reat favor to ye. Says I: ' Hinnissy an' Donohue,' says I, ' ye ar-re rayspictable wurrukin'-men, an' I will keep ye'er money f'r ye rather thin see ye spind it in riochous livin',' says I. ' As a gr-reat favor to ye I will take care iv these lithographs be lendin' thim to me frinds,' says I. ' If ye want th' money back ye can have it anny time between nine in th' mornin' an' three in th' afthernoon except Sundays an' holidays,' says I; ' but don't both come at wanst,' says I, ' or nayether iv ye'll get it,' says I. Well, ye lave ye'er money with me, an' I suppose ye think iv it lyin' safe an' sound in th' big sthrong box, where th' burglar boys can't get it. Ye sleep betther at nights because ye feel that ye'er money is where no wan can reach it except over me dead body. If ye on'y knew ye've not turned ye'er back befure I've chased those hard-earned dollars off th' premises! With ye'er money I build a house an' rent it to you. I start a railrood with it, an' ye wurruk on th' railrood at two dollars a day. Ye'er money makes me a prom'nent citizen. Th' newspapers intherview me on what shud be done with th' toilin' masses, manin' ye an' Donohue; I consthruct th' foreign policy iv th' govermint; I tell ye how ye shud vote. Ye've got to vote th' way I say or I won't give ye back ye'er money. An' all this time ye think iv that little bundle iv pitchers nestlin' in th' safe in me brick house, with me settin' at th' dure with a shot-gun acrost me knees. But wan day ye need th' money to bury some wan, an' ye hurry down to see me. 'Sorry,' says I, 'but I've jus' given it all to a lady who come out iv th' Chinese laundhry nex' dure an' said she was an aunt iv Jawn D. Rockefellar.' An' there ye ar-re.

"If iver I have anny relations with a bank, Hinnissy, it won't be in th' way iv puttin' money in. Were ye iver in a bank? Ye wudden't be. I was wanst. Wanst I was eighty-five dollars on me way to bein' a millyonaire, an' I wint down-town an' threw th' money into th' window an' told th' banker to take th' best iv care iv it. 'We can't take this,' says he. 'Why not?' says I. 'I don't know ye,' says he. 'Niver mind that,' says I. 'It's me money, not me-silf, I'm thryin' to inthrajooce to s-ciety,' says I. 'It's a very nice kind iv money, an' aven if ye don't like it now 'twill grow on ye,' says I. 'Or at laste I hope so,' says I. D'ye know, Hinnissy, he wudden't take th' money till I cud get Dorsey, th' plumber, to assure him that I was fr'm wan iv th' oldest fam'lies that had come to Archey Road since th' fire. Havin' satisfied himsilf that me money was fit f'r other people's money to assocyate with, he tol' th' polisman to

put me in a line iv people with blue noses, who were
clutchin' at postal-ordhers in front iv a window where
a young fellow sat. Th' young fellow was properly
indignant at havin' to take money fr'm sthrangers,
an' he showed it be glarin' at th' impydint depositors.
Whin it come me turn I wanted to tell him how I
hated to part with me little money; how long me
money an' me had slept together, an' niver had a cross
wurrud; how its slightest nod was a command to me,
but now I supposed th' time had come whin it must go
out an' see something iv th' wurruld, on'y I hoped
'twud be happy among sthrangers. An' wud he be
good to it, because 'twas all I had, an' not large f'r
its age.

"I felt very sintimintal, Hinnissy. F'r two years
I'd counted that money forty times a day. I knew ivry
wrinkle on it. I had what ye might call a legal ten-
derness f'r it. But befure I cud deliver me sintimintal addhress called, 'A poor man's farewell to his
roly-boly,' th' young fellow grabbed th' bundle, tossed
it over into a pile, hit me on th' chest with a pass-
book, mutthered 'Burglar' undher his breath, an'
dhrove me fr'm th' bank, penniless.

"As I passed be th' prisidint's office I found th'
great man biddin' a tearful farewell to Gallagher iv
th' fifth ward. Ye know Gallagher. He owns all
th' copper mines in Halsted Sthreet, has a half inthrest in Jack's tips on th' races, an' conthrols th'
American rights in th' Humbert fam'ly. 'Ar-re
ye wan iv us?' says I. 'Wan iv what?' says he.
'Wan iv us depositors,' says I. 'I am not,' says he.
'I've jus' dhropped in an' borrowed a thousan','
says he. 'What on?' says I. 'On a good thing this

afthernoon at Noo Orleens,' says he. 'Who vouched f'r ye'er charackter?' says I. 'Ye don't need a charackter to borrow money at a bank,' says he."

"How d'ye suppose that there lady fr'm Cleveland fooled thim bankers?" asked Mr. Hennessy. "Ye'd think they'd be too smart to be bunkoed."

"Don't ye believe it," said Mr. Dooley. "Nobody is too smart to be bunkoed. Th' on'y kind iv people that can be bunkoed are smart people. Ye can be too honest to be bunkoed, but niver too smart. It's the people that ar-re thryin' to get something f'r nawthin' that end in gettin' nawthin' f'r ivrything. I niver can burst into tears whin I read about some lad bein' robbed be a confidence game. Canada Bill, Gib Fitz, or Mrs. Chadwick niver got anny money fr'm square people. A man that buys a goold brick thinks he is swindlin' a poor Indyan that don't know its value; a fellow that comes on to buy f'r five hundherd dollars tin thousan' dollars' worth iv something that is so like money ye can't tell th' diff'rence is hopin' to swindle th' govermint; the foolish man that falls f'r th' three-card thrick has th' wrong card crimped f'r him whin th' dealer's back is turned; th' shell wurruker always pretinds to fumble an' carelessly show th' farmer which shell th' little pea is undher; an' th' lady fr'm Cleveland cudden't have got anny more money on Andy's name thin on mine if she hadn't promised to divide with th' bankers. I refuse to sob over thim poor, gloomy financeers anny more thin I wud over th' restless capitalist who loses his all in a wire-tappin' entherprise. Whin a man gets more thin six per cent. f'r his money it's a thousan' to wan he's payin' it himsilf. Whiniver annybody offers to give ye something f'r nawthin', or something f'r less thin its worth, or more f'r something thin its worth, don't take anny chances. Yell f'r a polisman."

"Th' wurruld is full iv crooks," said Mr. Hennessy.

"It ain't that bad," said Mr. Dooley. "An', besides, let us thank Hivin they put in part iv their time cheatin' each other."

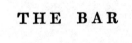

THE BAR

THE BAR

"IT ain't ivry man that can be a bishop. An' it ain't ivry wan that can be a saloonkeeper. A saloonkeeper must be sober, he must be honest, he must be clean, an' if he's th' pastor iv a flock iv poor wurrukin'-men he must know about ivrything that's goin' on in th' wurruld or iver wint on. I on'y discuss th' light topics iv th' day with ye, Hinnissy, because ye're a frivolous charackter, but ye'd be surprised to know what an incyclopeeja a man gets to be in this profissyon. Ivry man that comes in here an' has three pans iv nicissry evil tells me, with tears, th' secrets iv his thrade an' offers to fight me if I don't look inthrested. I know injyneerin', pammistry, plumbin', Christyan Science, midicine, horseshoein' asthronomy, th' care iv th' hair, an' th' laws iv exchange, an' th' knowledge I have iv how to subjoo th' affictions iv th' ladies wud cause manny a pang. I tell ye we ar-re a fine body iv men.

"Not that I'm proud iv me profissyon, or shud I say me art? It's wan way iv makin' a livin'. I suppose it was me vocation. I got into it first because I didn't like to dhrive an express-wagon, an' I stayed in it because they was nawthin' else that seemed worth while. I am not a hard dhrinker. I find if I dhrink too much I can't meet—an' do up— th' intellechool joynts that swarm in here afther a

meetin' at th' rowlin' mills. On Saturdah nights I
am convivyal. On New Year's eve I thry to make th'
ol' year jus' as sorry it's lavin' me as I can. But I
have no more pleasure in shovin' over to ye that liquid
sunstroke thin I wud if I had to dole out collars, hair-
dye, books, hard-biled eggs, money, or annything
else that wudden't be good f'r ye. Liquor is not a
nicissry evil. Hogan says it's wan way iv ra-alizin'
th' ideel. Th' nex' day ye'er ashamed iv ye're ideel.
The' throuble about it is that whin ye take it ye want
more. But that's th' throuble with ivrything ye
take. If we get power we want more power; if we
get money we want more money. Our vices r-run on
f'river. Our varchues, Hinnissy, is what me frind
Doc Casey calls self-limitin.'

" Th' unbenighted American wurrukin'-man likes
his dhrinks—as who does not? But he wants to take
it in peace. His varchues has been wrote about. But
let him injye his few simple vices in his own way, says
I. He goes to th' saloon an' rich men go to th' club
mos'ly f'r th' same reason. He don't want to go
home. He don't need anny wan to push him into a
bar. He'll go there because that's a place where wan
man's betther thin another, an' nobody is ra-aly on
but th' bartinder. There ought to be wan place
where th' poor wurrukin'-man can escape bein' patted
on th' back. He ain't so bad as people think. Wurrukin'-men don't dhrink to excess. Dhrunkenness is a
vice iv th' idle. Did ye iver see a la-ad sprintin'
acrost a joist two hundherd feet in th' air? D'ye
think he cud do that if he were a free dhrinker? Th'
on'y wurrukin'-men who dhrink too much ar-re
thruckmen, an' that's because they have so much

time on their hands. While they ar-re waitin' f'r a
load they get wan. Even some iv thim ar-re sober.
Ye can tell them be their hats.

" Somehow or another, Hinnissy, it don't seem just
right that there shud be a union iv church an' saloon.
These two gr-reat institutions ar-re best kept apart.
They kind iv offset each other, like th' Supreem
Coort an' Congress. Dhrink is a nicissry evil, nicissry
to th' clargy. If they iver admit its nicissry to th'
consumers they might as well close up th' churches.
Ye'll niver find Father Kelly openin' a saloon. He
hates me business, but he likes me. He says dhrink
is an evil, but I'm a nicissity. If I moved out a worse
man might come in me place."

" Ye ra-aly do think dhrink is a nicissry evil?"
said Mr. Hennessy.

" Well," said Mr. Dooley, " if it's an evil to a
man, it's not nicissry, an' if it's nicissry it's an evil."

THE END